DEADLY NIGHTSHADE

DEADLY NIGHTSHADE

Elizabeth Daly

FELONY & MAYHEM PRESS • NEW YORK

All the characters and events portrayed in this work are fictitious.

DEADLY NIGHTSHADE

A Felony & Mayhem mystery

PRINTING HISTORY
First edition (Farrar & Rinehart): 1940
Felony & Mayhem edition: 2013

ISBN: 978-1-937384-79-1

Manufactured in the United States of America

Printed on 100% recycled paper

Library of Congress Cataloging-in-Publication Data

Daly, Elizabeth, 1878-1967.
Deadly nightshade / Elizabeth Daly.
pages cm
ISBN 978-1-937384-79-1
1. Gamadge, Henry (Fictitious character)--Fiction. 2. Book collectors--Fiction. 3. Murder--Investigation--Fiction. 4. Detective and mystery stories. I. Title.
PS3507.A4674D38 2013
813'.52--dc23

2013019136

CONTENTS

The icon above says you're holding a copy of a book in the Felony & Mayhem "Vintage" category. These books were originally published prior to about 1965, and feature the kind of twisty, ingenious puzzles beloved by fans of Agatha Christie and John Dickson Carr. If you enjoy this book, you may well like other "Vintage" titles from Felony & Mayhem Press.

DEADLY NIGHTSHADE

CHAPTER ONE

Solanum Nigrum Linnaeus

ON FRIDAY EVENING, September the eighth, 1939, Mr. Henry Gamadge sat beside his open library window, doing several things at once. His left forefinger gently caressed a yellowed fragment of paper on which was scrawled a rusty signature; his eyes wandered from it to the big ailanthus tree outside the window, and his right hand conveyed spoonfuls of cantaloupe to his mouth. War news poured confidentially into his ear from a little radio beside him, turned low; a smell of freshly watered plants on the balcony, and of grass and shrubs in the yard beneath, came to him with the warm southerly breeze; which also brought him a murmur of subdued traffic, and the strains of *Norma*, played on a street organ. All his senses being occupied, Mr. Gamadge was (except for the war news) reasonably happy.

He was in his early thirties, but sometimes looked younger; his blunt-featured, rather colorless, amiable face being enlivened by intelligent gray eyes. He dressed well, but slouched in his chair and ambled in his walk; and he was apt when possible to efface himself in company. He did not object to his own society.

Having swallowed the last edible mouthful of cantaloupe, he screwed up his eyes once more over the brownish ink of the autograph beside his plate, and leaned back to glance as if for inspiration about his library. It looked very much as it had looked in 1873, when Gamadge's parents had furnished it, and when taste, though often excellent, tended to the grandiose and the somber. A worn Turkey carpet still lay on the floor, glassed rosewood bookcases towered almost to the molded ceiling, an ancestor in a brown coat and a tie-wig hung above the marble mantelpiece, solid furniture, chintz-covered, invited repose. On the low sill of the other window a big orange-tawny cat waved a dark-ringed tail.

The library was now also Gamadge's dining room. He had turned the whole first floor of the house (a relic among relics in the East 60's of the city of New York) into business premises, where he followed the occupation of consulting expert on old or pseudo-old books, manuscripts and autographs. He himself had written a book, intended for the trade, which had caught the fancy of the lay public; and his occasional articles, published in magazines, not only terrorized the unrighteous, but had been known to cause even the righteous a good deal of uneasiness.

Some people said that his book was better than a detective story; only once, however, and that no longer before than the preceding summer, had he been inveigled by circumstances into the rôle of practicing detective. The locale had been Maine, and his collaborator State Detective Mitchell, an elderly man of wooden-seeming personality whom he had liked very much.

He often thought of Mitchell; and as his eyes now rested on a little Japanese painting of blue waves dashing against a white rock, he thought of him again.

The telephone in the hall began to ring. It ceased, and Gamadge turned off the radio. An old colored man came in, carrying a coffee tray.

"Call for you, Mr. Gamadge," he said. "No, you sit there and take your coffee. I told them to ring again in ten minutes."

"I wish you wouldn't make these rules, Theodore. Did you bother to find out who it was, before you chopped them off?"

"Long distance. Now you don't need to jump out of your chair. They can call us up again. You get a private wire, like I ask you to, and you'll get all your calls, soon as they come."

"I want them all now, soon as they come. They may be clients."

"What about wrong numbers, wakin' us all up in the middle of the night? You mad enough then."

The telephone rang madly. Theodore went out, and returned to say in a discontented tone: "It's police, and she won't cut them off."

"Police!"

"Long distance. Maine."

Gamadge arose, and lurched in his ungraceful but rapid fashion into the hall. A colorless voice greeted him over the wire:

"Sorry to interrupt your dinner, Mr. Gamadge. Mitchell talking."

"Mitchell! I was just thinking of you. Where are you?"

"Ford's Center."

"Magic name. Wish I was there myself."

"I was going to suggest, why don't you come up for the weekend? It's the best time of year, now the summer folks have cleared out. You know how they get going by Labor Day."

"Very nice of you, but are you crazy? It's too far for a weekend. Nobody goes up there for a weekend."

"Easy as pie. You could take the ten o'clock tonight, and be here at seven thirty tomorrow morning. You could go back at ten P.M., Sunday, and be home Monday, early."

"I know I could, but why exactly should I?"

"Too busy, are you?"

"Busy listening to the radio. Aren't you?"

"No time for radio. I suppose you didn't see in the papers that we've been having a little trouble up here."

"Trouble? What kind of trouble?"

"Some children got hold of some poison berries. Deadly nightshade."

"Wait a minute; I think I did see a short notice, yesterday. 'Fatal accident,' it said. Were they on a picnic?"

"It wasn't a picnic. We don't know how they got hold of the berries. One of the children was Albert Ormiston's youngest boy; they're up at Harper's Rocks. You know who Ormiston is?"

"Certainly. The black-and-white artist."

"That's right. The little feller got over it, and he's all right again. Then there was the Bartram girl; Carroll Bartram was her father. Silk people, you know. She didn't get over it. We think perhaps one of the gypsy children had some of the berries, too, but they won't own to it."

"Why not?"

"Don't ask me why or why not, when it's gypsies; they never own to anything. Whatever he had, this little gypsy's getting along all right, too; he'll be as well as ever, pretty soon, they tell me. The little Beasley girl—farm people, the Beasleys are—she certainly had some of the berries; dropped some of 'em. We haven't found her. We think she must have wandered off and got in the marsh."

"Good heavens, Mitchell!"

"Her cat's gone, too."

"Cat?"

"Tortoise-shell cat, used to follow her around."

"Queer story. And I hate that *Trovatore* touch."

"You hate what?"

"The gypsy angle. There's something so exploded and fake-romantic about gypsies."

"Nothing romantic about our gypsies, Mr. Gamadge."

"What in the world has been going on up there? I didn't even know the stuff grew in this part of the world."

"It does, though. Half the community is out grubbing up what they can find of it, which isn't much, and the other half is about ready to start pestering the gypsies. We have the makings of a panic on our hands."

"Why are they putting it on the gypsies?"

"I'll tell you when you come up. I don't honestly know if they had a thing to do with it. Sheriff sends his regards, and hopes you'll see your way to making the trip."

"Thanks. But—"

"I can't recommend the Pegram House—that's where I'm staying; but there's a very good inn between Ford's Center and Oakport, on the main route. It keeps open late for the hunters. I could get you a room there."

"Do you mean Burnsides?"

"Yes. Food's good."

"Of course I know Burnsides. What I want to know is, why do you suggest my coming up?"

"We can't make out how those berries got around."

"But you people have the facts, and you know the circumstances. What good should I be to you?"

"We thought you might catch something we missed. You could talk to the families—"

"No, thanks! The last time I talked to the families, you know what happened. I haven't got over it yet."

"This is different. Besides, it would be a personal favor to me; I'm shorthanded."

"How's that?"

"You remember that state trooper, young Trainor?"

"Very well. Nice young fellow."

"He had to go and take a skid on his motorcycle that night, and get himself killed."

"What night?"

"Tuesday—the night it all happened."

Gamadge was silent for a moment or two. Then he said: "That's too bad."

"A good many people think so. He was a popular young feller."

The orange cat, trotting along the hall on some urgent private affair, stopped to rub himself against Gamadge's legs. Gamadge looked down at him thoughtfully.

"One of your race seems to be missing, old man," he said. "Shall I go up there and try to find out what's happened to her? It *is* a her, I'm told, if it's a tortoise shell."

The orange cat wound silently in and out between Gamadge's feet. Mitchell asked, uneasily: "Who're you consulting, there?"

"My familiar. He doesn't seem to advise my taking the trip. Not a mew out of him."

"That cat, eh? Well, you tell him this case is chock-full of cats; seven of 'em, so far. You tell him—"

"What about it, Martin?" asked Gamadge.

The cat suddenly reared up and clawed Gamadge's trousers, mewing sharply. Gamadge gently shook him off, and spoke into the mouthpiece with crisp decision:

"He's changed his mind. I'll take the ten o'clock."

"You will?" Mitchell was jubilant. "Then I'd better not keep you another minute. You probably want to do some hustling."

"Wait a second. I'd like to know—"

"Tell you when I see you. Good-bye till tomorrow morning, seven thirty."

Mitchell hung up. Gamadge replaced the receiver on its hook, frowning; thought for a minute, and then went back to the library. Theodore was clearing the round mahogany table, Martin at his heels; he had laid the autograph which Gamadge had been studying on a bookstand. Gamadge picked it up by the corners.

"Where's Harold?" he asked.

"Harold's in the kitchen, Mr. Gamadge, sir, cookin' up some mess, looks like glue. He say the labatory stove gone back on him. Athalie say he crowdin' her. Mr. Gamadge, this cat had his supper, five o'clock; you spoilin' him with all these snacks. He won't give us no peace now till he gets some cheese."

"Ask Harold to come here, will you? And pack me a bag for the weekend; I have to go up to Maine. No evening clothes. Tweeds, and a sweater, and a raincoat. No golf things. Put in a bottle of Scotch; they have local option there, now, and you never know where it's going to strike. Did you save the evening paper?"

Theodore produced it, and Gamadge found a short paragraph on an inner page. "Nightshade Poisonings in Maine," he read. "Community, Panic-Stricken, Seeks Plants." The rest of the item mentioned the Ormistons, the Bartrams and the Beasleys, but said nothing about the little gypsy; explained that the Ormiston boy had recovered; and devoted a few lines to a short biographical sketch of Mr. Albert Ormiston.

A short, pale young man with a morose expression came into the room. He wore white duck trousers, a black shirt, black-and-white shoes, and a red tie; and his dark hair gleamed oilily. There was a legend current among Gamadge's friends that he had been found, and dragged in, by the cat Martin; as a matter of fact he had appeared at the area gate one morning, two years before, asking for a job. Theodore, who happened to be suffering from an attack of rheumatism, and who had been disappointed by the cleaning man, engaged him. At noon he was given a meal, after which he fell asleep, exhausted. Gamadge wandered into the kitchen soon after he awoke refreshed, looked him over, and proposed another less physically strenuous job for him; and the end of the day saw him installed in a hall bedroom on the top floor.

Gamadge and Theodore (with some assistance from Athalie the cook) had kept him moderately busy ever since. He had begun by offering the dim explanation that he was "off a boat", and had at the same time given his name (Harold Bantz), and his age (seventeen). Gamadge judged from his manner of speech that he had been bred in greater New York, but—always incurious except in the way of business—had asked no questions. He had developed into a promising if taciturn assistant, who attended the courses of instruction marked out for him, and paid for, by Gamadge, without enthusiasm or complaint; and he had no marked peculiarities besides his lamentable taste in dress, and his aversion from Athalie's magnificent cooking. He preferred to consume the strange foods that he craved from the counters of eating houses and lunch wagons. Gamadge said he had a future in science.

He now pointed to the autograph in Gamadge's fingers, and said gloomily: "The ink's O.K., and the paper's O.K."

"Well, I want you to write to the client and tell him so. Tell him the thing's undoubtedly authentic, but I never saw another, and I can't prove anything without comparison. Tell him inquiries will run into money, more money than this will ever be worth, even duly authenticated." Gamadge handed it over, and went on: "Have you seen anything in the papers about some nightshade poisonings in Maine?"

"Yes; but there wasn't much."

"They call it here one of those tragic accidents. Two of the children got well, one died, one's missing."

Harold offered a fragment of his past: "I et a mushroom, once."

"But you recovered."

"Only just."

"There seems to be some mystery as to how these children got hold of the berries. I'm going up there tonight, and I'll be staying at a place called Burnsides. I don't know their number; if you want me, you can probably get me through the Ford's Center exchange. I'll be back early Monday morning; my train leaves the Grand Central Station at ten tonight. You have about an hour and a half to read up on deadly nightshade for me; make me a short précis, anything you can find in the books downstairs. Try the herbal, the botany, the medical books, the encyclopedia—I don't know anything about the plant."

"O.K.," said Harold.

"If I want you to get me any more information, I'll call you up, probably late tomorrow afternoon. I may use the code."

Harold's saturnine visage brightened, and was transformed by a boyish and candid expression of pleasure. He himself had imagined and constructed the code, without which he liked to think that his or Gamadge's life might someday be in danger. Gamadge affected to be amused by the code, but had sometimes found it useful.

"Don't let Martin sneak out," he continued. "Last time I had to pay eleven dollars for advertising, and a reward to that bakery."

"O.K."

"If you say that again, I shall go out of my mind. Have you absolutely no vocabulary?"

Harold asked in a colorless tone: "What vocabulary would *you* use, if you had to say 'yes' all the time?"

"Hanged if I know. Get to it, and let me put my affairs in order."

An hour and a half later, as Gamadge stood in the front hall, hat on his head and suitcase beside him on the floor, Harold brought him a sheaf of typed papers.

"Good for you." Gamadge ran through them. "Let's see. *Solanum Nigrum Linnaeus.* Also 'Black, Deadly or Garden Nightshade.' Also, *Atropa Belladonna.* That's the poison, is it?"

"Yes. I put some notes about atropine later on."

"I see you did. Plant grows practically all over the world, in shaded, woody places. I had no idea. 'Notation on Atropine.' Fatal stuff, isn't it? One-hundredth of a grain is the normal dose, and half a grain can kill; usually does, because you absorb it so fast that you don't get the remedies in time. You start with dryness of the nose and throat; you get lightheaded, and sometimes delirious; you fall into a stupor; and then, after some hours or—good heavens—some days, you die. Death results from failure of the heart and respiratory system."

"No pain," said Harold.

"No. That's a comfort; and children shake off the effects better than older persons do. One of these children didn't shake off the effects, though; probably didn't get the remedies soon enough. What does the plant look like?"

"I drew a picture."

"Good for you; here it is, and very nice too, if somewhat stylized. Where's the description? Grows quite tall—two and a half feet. Berries rather attractive: big, black, shiny, with a sweetish taste. But the plant has a disagreeable smell, and every part of it is poisonous. And some people grow it in their gardens! Ugh. Well, I'm off. Good-bye, and thanks for this, Harold. It's just what I wanted."

He seized his coat from Theodore, picked up his bag, waved a farewell to Athalie, grinning from the kitchen door, and stumbled over Martin, who was making every effort to get out of the house before his master did.

CHAPTER TWO

Black Berries

STATE DETECTIVE MITCHELL, a graying, stockily built man with sharp light-blue eyes, did not usually show or express emotion of any kind; but his wooden face beamed mildly when he shook hands with Gamadge on Saturday morning.

"You're a sport," he said. "Sheriff wants me to say he thinks he can get a requisition through for your expenses. That's only fair. The trip ain't cheap, and neither is Burnsides."

"Much obliged to you both," said Gamadge, laughing. "But where would the subsidy come from? The Village Improvement Society?"

"I guess you'll think we need some improvement when you hear the whole of the story. But I won't say a word about it till you've had some breakfast. My car's over here."

He wrestled Gamadge's bag away from him and led the way across the station platform to a well-worn two-seater. Gamadge sniffed the air, while Mitchell stowed the bag in the rumble.

"Don't worry about my expenses," he said. "I'm glad to have an excuse for getting up here again. I rather wish it was for golf, though; I'd like to hear the crows cawing. Hope you'll excuse me for saying so."

"It does seem a kind of a shame," admitted Mitchell. "I don't know that I blame you." They got into the car, and Mitchell started it. "You ever been up here this time of the year, Mr. Gamadge?" he asked. "We think it's the best time of all. Nothing like Maine in September."

"When the summer people go, as you so tactfully remarked last night. Yes, I stayed up over Labor Day, once. Glorious; but pretty cold at night."

They left Ford's Center and took the highway. It ran between stubble fields and pastures, with an occasional stretch of dark pinewoods, an apple orchard, a weather-beaten farm.

"Here's the turning down to Ford's Beach," said Mitchell. "We're halfway to Burnsides now."

A small, shiny coupé approached at a leisurely pace. It was driven by an elderly lady in black, who gave them a fixed, benevolent smile.

"Another early bird, and I think from her expression an addlepated one," remarked Gamadge.

"She's staying at the Pegram House," said Mitchell, "but I haven't the pleasure of her acquaintance."

As they neared a grove of towering pines a state policeman came riding slowly towards them on his motorcycle. He saluted, and Gamadge leaned out to wave at him. "That's young Pottle, isn't it?" he asked, peering after the dark, solemn-looking youth.

"Yes; taking day shift on the Gypsy Patrol."

"You're actually guarding them?"

"Thought we might as well; their men all went back to winter quarters in Boston last week, and there's nobody in camp but women and children. Feeling's running pretty high in the farms around here, and we don't want 'em molested. Besides, if they get a whiff of any kind of trouble, they disappear if they can. The ground kind of opens and swallows 'em. They can move awful quick for folks with their kind of transport; and you never know whether it's bad conscience or just gypsy. We want to keep an eye on 'em till we get this thing settled, one way or the other."

"They're really getting the blame for these nightshade poisonings?"

"Yes, they are."

The camp appeared, set in a ragged clearing among the tall pines. It was a dingy agglomeration of tents, rubbish heaps, and faded clothes hung out on a line. A neglected-looking horse peered out from behind a caravan, beside which stood a snub-nosed and ancient car, lopsided on its high chassis. A young woman with a baby in her arms sat on a box near the roadside, staring incuriously at the passers-by.

"Prettiest gypsy I ever saw," declared Gamadge. "Hang it all, Mitchell, they *are* going to turn out romantic, I know they are."

"They ain't romantic. You wait till you meet 'em."

Half a mile farther, Burnsides came into view on the right. Named locally in the plural for its two proprietors, it was a low, rectangular building, planted starkly in its bare and treeless yard, with a line of hardly less ornamental barns and garages behind it. No money had been wasted on outward show; but a wood fire burned on the hearth of the lobby, and Mr. Burnside was ready with a welcome. He was a lank, red-faced man, whose store clothes had not been altered to fit him.

"Right upstairs, Mr. Gamadge," he said. "You're the first of the late-season guests, and you can have your pick of rooms. I thought you'd like this back one, with bath."

"I do," said Gamadge.

"We don't have room service, but you can holler down the front or the rear stairs, if you want anything. Mis' Burnside says breakfast will be ready when you are."

"Give me twenty minutes."

Gamadge washed, shaved, changed into tweeds, and joined Mitchell in the barnlike dining room. Fat Mrs. Burnside and the hired help plied them with cereals, coffee, eggs and bacon, codfish cakes and homemade piccalilly. Gamadge, knowing her to be her own cook, praised everything, in the intervals of stuffing himself. She complimented him in return:

"You're a man worth cookin' for; you eat as good as the hunters do."

When they were comfortably settled in front of the lobby fire, Mitchell laid an open notebook on his knee and filled his pipe.

"You know any more about this business now than you did when I talked to you last night?" he asked.

"I've read up a little on nightshade and atropine—that's all."

"I'll start from the beginning, then, with the lay of the land. You know the two routes that take you from this vicinity to Oakport; the short cut just below here, which runs through a stretch of woods and comes out at the crossroads this side of Oakport Bridge; and the regular road, which branches off from the highway about a mile north of this, skirts the woods and marshes, and runs through the crossroads and on out to Oakport Point. State police headquarters are at the crossroads; and headquarters is probably where young Trainor was bound for when he took his skid. He was found about halfway across the short cut; it's a bad road, dark as pitch at night, soft where it isn't stony, and likely as not to have puddles between the ruts. He was in a hurry that night, and I guess he didn't use his best judgment.

"I don't have to remind you of that back road that runs up from Oakport, past Tucon, and hits the shore a little way south of Harper's Rocks. The Rocks is only a summer colony, as you know; most everybody clears out by Labor Day, because after that there are no deliveries from Oakport or the Center—you have to drive in, all of five miles, for milk and vegetables and ice. The Ormistons were the last to leave, and on Tuesday they were packed to go.

"The road turns as you pass the last cottage, and you drive due west for half a mile. Then you can turn north for Bailtown, or you can come back down past the Beasley farm, till you hit this highway, couple of miles above here. Between the east and the west road it's all thick woods, with a trail running through from Harper's Rocks—it comes out just below Beasley's. You can make it in a car, but you want to look out for snags.

"Got the layout? It's a horseshoe; five miles from Oakport to Harper's Rocks, half a mile around, five miles from the Beasley farm to the gypsy camp, say. Now, then; on Tuesday morning, at ten—"

"Just one moment," interrupted Gamadge. "Where were all these children, when they got hold of the nightshade? And why had they converged?"

"Converged?"

"Yes. They must have been together, I suppose."

"Together?"

"When they got hold of the berries," repeated Gamadge, patiently.

"They didn't converge. They were home."

"Home!"

"Unless the gypsies were on the road. You never can tell where they are; but they say they were in camp."

"Quite a stretch of territory in between the places."

"Quite a stretch. I'll start at Harper's Rocks, do it chronologically. At ten A.M., daylight saving time, on Tuesday, September the fifth, Tommy Ormiston was put out to play on his sand pile. The rest of the family was busy closing up the house for the winter. They have two cars and a trailer—sort of thing that looks like a grand piano; Ormiston totes his pictures and easels and things in it. The expressman was ordered for twelve noon.

"The cottage is high up on the cliff, with a front yard sloping down to the road. Halfway down the slope is a pine tree, and under the tree is the sand pile. Tommy Ormiston is the youngest child—there are two older ones. Mr. Ormiston was in his studio, packing sketches and things; the studio is on the ocean side of the cottage. Mrs. Ormiston was on that side of the house, too; or down cellar. The older children were upstairs, putting away their traps for the winter. Ormiston—you've heard of him, I think you said."

"Yes. Distinguished artist."

"He's a—" Mitchell consulted his notes—"a Social Perfectionist."

"What's that?"

"He didn't say. But he said if you are one, you can't have any servants. It's degrading to them, and to the employer. Anybody that works for you has to sit down and eat at the table with the family, and play word games in the evening."

"Word games?"

"Ormiston said word games. There must have been a lot of Social Perfection going on in Maine for a long time, but he seemed to think it was a novelty. Well, it's a good-sized cottage, so they need considerable help; and the way he gets round it is like this: he has young people come up and do the work for their keep. No wages—they're part of the family."

"That isn't a new idea, either; not by a long shot."

"Well, it results in some peculiar setups, as you can imagine. This summer the Ormistons' cook is—" Mitchell consulted his notes again—"a Miss Strangways; an artist. And a young feller named Breck, Davidson Breck—employed in the advertising business—he's the children's nurse."

"Is Mr. Breck making a success of it?"

"I don't see how he can be, because he's handyman and general dishwasher besides. He's badly upset about Tommy; says he never left him alone for an hour before, and wouldn't have this time, only Ormiston kept him nailing crates and moving trunks downstairs. He'd already closed up and fastened all the front shutters."

"I see."

"Yes; the front of the house was blind. It was nearly eleven before he had a chance to go out and look for the boy. He wasn't there. His pail and shovel were on the sand pile, and his hat, and a few of the berries; but Breck, not being country-bred, didn't notice 'em. He wasn't scared at first; strolled round the house, went up and down the road and a little way into the woods, along that cart trail; then he suddenly got into a panic, and sprinted back to the house to tell 'em the boy was gone.

"Miss Strangways came in about then—she'd been down on the beach, clearing out the bathing cabin they have there, and locking it up for the winter. Before that, she'd been in the studio, helping Ormiston. Soon as she heard about the boy she dropped everything, jumped in her little car, and went off to scour the roads. Breck did the rocks and beaches. Mrs. Ormiston—she's a calm sort of lady—she waited with the two other children till the expressman showed up, and sent him off again to get help. Their telephone had just been disconnected, so they didn't get organized till after the Beasley search was under way. Ormiston stayed home, hopping mad because his arrangements had been held up, and everybody had quit waiting on him.

"Tommy was found about one o'clock, by a state policeman. He'd rolled down into a little ravine in the woods, 'way up towards the north edge of 'em. He was half covered with leaves, and not a scratch on him. He was lightheaded, but he wasn't in that coma they end up with—luckily for him."

"Stupor," said Gamadge.

"Oh. Didn't know there was any difference. He came around wonderful under treatment, and now he's as well as ever; but the trouble is, we can't get much out of him. He says a lady in a car gave him the berries. Well, anything in skirts is a lady to Tommy Ormiston, and he don't know one car from another. He can't remember a thing about wandering off in the woods. No use taking him down and trying to get him to identify a gypsy; they all say he couldn't do it. He's only six and a half."

"A child of his size wouldn't see much, looking up at somebody in a car window."

"If there *was* a car window, or a car, or even a lady. He may have imagined the whole thing; the doctor says this poison makes 'em get mixed up afterwards, and likely to imagine things."

"Could he have found the berries himself?"

"There are some in the woods, near the edge of the trail; but if he went in there and picked 'em, he must have brought 'em all the way back to the sand pile, and then trekked off again. As for the ones he left behind, they were seen, and identified as nightshade, before he was brought home; luckily for him. The doctor knew just what to do for him. Doctor Dickson, it was; Ames—you remember Doctor Ames?—he's away on his vacation.

"Our next stop is the Beasley farm, which is a nice enough old place, but lonesome. Not a house near it for over a mile, and the tidal river runs in behind it, through the marshes, and cuts it off on the west. Sarah Beasley was one of nine children, but only three of them were home on the farm this summer—Sarah, about seven years old; a girl of fourteen called Claribel; and the baby.

"They have an old hay barn beside the road, screened off with trees and bushes. Sarah's tortoise-shell cat lived there, and brought up all her kittens there. She had six this summer; Sarah put in all her spare time with them. She'd bought six bells and six ribbons for 'em; different color for each cat. Let's see—" Mitchell consulted his notes—"Gold, silver, green, blue, red and purple. She kept 'em on a nail in the barn, and every time she went out to see the cats, she dressed 'em up in the ribbons and the bells.

"On Tuesday morning, few minutes after ten, she went out to the barn as usual. By eleven she hadn't come back, and Mrs. Beasley missed her and went to look for her. The six cats rushed out, the way kittens do, and they had on their ribbons and their bells—all but one; the white one. Her bell was red, and she didn't have it on; nobody's seen it since. Looks as though Sarah was interrupted before she finished the job.

"Well, Sarah wasn't in the barn, and the old cat wasn't there either. Mrs. Beasley looked around, wondering what had become of 'em; and suddenly she noticed some of the berries scattered around on the barn floor. She screamed so, Beasley heard her clear across the cow pasture back of the house, because she knew what they were. They found more of them on a bare knoll that rises up behind the barn, and slopes down in the direction of the marsh. We think Sarah wandered up there, lightheaded; the cat after her. It would complain when the going got rough, and Sarah would pick it up and carry it. If that's the way it was, and they got in the marsh, they won't be found."

Mitchell sucked at his pipe, removed it, and applied a match to it. When he had it going again, he went on:

"She may have gone into the woods, and met Tommy Ormiston, and got the berries from him; or he may have got them from her. But it's a lot of ground for a child of her age to cover, and Mrs. Beasley says she never went off the farm before in her life. Whatever those two children did do, they never walked those five miles to the Bartram house and back again; but some of the nightshade got there, sometime between eleven o'clock and noon.

"I guess you know the Bartram mansion, even if you haven't had a good look at it; you can hardly see it from the road now, the place is so overgrown and wild. Old lady Bartram—she died last spring—she wouldn't have the grounds touched, hardly, after her husband died, years ago. It's a fine old place, built in the days when the Bartrams owned sailing ships, and imported silk, instead of making it.

"There are two sons—Carroll and George. Carroll, the eldest, runs the silk mills; George sold out to him when the old man died, and went into the importing business abroad; Holland. He married there, and his little girl was born there, about five years ago. He had a nice house, nice business, all his money sunk in it; didn't mean to come back to this country till he retired, if then; but a couple of weeks ago the European situation got too much for him, and scared him out. He managed to get accommodations for his family on some ship or other, and they landed in Canada on Sunday. He bought a car and started for New York, where his partners are. They meant to take the trip in easy stages, stopping off at Oakport on Tuesday for lunch, to see his folks.

"It was a big day in the family, all of 'em except the two men meeting for the first time. Carroll Bartram wanted the two children to know each other. He lost his wife when this little girl Julia was born, seven years ago, their first child. He made a terrible fuss over her—too much of a fuss, Doc Loring says, and the nurse wasn't much better. This trained nurse, Miss Ridgeman, she's been with the little girl ever since she was born. Bartram kept the place open for 'em all the year round, put in a furnace, modern plumbing, I don't know what all. You couldn't beat those nurseries at the top of the house anywhere. He was scared to death of infections and accidents, kept running up here for weekends, spent nearly all summer here. He's kind of dazed by what happened, but I don't know whether I don't feel sorrier for Miss Ridgeman. I don't believe she'll ever get over it.

"What did happen was this: Bartram only keeps one regular indoor servant up here, an old cook; they'd engaged a girl to come in on Tuesday and help with the lunch. It's hard to get extra people for short jobs this time of year, and the girl couldn't come till twelve thirty, on that bus from York; so at twelve Miss Ridgeman put little Julia in her summerhouse, and went to lend a hand in the kitchen. This summerhouse is really a play-house, it's been enclosed by wire netting, and the child used to spend hours there; but she was never left alone in it for any length of time before. It's only a few yards from the house, and Bartram's study is on that side; he was there, looking out papers to show his brother, and he didn't hear or see a thing.

"The George Bartrams arrived about one, and of course the first thing they wanted, after they'd seen Carroll, was to meet little Julia. Miss Ridgeman went out to get her, but she wasn't in the summerhouse; the nurse couldn't find her anywhere. She came running back to the house, nearly crazy, to say the child was lost. Carroll started off through the east grounds, shouting. The Georges couldn't make out, at first, what all the fuss was about—they're used to chasing after this little Irma of theirs, and they didn't see anything to scare anybody in a child of seven wandering off for a short stroll on her own. But George went off through the back gate to the lane that runs behind the place, and Mrs. Bartram took Irma and began hunting around towards the west end of the place.

"As I said, it's very much overgrown, lots of hiding places for a child to crawl into. Mrs. Bartram and Irma went poking around among the trees and bushes, and finally they got right down to the southwest corner of the property.

"There's a big pine tree in that corner, with branches trailing on the ground. All of a sudden, Irma got down on her hands and knees and crawled under a branch; she backed out again, laughing and pointing, and Mrs. Bartram lifted up the branch. Julia was in there, looking as if she was asleep; she had a stalk of nightshade in her hand, and two of the berries were gone.

"She was in that coma, all right—stupor, I mean—although she'd eaten the berries less than an hour before. Mrs. Bartram got her out on the grass, and called the others; George Bartram recognized the nightshade, but nobody knew what poison it was. Miss Ridgeman's training showed; she calmed right down, carried the child into the house and started first aid, Mrs. Bartram helping. Their doctor—Loring—got there in five minutes; he lives in the village. He started in treating her for atropine poisoning, told them to call up clinics and hospitals in Boston to advise on remedies, and got hold of another doctor. He saw she was in a bad way, right from the start. Ames, as I said, is away, and young Dickson was up at the Rocks, by that time, working over Tommy Ormiston; so Loring telephoned to Cogswell, our medical examiner at Ford's Center. You know him. He arrived inside of half an hour, and stayed there right along. She died around half past two; Cogswell says she had an allergy for the poison, and nothing could have saved her.

"The George Bartrams stayed on, naturally. They're having the funeral this morning—early, to escape sightseers and newspapers. Carroll Bartram has been mighty decent about it all; it's pretty near wrecked him, but he helped us a lot, keeping down local excitement and throwing in his weight to protect the gypsies.

"As for them, they've got us licked. Cogswell and Loring went down to the camp Wednesday, to try and find out whether they'd been peddling in the neighborhood on Tuesday; they sell sweet grass and baskets, you know, besides telling fortunes on the beach. They don't go far afield, usually, because they have no transport except the caravan, and it's anchored for the summer—they sleep in it, some of them. But just now they have the use of that old car—you may have noticed it as we went by.

"Cogswell and Loring found that one of the children in the camp was convalescing from something or other; it might or might not have been from atropine poisoning. He's a little boy about seven, and the gypsies say he's had a cold. Cogswell thinks it may have been intestinal flu; and Doc Loring's looking after him. He's weak, and he's sleepy and languid; that's all the symptoms there are. Loring says you can't get a word out of him; cruel to try. He'll be all right in a few days, probably.

"The gypsies swear they were in camp all Tuesday till afternoon, and they swear they don't know what nightshade is like. But, as I remarked before, they'll say anything to keep out of a jam. They'd heard about the berry poisonings; Pottle told 'em. Everybody'd been warned to look out for some crazy person going round giving children poison berries.

"Well, that's the story, Mr. Gamadge. I'll be glad to hear what you think of it."

CHAPTER THREE

What Gamadge Thought

GAMADGE'S CIGARETTE, hanging forgotten between his fingers, had been sending a thin blue column of smoke up into the quiet air; he now remembered it, took a puff at it, and asked: "Cogswell an authority on poisons?"

"Not that I know of; but even if he was, he wouldn't let a thing like that go through without getting outside advice. He was right there on the spot, knew well enough what she died of, saw the evidence himself, had all the witnesses on the premises; besides which, the news about the other children had come through. But he persuaded Bartram to let him perform an autopsy, Loring as assistant. Bartram was willing, poor feller; he couldn't believe she'd died of those two berries, in that short time; especially as Tommy Ormiston was getting along all right. He wanted to know what had happened to her. Cogswell and Loring performed the autopsy there in the house, that same afternoon.

"By evening, Cogswell had got in touch with the best analyst in Boston; the analysis was begun on Wednesday, and we got the report yesterday. You ought to see it; I didn't know there were so many poisons in the world. And you ought to see the bill! Bartram paid it."

"Cogswell had a certain ruthlessness, as I remember him."

"He don't worry much about folks' feelings, when it's a question of keeping his records clear. The experts said she was allergic to atropine, and Cogswell and Loring signed the death certificate: 'Death resulting from failure of the heart and respiratory system, caused by the absorption of atropine from berries of the plant commonly called deadly nightshade.' Something like that. He finally let them bury the little girl today, as I told you."

Gamadge smoked in silence for a minute; then he asked: "Is there an official theory, or are you all waiting for evidence?"

"You can't call it a theory; we've made some guesses."

"I'm capable of doing that, anyhow. Let's see; the popular suspects are the gypsies, and of course they are the most obvious ones. What is the contention? That one of them decided to go on a peddling tour, taking that antediluvian bus." Gamadge paused. "Did you say they had acquired it recently?"

"It belongs to an old lady member of the tribe; she's visiting the camp just now. Pottle says they're always going and coming, you never know where any of 'em will turn up."

"In fact, they are nomads. Are they all at the camp now—the ones that were there on Tuesday morning?"

"Pottle says he thinks they are. He checked up on 'em Tuesday afternoon, when he went down there and warned 'em about the nightshade. None of 'em has left since. This old lady that owns the car, she's a fortuneteller down at Whitewater Pier; she's a cut above tents and caravans, now—lives under a roof. Puts on a lot of dog. Quite a character."

"Well, she or another takes the little gypsy who is recovering from something, and starts off on a peddling trip. Along the road that leads to the Beasley farm she lets him get out and play by the wayside, or in the woods. He picks a bouquet of nightshade, which she doesn't notice among his other botanical specimens. They don't stop at the Beasley farm—why don't they, Mitchell?"

"Farmers don't buy from gypsies—don't let 'em on their land, if they can help it."

"Of course not. Well, they see little Sarah Beasley in the barn; it's on the edge of the road?"

"Right on the edge."

"The gypsy is in the habit of sending the little boy to offer small wares to children. He offers Sarah a bunch of nightshade, in return for which she pays him—what? Would she have money in her pocket?"

"I doubt it."

"But somehow, she gets the nightshade. The gypsies drive on to Harper's Rocks, where all the cottages are found to be deserted. A little boy is seen, playing outside a shuttered house. He, also, gets a free present of deadly nightshade, and the lady in the car is all he remembers of the episode."

"You'd think he'd remember the boy."

"Hard to dogmatize, where children of that age are concerned. Her appearance may have been arresting."

"He and Sarah might have given the little gypsy some toy for the berries."

"Perhaps they did. Any bit of junk would tempt a seven-year-old gypsy. Well, the conveyance moves on—to the Bartram place. Is that a logical stop for it?"

"Matter of fact, it is. It's on the edge of town, before you go on out to the summer colony on the Point. It's only a little way beyond the entrance to that back road."

"And is there much traffic on the back roads just now?"

"Practically none. No deliveries, as I said, and the summer folks gone."

"Car mightn't have been seen by anybody. It stops at the back gate of the Bartram house, and the gypsy sees a child in the summerhouse. Could she have done so, Mitchell?"

"Not very clear, but she could."

"She sends the little gypsy in."

"I don't know why she should send him in. He hasn't made a sale so far, and besides, it's trespassing. They're deathly afraid of doing that."

"Shall I be maligning them if I suggest that the little boy might have been instructed to pick up any unconsidered trifle that he liked the looks of?"

"Well, no; I guess not."

"So in he goes. If he's seen from the house, it's only a little boy of seven. Do you know if the gypsies ever visited the place?"

"Old lady Bartram liked the gypsies—made rather a pet of one or two of 'em."

"Familiar ground! Of course he goes in. He hands over his own particular line of goods, and retires to the car. Is that lane populous, Mitchell?"

"It's hardly used at all, except by tradesmen, and Mr. Bartram. His garage is on it, opposite the gate."

"Then they have a line of retreat to Oakport Village. Would they be likely to get through to the short cut without being noticed?"

"Oakport goes more or less to sleep in the middle of the day, and this time of year it passes out entirely, except when the mails come in and the movies open and close. Anyhow, nobody saw any gypsies go through; we've asked, and we're going to go on asking."

"Once out of the cut, they'd have only a quarter of a mile or so to negotiate before they got back to camp; I suppose they weren't seen on the highway."

"Not so far as we can find out."

"Well, sometime along the route, the small boy samples his own wares. He's pretty much all in when they get back. His friends find the nightshade, and they know what's the matter with him; it's ridiculous to suppose that they aren't familiar with every herb and berry in this vicinity. They administer drastic first aid, which saves his life, but which leaves him considerably weakened; gypsy dosage must be awful. Perhaps they called in that old grandame to help cast a few spells over him, besides suggesting ancient tribal remedies."

"No, they didn't do that. She was here as far back as Sunday, Pottle says."

"I shouldn't have thought she'd leave Whitewater Pier, just now, with the whole rag, tag, and bobtail from Boston coming up there on Labor Day to get its fortunes told."

"She might have left to get away from the mob. She's pretty old, I should say, and she thinks a lot of herself. She's the rightful Queen of Scotland, or something; tells you about it first thing."

"I'm glad you warned me of that. Well, there isn't a hitch in the theory, except Tommy Ormiston's failure to report a little boy. I assume that you've all considered it; doesn't anybody feel like adopting it?"

"Sheriff does, I can tell you. If he can lay it to the gypsies, and run them off the premises, and promise not to let 'em come back, folks will stop barricading their farms and keeping the children indoors. School starts next week; we've got to raise the siege, or we'll be in all kinds of a mess. Cogswell wants the gypsies to take the rap; he says the little gypsy certainly had some of the berries, and it's a closed case. It makes him tired, the way they won't co-operate; and he'd like to get rid of 'em."

"Have they been camping there for long?"

"Since before my time. Half a century."

"And never done anything worse than a spot of pilfering, now and then?"

"The children pick things up when they find 'em lying around; the older ones toe the line pretty careful."

"Are you the only person standing out for pure reason, as against guesswork and the undistributed middle?"

"No. Bartram don't want 'em pestered. He's been used to treating 'em like human beings; old lady Bartram, as I said, used to like 'em. Had 'em up to the house, before she got so sick, to tell her fortune. Bought dozens of baskets from 'em. Some of their baskets are first-rate, you know; they cost quite a lot. Old Mrs. Bartram had a collection, and gave 'em to people for Christmas."

"Any of her protégés still in camp?"

"I don't know. Wait, though; that Martha—the one you saw with the baby—I think I heard Mrs. Bartram was quite interested in her, when she was a little girl. Kept her in decent clothes and shoes. So she married a Yankee, as they always call us."

"I thought they weren't allowed to marry gentiles—as they also call us."

"They do it all the time, around here. Yes, Loring says old Mrs. Bartram was interested in Martha Stanley."

"Good old tribal name."

"I never knew a gypsy that wasn't called Stanley."

"Is her husband a member of the tribe, in good standing?"

"No, he's dead. Died of pneumonia last winter. He was a friend of Pottle's, and that's why Pottle don't want the gypsies blamed unless we get evidence against 'em."

"Have they any other influential friends?"

"Doc Loring. He's taken care of 'em for years; gives 'em a call now and then to make sure they haven't any infectious diseases in camp, and that they keep the place reasonably clean. He says they're the most harmless bunch of half-wits in the community, and don't do anywhere near as much damage as the village and farm people do. He says they get blamed for everything, from forest fires to chicken stealing, and all because they ain't Aryans. He says if he was mosquito-proof, the way they are, he'd like to be a gypsy himself. He says they're innocent but astray; something like that. He's quite a comical feller."

" 'An innocent life, yet far astray'; don't tell me you have the Last Wordsworthian dispensing pills over in the village of Oakport!"

"Ormiston thinks it was the gypsies; but he talks so much, you don't hardly know what he really thinks. Mr. and Mrs. Beasley, they don't think anything."

"Well, let's tackle the other comforting possibility: a lunatic lady in a car."

"You think that's a comforting theory, do you?"

"Yes, because it assumes irresponsibility on the part of the agent."

"A crazy woman may be planning to distribute some more nightshade berries, and how are we going to prevent it?"

"She won't do it again if it was just an unfortunate blunder. I assume a well-meaning half-wit, confusing nightshade berries with huckleberries."

"Even a half-wit would come forward, if she was well-meaning."

"Would she, indeed? If I were in her shoes I might come forward; but not in person, Mitchell—not in person! I should send you a letter from the uttermost fringes of the jungles of Central America. But as she is a mere wisp of conjecture, let's eliminate her for the moment. You know what we are now up against?"

"Oh, yes; I know," growled Mitchell. "Premeditation, and motive; but you tell me what these families had in common, for anybody to get at 'em through their children."

"I'll tell you two things the children had in common. First, their age. They were all approximately seven years old; but of course that may mean no more than that seven-year-olds are just old enough to be allowed to play alone, and just young enough to accept berries from strangers. The nightshade was pretty well advertised, wasn't it?"

"Advertised?"

"Deliberately or not, who can say? There were berries on Tommy Ormiston's sand pile, in the Beasley barn and on the slope behind it, in Julia Bartram's hand; which makes it even more likely that mass murder was not intended. I mean, the two children who were found got treatment for atropine poisoning almost immediately, and Julia Bartram died only because she was allergic to it. We are to suppose that if Sarah Beasley had been found she might well have recovered, too."

"The berries were left there on purpose, so some of those children could be cured?"

"Let us charitably hope so."

"Then we have three reasons, anyway, why nightshade was used. First, the children would like the look of the berries, and be willing to eat 'em; second, they'd advertise the atropine; third, they'd make the whole thing look like some kind of an accident, and perhaps keep us on that tack—where we still are, come to think of it."

"There's another reason, of course—atropine confuses, and makes the wits to wander. Nobody quite knows whether Tommy Ormiston really saw a lady in a car, or merely dreamed it. There may be other reasons still."

"You said the children had something else in common."

"They were alone that morning by the merest chance. Sarah Beasley had no fixed time for visiting her cats, and no exclusive rights in the barn. Tommy Ormiston was abandoned on his sand pile for an hour because it was moving day; the rest of the family was engaged elsewhere; and Mr. Breck happened to have closed the shutters, so that he could not be watched or overlooked from the front windows. Julia Bartram was left alone in her summerhouse for about the same length of time, because of an unprecedented family occasion—the unexpected arrival of her uncle, aunt and cousin from Europe. Her case is also complicated by the fact that the extra help which had been engaged arrived late; otherwise, the nurse would not have stayed so long in the kitchen.

"We are confronted with coincidence, here; unless we accept the theory that the nightshade was distributed by somebody whose wits were in good working order, and who was to some extent acquainted with these households, their habits and their plans."

Mitchell shook his head. "I tell you there ain't any motive in the world that could include the Bartrams, and the Ormistons, and the Beasleys."

"I'm inclined to agree with you. Let us suppose then that one of these children was to be eliminated, for reasons of gain, revenge, we know not what; the others were therefore given the berries for purposes of camouflage—to distract our attention from the family under attack."

"The Beasleys were camouflage, then. They just haven't got an enemy in the world, and nobody has anything to gain by poisoning one of their children. We know all about the Beasleys."

"Who knows all about anyone? I'm inclined to think you're right, though; the Beasleys look very much like camouflage, poor souls."

Mitchell sucked gloomily at his pipe. "Well," he said, "I asked you to come up and meet the families."

"But why should they meekly submit to meeting me?"

"Loring knows who you are, and he's told the Bartrams; they want to see you."

"How about the distinguished Ormiston?"

"He's heard of you, too. He said I could bring you along."

Gamadge looked at Mitchell rather wanly. "I sometimes wish," he said, "that I did not feel myself under an obligation to you, my dear Mr. Mitchell."

"You ain't; but if you was, you'd work it all off between now and Sunday night."

CHAPTER FOUR

The Companion of Sirius

"WE'LL START WITH the gypsies." Mitchell turned his car out of the Burnside precincts, and drove south. "Then we'll go to the Bartrams, by way of the short cut; from there to Harper's Rocks, and around to the Beasley farm."

The tall pines of the gypsy encampment towered ahead of them, and on their left a narrow dirt road wound between cornfields, and disappeared into the dark mouth of the woods beyond. Mitchell stopped.

"Here's the entrance to the short cut," he said. "Trainor used to take this way home, sometimes, when he was bound for headquarters. He reported there before he went off duty."

"What time?"

"No special time—usually about seven. He was late on Tuesday, account of all the extra trips to Beasley's. He was seen about seven fifteen, out Bailtown way—his regular beat. He lived in Oakport, and they were expecting him there for his supper. Cogswell says he could have died around eight."

"Who found him?"

"Farmer going through the cut, about six on Wednesday morning."

"Nobody miss him before that?"

"Yes, but lots of things can keep a trooper from coming home. Car trouble, accidents. They don't always report in. Use their judgment."

"Both he and Pottle were on this beat?"

"Yes, but Pottle was doing night work. He got shifted to day duty after Trainor was killed."

"He seems to have been on day duty last Tuesday afternoon. You said he came down here to warn the gypsies about nightshade carriers."

"He got routed out to help search for Sarah Beasley."

"Why did Trainor come down as far as this, instead of using the upper road?"

"Just patrolling the routes, I suppose; or giving the gypsies a look-in."

"Do they say he gave them a look-in, or haven't you asked them?"

"They say he didn't; but they wouldn't own up to seeing him last thing before he got killed in the short cut."

"Very annoying, they must be. Here comes Pottle; let's wait for him."

Officer Pottle rode up, and stopped beside the car. "Glad to see you back, Mr. Gamadge," he said. "Did you hear about Trainor?"

"Yes, and I'm awfully sorry. Mitchell thinks he may have ridden down on Tuesday evening to look in on the gypsies."

"He may have. We kind of get them on our minds, after their men go back to Boston; there are children in the camp. These gyps ain't afraid of anything on earth except jail and their own menfolks, but we like to keep an eye on 'em."

"He was late getting back to headquarters, Mitchell says; you didn't wait for him?"

"No, I started off as soon as I had my supper—went to Beasley's by the upper road."

"Who's taking his shift now?"

"Bowles."

"Queer, about Trainor getting killed that way in the short cut. He must have been well enough used to it."

"I wish somebody'd explain to me how it did happen. Last thing I would have expected, for Trainor to fall off his bike. He could loop the loops on it."

"There's always a last time, if you fellers will take chances," said Mitchell, irritably. "Is the whole family in camp today?"

"All there. I guess they'll be glad to get rid of the old lady; she rules the roost, all right. She's goin' back to Whitewater, Monday. Thinks she'll take the little sick feller with her, cure him up at the shore."

"I understand that she has delusions of grandeur," said Gamadge.

"You bet she has."

"Do you know these gypsies at all well, Pottle? Understand their mental processes, that sort of thing?"

"They haven't got any mental processes; I told Charlie Haines he was a fool to marry that girl Martha; but some fellers don't seem to want their wives brainy."

"Do you think they might make some kind of mistake about a thing like this nightshade? Mix it up with some other kind of berry?"

"No, I don't. I bet they know all the poisons in these woods, and a few more."

"Even the children?"

"I bet Martha's baby would have the colic if anybody showed it a poison berry of any kind. Don't forget they make their livin'—if you can call it a livin'—out of these woods and swamps; that sweet grass they make their baskets of, and all the rest of it. And the kids pick berries for sale before they're hardly able to talk."

"According to your ideas, they can't very well be responsible for this nightshade business, then."

"I don't know if they are or not; but if I had any say about it I wouldn't run Charlie Haines' wife and baby out of town without any more proof against 'em than a kid with hang-over from grippe."

"How about coming along and introducing me? Tell the old lady I want my fortune told?"

"Glad to." Pottle turned his machine and preceded them to the camp in a stately and official manner; with the result that when they arrived, no gypsy was to be seen. The old horse champed stoically at the hay in his nosebag, and ragged clothes flapped on the line; otherwise there was neither sound nor motion, and the pines crowded darkly up like an army. Pottle raised his voice:

"Hey, come out of it, everybody; I brought a gentleman to call on you." And as this brought no response, he added: "Wants Mrs. Stuart to tell his fortune."

Three women and a boy materialized suddenly from the gloom in the background, and stood gazing blankly, but with alert eyes, at the visitors. Gamadge had never seen passive resistance so perfectly illustrated. He took a good look at them.

The women, as is the wont of the modern tribes, managed to look both outlandish and dowdy. There was a very old one, an octogenarian, perhaps, although her hair was coal-black, and her spine a good deal straighter than Gamadge's own. She wore a long black silk dress with black lace ruffles at her neck and wrists, gold hooped earrings, and a long gilt chain, the ends of which were tucked into her belt. A black net veil was arranged on her head with a corner of it coming well down on her forehead, which gave her an air at once regal and nunlike. She stood immovable, her yellow hands clasped across the middle of her fitted basque.

A forlorn hag wavered irresolutely near the matriarch; she was ochre-skinned, almost toothless, and of uncertain age, and she wore a gray calico dress, a large black straw hat trimmed with poppies, and a Paisley shawl of unimaginable antiquity. Beside her stood a boy of nine or ten, who resembled any barefooted, undernourished country boy; except that he was dark beyond sunburn, and that his thin face wore an uneasy scowl.

Martha, without the baby, looked about eighteen. She was slim and neat in a faded pink gingham dress, the exotic note in her case being supplied by somebody's red satin evening shoes, and somebody's West Indian bandanna. The bright colors set off her pale skin and soft eyes to an extent that accounted for Mr. Charlie Haines' experiment in exogamy.

Gamadge took off his hat.

"I'm very glad to find you here, Mrs. Stuart," he said. "I think you tell fortunes at Whitewater. Pottle said you might be willing to tell mine. Pottle, will you introduce me?"

"Mr. Gamadge," said Pottle. "Mrs. Stuart, Georgina Stanley, Martha Stanley, and William Stanley."

Georgina, Martha and William Stanley stared; Mrs. Stuart bowed, in a formal and condescending manner.

"I will tell your fortune, gentleman," she said. "Come into the tent."

"Why not do it out here? It's such a nice day, and I don't at all mind an audience." Gamadge picked up a soapbox, placed it in friendly juxtaposition to a stump, and asked: "What is your fee?"

"Fifty cents, gentleman." Mrs. Stuart sat down on the soapbox, and Gamadge, adjusting himself to the top of the stump as best he could, produced two quarters. These he placed reverently in the old lady's hand. She drew a quick, complicated sign in the air with them, placed them in a bag that hung from her waist, and fixed Gamadge with a glittering eye, as bright and as black as jet. It seemed also to be as shallow as jet, but there was an unfathomable sharpness to it. She made no attempt to take his hand.

"You were born under a dark star, gentleman," she said, indifferently, her accent a strange combination of cockney, Scottish, and something vaguely European. Gamadge, looking interested, nodded.

"Curious," he said. "I beg your pardon, Mrs. Stuart—did I understand that you have Scots blood?"

"I am descended in direct line from King James of Scotland, Mr. Gamish."

Feeling obscurely Levantine, Gamadge continued: "Then you have second sight, no doubt, as well as the usual gifts of the gypsy."

"I have the second sight; and I am also the seventh daughter of a seventh daughter, Mr. Gamish."

"No wonder you saw at once that I was born under a dark star. But do you know its name, Mrs. Stuart? Do you know its name? Ah! I see that you do not." For the old lady, slightly taken aback, was looking at him with some annoyance.

"I cannot tell the name of the star," she said at last, with insufferable condescension, "until I know the day and hour of your nativity."

"Then I'll tell it to you," said Gamadge, "and save you all the trouble of figuring it out. It's the companion of Sirius."

Mrs. Stuart continued to fix his eye with her stony black one; he continued:

"There is no darker star in the heavens. It is so dark that no mortal eye has ever seen it; no, not with the biggest telescope ever fashioned by the hand of man. It is an astronomer's guess, Mrs. Stuart; a heavenly inference. Can there be a darker star than that? I don't think so."

William Stanley spoke, from the shelter of Georgina's skirt: "How do they know it's there?"

"They know it's there, William, through the perturbation of orbits. If you are interested, I shall explain fully some other time. Just now, I want to explain to this gifted lady exactly what it is that my nativity means to me: it means that I was born to perturb the orbits of others, myself remaining unsuspected and unseen. I will make a confession to you, Mrs. Stuart: I came here to find out whether you really had extra-sensory perception; I see that you have, and that I can discuss this nightshade mystery with you on equal terms."

The old lady, staggered to find her dupe endowed with a line of patter even more outrageous than her own, surveyed him steadily; in fact, the glance they now exchanged somewhat resembled that of two Roman augurs. But Mrs. Stuart found nothing to antagonize her in the personality of the eccentric in well-tailored tweeds who sat quietly in front of her, hands in the pockets of his coat, face serious, legs crossed, one shoulder higher than the other, eyes screwed up against the sun. His blunt features looked amiable; he was not the sort who ever came into her booth at Whitewater Pier, even on a bet. She said politely, and with apparent candor: "We know nothing about the nightshade, gentleman."

"If you say so, I believe you, of course. And none of your children here got any of the berries, because they know all the poisonous shrubs. You wouldn't pick nightshade, would you, William?"

He swung around on his stump to toss this question casually in William's direction. William, accustomed to blanket negation on all subjects, shook his head; adding for good measure: "Or the speckled mushrooms; or the poison ivy; or the poison sumac."

Gamadge, feeling rather than hearing a slight stir behind him, where Mitchell stood, continued with some haste:

"And you wouldn't take such things as poison berries from a stranger, either; not even from a lady in a car."

William lapsed still further; he became informative: "She only gave me a piece of candy, and started to take my picture."

"Oh." Gamadge was again conscious of that slight, involuntary shuffle of feet behind him. He said: "Started to take your picture, did she?"

"Yes, and she had the littlest camera I ever saw."

"When was this?"

William suddenly became aware of a certain tenseness in the atmosphere about him. He looked around him at the expressionless faces of his relatives, kicked the pine needles beneath his feet, and shook his head.

"Yesterday? The day before?"

Silence.

"Can you tell me what she was like, William?"

Silence.

"Or what kind of car she drove?" Gamadge waited a moment, and then said, rising: "Not that it matters; but here's a quarter for answering my questions; some of 'em, anyway. And if you can remember anything more about that lady, there's a reward out."

William's disinherited face was turned up to him hungrily.

"A reward," said Gamadge. "Grown people get money; boys get anything within reason that they happen to want most. Have you a bicycle, William?"

Poor William almost sank under this question; he glanced at Mrs. Stuart's forbidding countenance, and back at Gamadge. His shake of the head was desolate.

"Well, you think it over, and talk it over with your family. See if you can't remember something about this kind lady that gave you candy and nearly took your picture. Why didn't she entirely take it, William?"

But William's informative mood had definitely passed. He now looked as witless as the rest of the tribe did. Gamadge turned to old Mrs. Stuart.

"Too bad about the little Bartram girl, wasn't it?" he said. "Did you know old Mrs. Bartram, Mrs. Stuart?"

Mrs. Stuart raised two fingers in a pontifical gesture, lifted her eyes to heaven, and said: "Mrs. Bartram was a spirit!"

This encouraged William to make another desperate bid for favor. Associating all proffers of information, relevant or irrelevant, with currency, he said in an eager tone: "She gave Grammer that dress and that chain."

Georgina coughed. Gamadge ignored William's remark, and addressed Mrs. Stuart cheerfully:

"Well, it's been a great pleasure meeting you all. I don't see the baby, though; and I don't see your other grandson.

I meant to leave a little souvenir with each of them. Here's William's."

He placed the promised quarter in William's hand. Mrs. Stuart said, equably: "Take him into the tents, Georgina."

"I won't disturb them?" asked Gamadge.

"No, gentleman."

"I understand that you're taking the little fellow who had flu to Whitewater Beach with you."

"On Monday, if Doctor Loring says he is strong enough."

Gamadge followed Georgina to the farthest tent, the flap of which had been fastened back. It was hot inside, and the dark-eyed, crop-haired little boy who lay on a comfortable-looking cot within had pushed off his coverings. The woollen bathing suit he wore revealed him as sturdily built, and far from emaciated by his illness. He lay relaxed, staring peacefully at nothing.

"He'll do," said Gamadge. "What's his name?"

Georgina mumbled, as well as she could for lack of teeth: "Elias."

"Hello, Elias." The dark eyes turned to him, and wandered sleepily away again.

"Sleeps most of the time," lisped Georgina.

"Very wise of him. I know what one's like after flu—a rag. Well, thank you very much, Mrs. Stanley. See if you can persuade William to remember something about the lady in the car. Just a tourist, I suppose, but even if she was, my offer stands. I'll give the baby a miss, but here's its lucky piece."

He placed a quarter in Georgina's hand, which instantly became a claw to receive it, and laid another on the listless palm of the invalid. No attention was paid to this gift by the small dreamer, who continued to gaze at nothing with every appearance of dreamy contentment.

Mitchell awaited Gamadge in the car, and Pottle stood with a leg over his machine. Gamadge, with his foot on the step, turned to make his farewells.

"I miss young Trainor around here," was the form they took. "Miss him very much."

The gypsies all looked deeply concerned. William said, in a low voice: "He fixed my toe."

Martha spoke for the first time, in a thin, childish voice: "He went to school with Charlie."

"Too bad; and so unnecessary." Gamadge climbed into the car, and they drove off; Pottle escorting them, and the gypsies watching their departure with interest. At the entrance to the short cut Mitchell stopped.

"See if you can't get something out of the boy about that woman in the car," he admonished Pottle.

"The minute I start asking them anything, they freeze up. *I* can't throw quarters around." Pottle was annoyed. "And that reward of yours is going to get you a fine crop of lies from those gypsies, Mr. Gamadge. They'll do anything for money."

"Well, I hadn't offered anything when William came through with his information," replied Gamadge, mildly.

"He certainly gave those women away! I knew they knew all about nightshade."

"Whatever he told us doesn't matter to the gypsies. You can be pretty sure of that. They hadn't warned him off any of those subjects, and I don't think they'd ever heard about the woman in the car before. Wild horses wouldn't drag a family secret out of William Stanley. I don't believe," he added, "that they know a thing about the nightshade poisonings; if little Elias handed any of it around, they aren't aware of it."

"Who in time is Elias?" demanded Mitchell.

"The sick boy. I don't think he's had a long or serious illness, but he's not talking yet. When he is, I think he'll have forgotten all about the nightshade, if he ever knew about it. It's a long lapse of time for a child of that age."

"You handed the old lady a new one," remarked Pottle, starting his machine. "After this, all her customers are going to be companions of Serious."

"I hope it will be good for trade."

"What'd you think of Martha?"

"Very attractive."

"She's sixteen years old. When she gets to be Georgina's age—twenty-five, I think—she won't have any teeth, either. Well, so long."

He rode off, and Mitchell turned into the short cut.

CHAPTER FIVE

"A Curse on the Place"

"LADY IN A CAR! Lady in a car!" grumbled Mitchell. "Of course she was a tourist. I bet Tommy Ormiston saw her, and got her mixed up with everything else that happened to him on Tuesday morning."

"She certainly does keep cropping up, doesn't she?"

"You brought her up, this time. I don't butt in on your system—not any more; but I should think you could have got something a little more definite out of William Stanley."

"It was no use trying, with his family standing around like basilisks. They didn't know what I was getting at. Let them think it over, and perhaps they'll let William earn his bicycle."

"You going to buy that boy a wheel?"

"I saw a very nice little one in a window as we went through the Center; marked down. Secondhand goods. It was only seven dollars."

"We won't let Bartram offer any rewards, yet. We knew he'd get a lot of fake information and crank letters."

"The gypsies won't write us any letters, whatever else they may do."

"I wouldn't be too sure."

They passed abruptly from dazzling sunlight to a glimmering dusk; trees met overhead, branches swished wetly against their mudguards, tires sank into watery channels between the ruts. Mitchell observed that it was hardly ever dry in here. Gamadge braced his feet, enduring the bumps in silence. A wagon track on their left disappeared into what looked like virgin forest.

"Where does that go to?" he asked.

"No place, unless it comes out on the upper road. Wood choppers use it, I guess. Here we are."

Coarse grass on both sides of the road bloomed with the bright colors of wild orchids, fireweed and lady's-eardrops. Mitchell stopped the car, and they got out.

"There's where he was found, just where that rock sticks out of the bank. He pitched onto it, smashed his head. Brake was on, and his legs weren't clear of the bike."

Gamadge walked to the spot, and stood with his hands in his pockets, glancing about him. "Looks as if about six cars had skidded," he said.

"There was a good deal of trampling before we got here."

"I see that; but there's a great swipe smoothed over."

"Yes; it does seem to run pretty continuous under the tire marks and the footprints."

Gamadge and Mitchell were not fond of wasting words in vain surmise; moreover, they were usually able to communicate, when facts confronted them, without any words at all. Neither of them said anything more about the great swipe; it extended from motorcycle tire marks that stopped abruptly beside the road, across the ruts, to the rock itself. The place was a mass of churned mud and leaves, but this wide swath was clearly discernible.

"Obviously a skid," said Gamadge.

"Troopers ain't supposed to have such accidents."

"All part of the Tuesday upset, no doubt." As Mitchell said nothing, Gamadge asked: "What was the verdict? Misadventure?"

"What else could it be?" Mitchell spoke with unaccustomed sharpness. "I went over this place on my hands and knees, almost. It's a bad road, but it's used as a highway; and it's always in a mess. You can see how the tires cut it up and splash the water, and the dead leaves drift across. And there's all this grass in the middle."

"I can see what it's like. Was Trainor's lamp working?"

"It was in working order; but it got smashed when he did—only part of his machine that did get smashed, naturally enough."

They returned to the car, and drove on amidst a delicious fragrance of pine, spearmint, dead leaves and wet earth. The road widened and became smoother, and the car emerged from the woods and rolled along between stretches of russet marsh. Farms and cottages suddenly sprang up on the left against a background of dark trees, their gardens blazing with dahlias and asters. They passed a filling station, and a neat white house just beyond, which Mitchell pointed out as state police headquarters.

"But of course you know it," he said. "Here's the crossroads."

Beyond the crossroads weather-beaten sheds and wharfs prepared the traveler for the fish-laden atmosphere of Oakport Village. The car rumbled over an ancient wooden bridge, and entered a somnolent and ever-dusty square.

"Everything but the post office and Picken's drugstore kind of folds up from now on," said Mitchell. "The village caters mostly to summer trade. If you want city goods, you have to go to Ford's Center."

"Do the doctors fold up, too?"

"Young Dickson goes south—he has a connection somewhere in Florida. Ames and his family live in Bailtown; they're there except three months in the summer. Loring stays right here. He says it's just what he likes—plenty of doctors at the Center to take care of the farmers, and nothing for him to do but play chess with his cronies, and write pieces for the magazines. He isn't exactly what you'd call lazy, I guess, but I wouldn't say he had much ambition."

"Perhaps he's ambitious as a writer. What sort of stuff does he write? Medical? Philosophical? Or just plain whimsical?"

"I don't know."

They left Oakport Village behind them, and entered a broad, elm-shaded street lined on both sides with stately houses, pillared and green-shuttered.

"Seafaring people built those." Mitchell waved his arm. "This was a big port, once; China and India trade. The Bartrams owned a good deal of property here, and they kept enough of it to protect 'em from close neighbors. Here's their place now."

For the last few minutes they had been climbing, steadily if gradually. Mitchell turned the car left, and they entered a narrower road, bordered on the east by a hilly meadow of goldenrod, scrub oak and sumac, and on the west by a picket fence and a high privet hedge. Behind these, straggling lilac bushes and tall trees formed a screen for the big white house that could be dimly discerned, a pattern of light and shade, beyond.

The car rounded a bend in the road, and Mitchell stopped it in front of a gate. "Here we are," he said, sliding out from under the wheel. Gamadge also descended, to follow him up a long flagged walk, bordered with flower beds that would have been the better for weeding. The façade of the house rose before them; wide and low, of white-painted brick, with the inevitable green shutters. A broad, shallow flight of steps led up to a portico with fluted columns, and a door with a handsome fanlight. Mitchell climbed the steps, but Gamadge paused on the flagged walk to glance about him.

"Lovely old place," he said. "I haven't seen a trellis like that in years; and the red honeysuckle on it—I bet that's been growing there for the best part of a century."

He strolled eastward, where flower beds of which the plants had ceased to flower stood up like immense pincushions from the coarse grass of the surrounding turf. Little ornamental wire railings enclosed them, and bordered the winding gravel paths. Ironwork seats and settles, with grapevine backs and arms, rusted under the syringa bushes and mountain-ash trees; and a thick box hedge, dying in patches, was designed to conceal the kitchen garden and drying ground.

"Coming?" asked Mitchell, his hand on the old-fashioned brass bellpull.

"Just a minute." Gamadge crossed the walk, and wandered a few paces to the west of it. Here the trees—evergreens and maples—grew thickly enough to form a grove. He could see glimpses of sunlight beyond, but he did not penetrate to it. He stood quietly sniffing the air.

"Smells good," he explained. "There's a tang of salt in it."

"The shore isn't far off."

"I've never been up this way before. Lovely old place—lovely. Dozing, isn't it? They've let it run right to seed. Too much greenery, besides. Just a little too damp and dim."

He joined Mitchell at the door, on which a brass plate bore the name BARTRAM in rubbed letters. Mitchell pulled the bell; they heard a far-off tinkle, and after a while the door opened a crack.

"The family is out," said a quavering voice.

"All right, Annie; you know who I am. Let us in," said Mitchell.

The door opened halfway. Gamadge saw a scared, wrinkled face, pale-blue eyes, and a small bent figure in dark blue, with a white apron.

"The family is not at home," Annie repeated.

"None of 'em?"

"Only the nurse and the little girl."

"Where are they all?"

"They're at the funeral."

"Funeral! I thought they were going to have the funeral early."

"A grand Boston funeral. Late, it was—an hour late."

"I hope they didn't find much of a crowd at the cemetery."

"'Twill be like a fair."

"Not so bad as that, I hope."

"But Ormiston will not be at the graveyard."

"Never you mind that; let us in, will you? I want my friend Mr. Gamadge to meet Miss Ridgeman, and he may like to have a word with you."

The door opened wide. As he entered the square hall Gamadge turned to the small creature at his elbow, and asked: "Was Mr. Ormiston expected at the funeral? I didn't know the Bartrams knew him."

Annie replied in a grudging tone:

"They know him, but it's little or nothing we've seen of him since the old gentleman died. Didn't he telephone down, though, on Tuesday, when he didn't know if his little b'y would get well, and ask the master would we have him in our graveyard?"

"Have Tommy Ormiston in the Bartram graveyard?"

"I took the message meself."

"What in the world did he do a thing like that for?"

"Ormiston has no graveyard. Where would he put the little b'y? And wouldn't it be like him to borrow a grave?"

"I suppose it would, if you say so."

"Mrs. Ormiston is a good, kind woman. She was down here, askin' if she could help us; and she's at the funeral now. It was herself told Mrs. George that Ormiston couldn't wait to get back to the city to his paintin', and he was half crazy with the delay. What's a little b'y to him?"

"You seem to have it in for him, all right," said Mitchell.

"Mrs. Ormiston is a kind woman. I said to her: 'Take your children away from here, before worse happens to them. Take them away,' I said. 'There's a curse on the place.'"

"I know; you've been saying so right along. But things happen in most places; this isn't any worse than any other place."

"And I said the same to Mrs. George Bartram. I said: 'Take your child away from this dreary seacoast.'"

"You must have been a big comfort to 'em. Anything you'd like to ask this old lady, Mr. Gamadge?"

Annie turned vague eyes on Gamadge, in which he read a vast bewilderment, and a definite fear. He said: "You can't see the summerhouse from your kitchen, Annie; I know that. Can you see it from your bedroom upstairs?"

"Me room upstairs?"

"Yes. Is it on the west side of the house? Can you see the summerhouse from the window?" As she continued to look at him blankly, he went on: "I wondered if you had happened to go up there on Tuesday, between twelve and one. If you had seen anything unusual going on in the garden you'd have mentioned it—I know that; but I thought you might have seen something that you didn't think important at the time, but that might interest us."

She drew away from him, looking very much frightened.

"*Did* you look out of your window?" persisted Gamadge.

"I have not climbed a stair in this house since the stiffness got into my knee, a dozen years ago. The old madam gave me the little room next the kitchen for my bedroom, and she put a bathroom for me where the old scullery used to be."

"Which side of the house are you on?"

"The east side, and me windows are choked up with vines. It's strangled we are with the trees and the bushes, but the old madam would not have them cleared away. 'Annie,' she told me, 'the old master liked the shade. We'll cut nothing down while I live.' That was when young Mrs. Carroll wanted the landscape artist to come in and make a garden among the rocks."

"So if that little gypsy had wandered in through the gate on Tuesday, at noon or thereabouts, you wouldn't have seen him from the kitchen door, or from any window."

"Thank God, not a thing did I see."

"You were pretty busy that morning, weren't you?"

"I was; and the new girl never came until most of the work was done. By the front door she came, like a visitor; 'It's Miss Gibbons I am,' she says. And I pushed her back into the kitchen before she had her hat off."

"So she never had a glimpse of the summerhouse."

"It's many a glimpse she's had of it since; and didn't she try to bring her young man in yesterday, to have a look at it. And hasn't she gone off to the funeral this morning, like one of the family, in the dry cleaner's van."

"But on Tuesday morning she came in by the front door, and didn't see a thing. Meanwhile, Miss Ridgeman was helping you in the kitchen. What time was it when you asked her to come in and lend a hand?"

"It's not for me to call a nurse away from a child. Nobody can say I did a thing like that."

"Of course not. I mean, what time did she come?"

"It was after twelve when she looked in on me and saw the dishes from the top shelf of the pantry waiting to be washed, and the vegetables wilting in their skins. 'Annie,' she says, 'you'll kill your knee entirely,' she says. And not a step did she take out of the kitchen until the doorbell rang and the company came. It was kind of the woman, tired as she had a right to be herself, with cleaning the upstairs."

At this moment a nurse in a white uniform appeared in the hall above, holding a little girl by the hand.

"Good morning, Miss Ridgeman," said Mitchell. "I hear the family's been delayed."

"A little." She came down, the little girl eagerly stepping from stair to stair beside her. "They'll be here any minute now, and I know Mr. George Bartram will want to see you, even if Mr. Bartram isn't up to it yet."

Annie disappeared through a baize door at the end of the long hall, and Miss Ridgeman assisted her charge down the rest of the stairway. Mitchell introduced Gamadge, who shook hands gravely with the nurse and with Miss Irma Bartram. The latter swung on Miss Ridgeman's hand in a carefree manner; she was a jolly-looking little girl, with thick, curly brown hair and round brown eyes, whose short white dress and blue jumper gave her the appearance of being about seven eighths leg. Miss Ridgeman was a square-built, rather homely woman, darkish in coloring, with a face and manner that expressed practical common sense. This had been overlaid at the moment by a dryness and constraint that might well have been the effects of a great shock. Even her voice was subdued, as she said:

"Come into the sitting room. I should like very much to talk to you, and Irma can play chess. Can't you, Irma?"

Irma nodded, and ran into the sitting room ahead of them. She skipped to a low table at the farther end of the long parlor, and opened a rosewood box. From it she began to take out big red-and-white carved ivory chessmen, which she ranged in two rows.

Miss Ridgeman led the two men to a bay window overlooking the front garden.

"It's just as well that we have young company with us at present," she said, in that dry, strained voice. "We have to pretend to be cheerful, and that's just what we all need."

"You've been fine, Miss Ridgeman," said Mitchell. "I'll have to hand it to you."

"Fine?" The nurse's face hardened. "That's hardly the word to describe my behavior, I'm afraid. If I can help them in any way now, I'm thankful for the chance."

"Don't feel that way. I wish you'd tell me something; is that old cook of yours all right in the head?"

"Annie? Oh, yes. It's been a frightful shock to her, that's all. Has she been telling you there's a curse on the place?"

"Yes, she has."

"Nobody can quite make out what she means. I suppose you could call what happened a curse."

"But she don't know what really did happen, you think?"

"Absolutely not. She never notices what goes on. I wanted to ask you if you'd had any news—about that little gypsy boy, for instance."

"No news about him at all."

"I do hope they can prove that he wasn't responsible. Doctor Loring and I want Mr. Bartram to take him."

Mitchell was astonished. "Take him?"

"Yes."

"For good, you mean?"

"Yes."

"You mean—right away?"

"It would be the best thing in the world for Mr. Bartram."

"For the kid, too, I guess; but it isn't everybody would adopt a gypsy, let alone this gypsy."

"Mr. Bartram isn't everybody."

"But it would keep the whole thing right in front of him all the time."

Gamadge said: "Just the kind of thing you New Englanders are supposed to be willing to tackle, isn't it? Now later immigrants, like Annie and myself, might balk at it; but you are made of sterner stuff, and ought to take it in your stride."

"I'm not a New Englander," said Miss Ridgeman, faintly smiling, "but I can easily imagine myself doing it. His grandmother wants to take him back with her to Whitewater Beach; I understand that she has some kind of decent place to live, there, but I wish he didn't have to go. Have you seen him, Mr. Gamadge?"

"Yes; nice little fellow. They seem to be making him comfortable enough."

"Doctor Loring saw to that. The gypsies still cure people with spells, he says."

"But would his folks give him up?" asked Mitchell.

"I understand that his father and mother are dead. Doctor Loring thinks his grandmother might be glad to 'give him up,' if you can call it that."

"Sell him, most likely."

"I'm afraid so. It would be the saving of Mr. Bartram to get up an interest in another child; and this one needn't be any burden on him at all. The house is big, and I should be only too glad to stay on and look after him. Only..."

She paused, and was silent so long that Mitchell asked: "Only what, Miss Ridgeman?"

"I hardly like to offer."

"In the name of goodness, why not?"

"After what happened, Mr. Bartram may not think that I'm capable of looking after a child. I shouldn't blame him if he didn't."

"Now, Miss Ridgeman—" Mitchell was concerned.

"He can't bear the sight of me." Her self-possession had cracked a little, but she went on, calmly enough: "I ought to leave the house; I would, only they need me badly just now, on account of Irma."

"Mr. Bartram hasn't said a word about your being to blame. Nobody blames the Beasleys, or the Ormistons."

"Indeed people do blame the Ormistons."

"Annie seems to be down on him. Do you know why?"

"No, I don't, Mr. Mitchell. He's never been inside this house, to my knowledge, since I came here myself, when Julia was born. I think the families used to know each other in Boston. Perhaps he was a disagreeable boy."

"He's an eccentric kind of a feller now. Funny thing he did—asking Mr. Bartram to let him bury Tommy in the Bartram lot; and the boy wasn't even dead!"

"Annie can't get over it; but in a way it isn't so queer. The Ormistons have always lived in Europe a good deal, and I suppose they probably just get buried anywhere they happen to die. Annie thinks it's more important to have a graveyard than to have a home."

"And in France," said Gamadge, "families often share burial lots; lack of space, I suppose, as well as frugality."

"Still, he was a little casual about it all. But they were terribly upset in every way. They are now. They're half packed, with their things in crates and boxes, all alone in that deserted place. Of course he wants to get home."

"An artist with all his materials in crates must be a pathetic object," said Gamadge.

"I can sympathize with him in a way, because we're so upset ourselves. We weren't prepared for three house guests, and one of them needs a good deal of attention." She glanced down the room at the absorbed Irma, and went on: "Annie's lame, and the new girl isn't much of a treasure. I haven't been able to do any marketing. I'd take Irma with me, only both the cars are out." Her haunted eyes turned towards the world that glimmered with light and shade outside the windows.

"I'd be glad to run you down to the village, Miss Ridgeman, and tote the parcels back in the car," said Mitchell.

"You would? Oh, thank you—but I can't leave Irma. Annie isn't able to keep after her."

"Leave her to me," said Gamadge.

"You really wouldn't mind?"

"Certainly not."

"I'd telephone for the things, but the deliveries are so late, and there isn't much in the house for lunch."

"Go ahead; it will be a pleasure for me," Gamadge assured her.

"The nurses in Holland must be quite strict, I think; she's very good; really no trouble at all."

"You relieve my mind tremendously."

Miss Ridgeman went out into the hall, Mitchell following her. She seized a cape from the rack under the stairs, and they hurried off. Gamadge heard the car drive away, and then, after lighting a cigarette, joined Irma at her chess table.

CHAPTER SIX

Old Iron

"ALONE AT LAST with the witness in chief. I've been looking forward to this," said Gamadge. He sat down and contemplated Irma thoughtfully. "We must have a talk; the subject will be cats."

Irma looked up.

"What a subject!" Gamadge spoke with feeling. "We must give it our undivided attention. May I help you put the chessmen away?"

They accomplished the job in silence; Irma placing each piece carefully on the wrong peg, and Gamadge removing it and shifting it to the right one. This took some time; but at last the rosewood box was closed, and he assisted her into a large chair opposite his own. He then said briskly:

"Cats. Everybody ought to have a cat. I have a very large yellow one, whose name is Martin. Have you a cat, Irma?"

Irma's mouth drew down at the corners. She stretched her right arm as far outwards and backwards as it would go, and made a circle in the air with her forefinger.

"I never in my life saw anything so graphic," said Gamadge. "The map of Europe unrolls before me, and I know the very spot in the Netherlands where that animal now lives as best it can. You had to leave it behind."

Irma nodded, her face the picture of gloom.

"But luckily there are many other cats in the world. For instance, I know a place not far from here where there are six kittens, one of them white. It just occurred to me that I might be able to get hold of it and bring it back here this afternoon. Mind you, they may not let you keep it."

Irma's face had become radiant. She paid no attention to Gamadge's warning, but placed her hands on the arms of her chair and bounced up and down.

"If I do that, will you do something for me?"

Irma, who seemed to be only too well acquainted with this ominous gambit, became very grave, and looked at him doubtfully.

"I just want to know how you came to dive under that pine tree," he went on. "The other day, you know; when you found your little cousin. Your parents are used to your flighty ways, and they seem to have thought nothing of it; but I wondered whether you hadn't some reason for crawling under that big branch. Had you a reason?"

Irma, gazing at him fixedly, seemed to ponder the question. At last, and very slowly, she reached down into the breast pocket of her woollen jumper, fumbled there, and withdrew her hand, clenched into a fist. She extended it, opened it, and disclosed to Gamadge's incredulous stare a little red bell, attached to a wad of very dirty red ribbon.

Gamadge eyed it for some moments in silent fascination. He then advanced his own hand, but Irma withdrew hers in alarm. She replaced the bell in her pocket, fumbled there again, and produced something else. This, when exhibited on her palm, proved to be a small, shriveled object, black and vaguely spherical. Gamadge snatched it, without pause or ceremony. He examined it closely, gave an exclamation of loathing and dismay, and dropped it into his pocket.

"Little ball," protested Irma, speaking for the first time in their acquaintance.

"You can't have it. I'll get you another little ball, one that you can play with. Good heavens," he said, staring at her, "you must have a charmed life. Did they teach you in Holland never to put anything you found into your mouth?"

Irma nodded.

"They made a good job of it. Good heavens," repeated Gamadge, "what an extraordinary child you are. Shall we go and look at the place where you found these things?"

Irma nodded, slid from her chair, and rushed into the hall. Gamadge followed her down the hall, past the stairs, and round them to a short passageway that ended in an open side door. Irma ran out, jumped down two shallow stone steps, and stopped to hunt in the depths of a low bush that grew to the right of them. She pulled forth a rusty little iron shovel, brandished it playfully at Gamadge, and dashed off across the lawn.

Gamadge, striding at her heels, inquired: "May I ask where you got that coal shovel? It's a sensible plaything, I grant you; but it's rather dirty. Doesn't it belong in the kitchen?"

"Annie gave it to me."

"Did she, really? All right; lead on."

They passed the summerhouse—a rustic affair, once picturesque, now enclosed in stout wire netting—and crossed an expanse of green, tended lawn. A narrow path led them suddenly into a sort of maze, where bushes higher than Gamadge's head almost met across the trail. Trees, rising high above, shut out the sun. They were in a wilderness—out of the world.

"It's a jungle," muttered Gamadge, pushing long twigs of lilac away from his face. Irma moved confidently on, turned a corner, and was out of sight in a moment. A rustle in the shrubbery behind him made Gamadge stop and turn; Annie hurried up, limping, and breathing hard.

"Oh," she said, when she caught sight of him. "You're with the little girl."

"Very much so," replied Gamadge. "Were you worried about her?"

"I saw the nurse drive off, from the dining-room window, and the child was not in the lower part of the house. I wondered was she alone in the garden."

"I'm not surprised that you're nervous about her."

"Who wouldn't be, in this place?" She glanced to right and left with an indescribable air of repulsion. "'Tis no place for children."

"She has her shovel with her," said Gamadge. Annie gave him a quick, rather frightened look, but made no reply. "You like her to have a bit of old iron along when she plays out here, don't you?" he persisted. As she remained silent, he asked: "Don't you feel like telling me why you think the place is dangerous—in that way?"

"I wouldn't speak of it. The gentry wouldn't want me to be talking," said Annie, faintly.

"You're not referring to the Bartrams, are you?"

"No, I am not. I'll say no more; they'd think me out of me wits."

Gamadge studied her, looking thoughtful. Presently he said: "You're on the wrong tack, Annie. Why not tell me about it? Perhaps I could explain."

She shied away from him, and hurried off along the path.

Gamadge, frowning, turned back and realized that Irma was out of sight. He called her at the top of his voice:

"Hi! Irma! Where has the child got to? I believe I have the jitters myself now. Irma!"

She bounded into view at the turn of the path. Gamadge addressed her fretfully: "Don't you go rushing off alone, shovel or no shovel. Where's that pine tree? Let's have a look at it, and get out of this place—it gives me goose flesh."

The tree was some distance ahead, off the path and in a corner of the high picket fence. Irma pointed to a wide branch, laden with cones, that trailed on the bare ground.

"Where did you see the little bell?"

She bent down and poked her finger into a spot just under the edge of the bough.

"How about the dear little black ball?"

Irma shook her head, and indicated by a gesture that it had been lying on the path, some distance away. Gamadge lifted the branch, restrained her, by a powerful clutch at her skirts, from diving under it again, and glanced below.

"What a nice little house," he said. "You'd like to play there, wouldn't you? Well, you've been a good child. I shall try to do something effective about the white kitten. But we still have a delicate bit of business to transact." He lifted her to the top of a stump, steadied her with a hand hooked into her belt, and continued persuasively: "Now, don't go off the handle; I want to borrow that little red bell."

Irma looked horrified, and made as if to leap off the stump into space; but his hold on her belt restrained her.

"I said borrow," he insisted. "Wait a minute! You don't know what that red ribbon is—it's the white cat's necktie. Or at least I think it is; and if it fits, the animal probably belongs to you. Here—you needn't choke me to death." For she had seized him about the neck, and seemed bent upon strangling him. She suddenly released him, dug into the pocket of her blouse, dashed the bell and ribbon into his hand, and with his assistance leapt to the ground. Gamadge followed her along the path, through the maze, and back to the lawn. Here she began busily to dig with her shovel in a hard flower bed, while Gamadge strolled about the summerhouse, strolled to the back gate, returned, and lighted a cigarette.

Mitchell found him sitting on a fragile-looking iron bench, watching his charge with an air of benevolent detachment. He joined him on the bench, and got out his pipe.

"All serene?" he asked.

"Not so very. I have two pieces of information for you, both rather curious. In the first place, Annie thinks she knows how the children got the berries."

"No! I had an idea she was worrying about something definite."

"Very definite. You can't do much about it, though. Her idea seems to be that it was done by some sort of witchcraft."

"Bother the silly old thing. We can't—but see here: if she thinks that, she must have seen something."

"Well, not necessarily; it may be nothing but an idea. And the trouble is, even if she did meet what she thought was the uncanny, and in some far from agreeable form, she'll never dare talk about it. We won't know what she saw, nobody will ever know; unless I can prove to her satisfaction that she's mistaken."

Mitchell glanced about him as if he expected to see a phantasm of the Celtic twilight gibbering at them from behind a tree or a bush.

"She even provided Irma with a charm to ward the gentry off with," continued Gamadge, who did not seem to be amused. "Old iron does it. She gave Irma that shovel. Well, it's an unproductive subject, at present; let's drop it and go on to the other one."

"I would have said she was telling the truth, when she told us she didn't see anything, that morning," said Mitchell.

"So should I. Now, Mitchell, please look at this." Gamadge extracted the red bell, with its wad of ribbon, from his inside pocket. Mitchell gazed at it, openmouthed.

"It's one of 'em!" he exclaimed. "I saw the others; it's one of 'em! Where in time..."

Gamadge told the story of Irma, the pine tree, and the black berry; which he also produced for Mitchell's inspection. That individual seemed able to do little more than stare, until Gamadge had finished. Then he said in a low voice:

"That settles it. The little gypsy was here. He got that bell from Sarah Beasley in exchange for the nightshade—"

"A poor sort of swap, though, don't you think?"

"We don't know what else he gave her for it. When he was here, he dropped that bell. Julia Bartram got hold of it, and she kept hold of it—till she went in under the tree. She must often have played there. That settles it," he repeated. "It's that little gypsy." He lighted his pipe, and had it going before he suddenly spoke again—this time with an almost ludicrous expression of dismay on his ordinarily calm and expressionless face. "Unless—my gracious heavens!"

"You see another explanation, do you?" Gamadge was watching him closely.

"But my gracious, it can't be so! The George Bartrams! I never even checked up on that trip of theirs; they might have got here any time. You *can't* check up on a motor trip, in a private car! It never entered my head. See here: if he had to leave his business over there in Europe, he may be out of a job."

"So he may." Gamadge's face was blank.

"And they ain't picked up so easy over here, now; I've known men better fixed than George Bartram is, lose a job and never get another one. But, my heavens! Well, I can test some of it. You want to come over here a minute, little girl?"

Irma looked up, planted her shovel in the flower bed, and arrived in a confident and trustful mood. Mitchell, plainly endeavoring to conceal his extreme discomfiture, said cheerfully: "You came down here by way of the shore, didn't you, Irma? Tuesday, I mean. Motored down along the beaches. Waves, rocks, sea gulls."

Irma thought for a moment, and then nodded, violently.

"But you all got out of the car, sometimes, looked at the view, picked flowers in the woods."

Irma responded more quickly this time; she nodded like a mandarin, and Mitchell, looking at Gamadge, asked: "Don't she ever talk?"

"Seldom."

"Well, Irma," Mitchell proceeded, as if with a certain distaste and reluctance. "You came past a barn, and there was a little girl playing there; perhaps she was playing with a cat. White cat."

Irma's eye fell upon the red bell in his hand, and she nodded—slowly and reflectively, this time.

"She gave you this little bell, and you gave her a bunch of berries for it. That so?"

Irma nodded.

"And then," Mitchell went on, "Your folks drove the car through the woods up there, and they saw another—they saw a little boy playing in front of his house—"

"Just a moment, Mitchell. May I take the witness?" asked Gamadge.

"Go ahead."

"And then," said Gamadge, "you caught a very large butterfly."

Mitchell stared, but Irma nodded as if trying to dislocate her neck.

"You jumped on its back, held tight to its horns, and flew over the woods down to Oakport. Didn't you?"

"Yes, I did," shouted Irma. She spread out her arms, flapped them wildly, and sprang into the air.

"Irma!" called Miss Ridgeman, from the side door. "Come and get your crackers and milk."

Irma seized her shovel and fled; pausing at the bush beside the house steps to plant it faithfully deep down among the roots.

"It's no laughing matter." Mitchell turned upon Gamadge with a look of reproach.

"I know; can't help it. Irma's pantomime is always so graphic."

"She'll say anything!"

"That's what you get for leading the witness."

"We don't know where she found this thing. Can't depend on a word she says."

"You can't depend on any of these children as witnesses, Mitchell; surely you know that. On Irma least of all—she's only five."

"She must have found this bell somewheres."

"Or had it given to her. She may quite well have picked it up on the Beasley road."

"I'll have to ask these people some questions. I don't even know whether the little Bartram girl had an estate of her own, or who it goes to. I do know her father's mills are all right; they went through some tough times, of course, but they've picked up pretty well since Bartram brought himself to making artificial silk. George Bartram—he could come in here without worrying about being seen. He knows the place, and he knows the back way."

"Meanwhile, what is his wife doing? Or is it a conspiracy?"

"We'll try to find out."

A tall, broad-shouldered man and a pretty little woman came around the side of the house.

"Here they are," said Mitchell.

CHAPTER SEVEN

Bartrams—Cadet Branch

MR. GEORGE BARTRAM'S handsome, rosy countenance and spreading waistline bore witness to good living; his keen eyes, long, sharp nose and determined jawline seemed to announce the fact that he meant to go on providing comfortably for himself if he could. He was well, if not quietly, dressed in brown checks, a lightweight brown overcoat, and a soft brown hat. He was talkative.

"Glad to meet you, Mr. Gamadge," he said, shaking hands without waiting for an introduction. "Loring says you're a great man. I know you're a busy one, and I'm speaking for my brother as well as for myself, when I say that we don't propose to let you spend your time on our troubles for nothing. You'll take the suggestion as a matter of business; Carroll wants you to send him in a bill for your services."

"Oh, thanks very much indeed," answered Gamadge. "It's quite impossible; I'm in no way qualified. Mitchell likes to have somebody to talk to when he's on a case, and as he was very kind to some friends of mine who got into trouble, last summer, I'm only too glad to oblige him."

"Well, that's that. My brother is very anxious to talk to you, whether you're qualified or not. Loring's given him a pick-me-up, and he'll be ready to see you in a few minutes."

"I really do think we ought to put off our talk until tomorrow."

Mrs. Bartram reassured him in bright, decided tones:

"Oh, no, Mr. Gamadge; it's just what he needs. Doctor Loring says it will be the saving of him to see somebody new, and keep up an interest in outside things and people."

"Well, but this investigation, for what it's worth, won't divert his mind, exactly, will it?"

"*You* will, though, Mr. Gamadge. He's interested in you. Oh, I'm so sorry for him. I hope we'll be able to take him along to New York with us on Monday. He ought to get away from this house. And you know," continued Mrs. Bartram, who seemed to be as chatty as her husband, "I won't be sorry to go, either. And I was looking forward to seeing the old family place so much."

"It's been a tough experience for you, Mrs. Bartram. Are you familiar with this part of the country?" asked Gamadge.

"No, I've never been East before—except when we went through on our trip to Europe, ever so long ago. I didn't think then that I'd come back married, and with a little girl! I come from Ohio."

"Just a tourist, weren't you, Dell?" Her husband contemplated her with affection. She was a conservative, Gamadge noted; her dark-green suit was longer in the skirt than the fashion of the moment decreed, and her smart green felt hat fitted her head with uncompromising snugness. Blond hair, tightly waved, covered her ears and was pinned into a large neat roll at the back of her neck. She had Irma's pink cheeks and round eyes, but there was a suggestion of primness about her that the expansive Irma did not, and never would, possess.

"Traveling with Famous Cruises, in The Hague," she told Gamadge. "I met Mr. Bartram at The House in the Bush. So pretty, isn't it? Or haven't you been there, Mr. Gamadge?"

"I have. I liked Holland ever so much."

"Isn't it a wonderful place? We did hate leaving, so!"

"We did," agreed her husband, grimly. "I settled right down there, you know, Gamadge; never left the country except on business trips—the Dutch East Indies, and so forth. Before Irma was born. Those were the days, weren't they, Dell?"

"They were wonderful. Have you ever been to Java, Mr. Gamadge?"

"Never, I'm sorry to say."

"And to think it's all over, perhaps forever! I can't believe it. It was just like a bad dream, crowding in on that awful little boat. No conveniences. I didn't realize there *were* such boats any more as the *Alberta*."

"I pulled every string I could get hold of, trying to wangle a passage on the *Nieuw Amsterdam*," said Bartram. "Couldn't make it; she was jammed. We were lucky to get anything. Rough trip, too. We docked on Sunday. That reminds me, Mitchell; believe it or not, I never realized until last night that we drove down that road past the Beasley farm on Tuesday morning, just before everything happened up there."

"No!" Mitchell's face was wooden.

"We did. Truth is, we were so tied up with our own troubles here that I hardly paid any attention at all to the other cases. I didn't take in where the other poisonings had happened. And then somebody said something about the Ormistons, and I remembered the locality, and figured it out. But we came through early—around ten."

"Too bad you weren't an hour later."

"Might have seen something, mightn't we? Quite a trip, we had. We wired to Carroll from Montreal on Sunday morning, and said we'd be dropping down for lunch on Tuesday. Was he surprised! You can imagine, after all these years. He's kept at me, of late—wasn't I getting nervous over there? Wasn't I thinking of coming home? I said, certainly I wasn't; swore I'd stick it out. I thought Holland was as safe as Boston, and always would be. But Adèle began to worry, this summer; she's a good sport—so's Irma, for that matter—but the Americans started to clear out, and you know what mass suggestion is. Well, I went out on Sunday morning and bought the Cadillac; and if anybody had told me even three weeks ago that I'd be buying it in the slightly used department—"

"Now, George! You said you were going to stop talking that way."

"I know; fact is, let's hope it's temporary, but just now I'm hanging on to my cash. Well, I finished sending my telegrams—I forgot to say that I couldn't send any radio messages from that damned *Alberta*; something had gone wrong with their wireless, or so they said. I never could make out whether it was really a breakdown, or whether they had orders not to send out anything; it was all very hush-hush, even then.

"I got the car, and as soon as Dell had pulled herself together—"

"I was sick almost all the way over," said Mrs. Bartram. "Ten days."

"Sick as a dog; Irma wasn't, though. Gad, you should have seen that child eat! Rotten food, too; nothing any good but the cheese. You know that Canadian Cheddar? Wonderful. Well, Dell wanted to see something of the country, so I doped out a route, and we started down. Spent Monday night in a little town called Haverley, not far up the line from here."

"How'd you like the Beaulieu Tavern?" inquired Mitchell, with assumed interest.

"Didn't stay there. Stayed at the Stone Ridge House, and a one-horse place it was. Canary-bird dishes for the canned vegetables, and no private baths."

Mitchell, in his satisfaction at having extracted the name of the hotel from George Bartram without asking for it, was about to commit the faux pas of wondering aloud why the Bartrams had not stayed at the Beaulieu; but remembered in time that it was a resort, and expensive.

"Tuesday morning we started early," continued Bartram, "and we struck Bailtown just before ten. I wanted to go around the other way, but Dell and Irma were crazy about the shore, so we stuck to the coast road. When we got to the Point up there above Beasley's we came right down past the farm, and went on through to Ford's Center."

"Went to the Center first, did you?"

"Yes. I'd told Carroll we'd turn up at one, so we had lots of time; and poor Dell was going crazy about the state of her hair."

"Of course I wanted a wave, George; I wasn't going to meet your brother for the first time looking like I don't know what; and Irma needed a shampoo. We couldn't get anything done on the boat, and it was Sunday in Montreal, and Labor Day in Haverley. So George decided to drive down early on Tuesday and try to find a hairdresser in Ford's Center. We didn't tell Carroll; we were afraid he might feel hurt about our not coming here right away. He doesn't know yet."

"Well, the point is that we passed the Beasley farm—and it hadn't changed by so much as a lilac bush since I saw it last—we passed it shortly after ten."

"You didn't see anybody, I suppose, or meet a car?" asked Mitchell wistfully.

"Not a soul."

"No gypsies on the road?"

"Not that I noticed; there was no traffic at all until we got to the Oakport branch, and not much after that. I parked my wife and Irma at a moth-eaten place—"

"The funniest hairdresser's I was ever at," said Mrs. Bartram. "It didn't even look sanitary. They gave me a very nice wave, though."

"I see that they did." Gamadge glanced respectfully at the petrified-looking ridges on either side of Mrs. Bartram's round face.

"And it stayed in very well. So George went off, and he never came back for us for two solid hours."

"Having a shave, haircut, massage and general brush up of his own, I suppose," said Gamadge, carefully avoiding Mitchell's gleaming eye.

"No, I managed to do what had to be done in that line at Haverley. I just went for a drive over the old territory, down the shore a way, around towards the west."

"Look up any old cronies?" asked Mitchell.

"I haven't any old cronies around here, any more."

"Ormiston?"

"Ormiston! He was never a crony. Anyhow, we got to Oakport by one. My God, what a thing to run into! I was the one that saw the nightshade, you know. 'Carroll,' I said, 'my God, that's nightshade!' They have lots of it in Europe, you know—much more than here."

"It was terrible. Oh dear, I can't bear to think of it," said Mrs. Bartram.

"That nurse has her wits about her."

"But your brother ought to pension old Annie, George. She really isn't right in the head."

"You and your pensions! My dear child, do you know how much capital it takes to pension anybody?"

"She could probably live in Ireland somewhere for five dollars a month."

"I hope I'll never have to see you or Irma living on five dollars a month somewhere. And do you realize that poor old Carroll has been supporting that Mike of hers since 1922, or whenever it was? Her son was ambushed and shot in the Troubles, as she calls them," he explained to Gamadge, "and he's an incurable in some Irish hospital. Father started paying his expenses, and then Mother took it on, and now Carroll has the job."

"You've noticed that Annie seems a little odd?" Gamadge addressed Mrs. Bartram, who replied with vivacity:

"She's been odd ever since it happened. After Miss Ridgeman and I got poor little Julia into bed, and the doctor came, I rushed down to the kitchen for things he wanted, and I told Annie about it. She hadn't heard a thing, and Adelaide was down cellar, freezing the ice cream. 'I'm Mrs. George Bartram,' I said, 'and poor little Julia has eaten some nightshade berries. Miss Ridgeman and I have got her to bed, and the doctor wants hot water and coffee and mustard.' She sat on her chair staring at me with her mouth open, and she never moved. I had to call that Adelaide to help me find things."

"You're sure you mentioned nightshade to her?"

"I'm almost sure I did. Why? Oh, you think it gave her a shock. Well, she never even said anything. Adelaide and I—oh, I'll never forget that day!"

"Yes, you will, Dell. I ought to take you and Irma out of here."

"We can't consider ourselves at such a time. Annie does rather scare me, Mr. Gamadge; she keeps telling me to take Irma away, and she said the same to Mrs. Ormiston. We don't know what to make of it."

"Don't make too much of it, Mrs. Bartram."

"That's what I say," agreed George Bartram. "The Irish always get some wild idea in their heads. Annie hasn't been right since the Troubles. Let's talk about something else. Who do you suppose that funny-looking old bird was, Dell—the woman sitting on the cemetery wall, this morning?"

This peculiar attempt on the part of her husband to take Mrs. Bartram's mind off gloomy subjects did not seem to strike that lady as strange. She responded with a matter-of-factness that Gamadge found rather touching; her immunity to the absurd made her immune to her husband's absurdities.

"That elderly woman, dressed in black? I thought she must be one of the Bartram connection."

"We have no connections, and if we had they wouldn't look like that old girl. Who was the fellow in steel spectacles and the pepper-and-salt suit, talking to Mrs. Ormiston?"

"I don't know. Didn't he come with the sheriff?"

"Hear about Ormiston asking to bury his boy in our lot, Mitchell? Cool, wasn't it?"

"Now, George, please don't get started on that again!" She looked as if the subject upset her, and Gamadge created a diversion:

"I hope you won't be annoyed, as you might very excusably be with me, Mrs. Bartram; I've promised Irma one of the Beasley kittens."

"How awfully kind of you, Mr. Gamadge! It will be just the thing for her. It isn't so easy to keep her happy, when we're all so—"

Her husband interrupted with a chuckle. "I'd like to see anything get Irma down; or keep her down, for more than three minutes."

"Well, you know," said Gamadge, "I think she still misses the cat she left behind her in Holland."

"Of course she does," agreed Mrs. Bartram. "I'm so glad she's going to have another one."

"She'll have one if I have to telegraph to the Bide-A-Wee in New York for it; but I think the Beasleys will probably be glad to get rid of one of theirs."

Irma shot out of the side door, and pranced up to them.

"Uncle Carroll wants you all to come right in the house," she shrieked. "He has a present for me, and he wants you for winches."

The witnesses trooped obediently back in her wake, Mitchell falling behind to mutter in Gamadge's ear: "Most confiding feller I ever met in my whole life."

"He is; it just boils out of him," agreed Gamadge.

"He ain't overcome with sympathy for his brother—would you say so?"

"Mr. George Bartram will never be overcome with grief for anybody except himself, his wife and his offspring."

"In the order named?"

"In the order named."

CHAPTER EIGHT

Estate of Julia Bartram

THE BARTRAM SITTING room or parlor was long and low, with two windows on the west, and the big bay on the south. Between the side windows a white mantelpiece, delicately carved, rose above a smoky brick hearth; a mellow landscape in an old gilt frame hung above it. The mahogany furniture might have been brought from England, in the mid-eighteenth century, by one of the Bartram ships; but the glass and pottery, and the big gilt and lacquer box that stood on a console below the mirror on the north wall, had made a longer journey—they were all from China. The pale Chinese rug was hardly darker than the old white wallpaper, striped with gold, which had suffered with the passing of time; it showed blotches of damp near the ceiling, and a torn strip had been replaced beside the door.

Carroll Bartram sat on a davenport before the fire. His arm lay along the back of it, and his long, fine hand clasped and unclasped the carved rail. A clever-looking, beak-nosed little man stood behind him, and Miss Ridgeman hovered in the rear. She was holding a tray with a tumbler on it, and she looked as if she were afraid to advance and offer it to her employer.

George Bartram led Gamadge around the end of the davenport.

"Let me introduce my brother," he said, "and Doctor Loring. Carroll, this is Mr. Gamadge."

Carroll Bartram leaned forward to shake hands with Gamadge. "I hope you'll excuse me for not getting up," he said, pleasantly. "I'm all right, but for the moment something seems to have got me in the legs."

"That will go in a minute." Doctor Loring watched his patient, smilingly. "You're better already."

"I really feel—" began Gamadge, but his host interrupted him:

"No, I want to see you. How are you, Mitchell? Do sit down."

Chairs were drawn up, but Loring and the nurse remained where they were. Gamadge took advantage of the few moments while people were getting settled, and hastily studied his host. The older Bartram looked younger than his brother George in all ways but one. His expression was that of a man profoundly shocked, who is still struggling against fact, and in the process of resigning himself to it; and the strain had for the time being aged him; but his face, Gamadge thought, was a naturally smiling one. He was taller than George Bartram, slender, with a clear, tanned skin and wide-set, fine, dark eyes. His long nose had escaped sharpness, and his mouth was too amiable for determination.

"Not a businessman by nature," thought Gamadge, "and not an intellectual. Sports and games; I bet he's good company. He can't stand up to trouble like this—it knocks him endways. He'd run away from it if he could, but he knows how to control his feelings."

Bartram said: "I hear you've met the little gypsy, Mr. Gamadge."

"I have."

"Glad you had a look at him. Well—what did you think of him?" Bartram glanced about at the others, and back at Gamadge, and the corners of his mouth curved up a little. "What do you think of him?" he asked again.

"Nice little fellow."

"Loring says he probably has a lot of Yankee blood in him."

"Oh, undoubtedly." Doctor Loring smiled broadly. "Good, strong physique. Not a scarecrow like young William."

"Perhaps he's a Young Pretender," said Gamadge. "Scottish royalty."

"You met the old grandmother, did you?" Loring's smile widened. "Great character, isn't she? You ought to try to pin her down, sometime; ask her which James is her forefather. She'll begin to hedge, get on her dignity, imply that it's a question of world politics, and snub the life out of you."

"Thrones would shake if she told all she knew?"

"They would; like jelly."

"Loring ran me down there after—afterwards, to look at the boy," said Bartram.

"So that's where you got to?" George's face expressed surprise. "We couldn't imagine—"

"Yes. He would do it. I don't think that's much of a place for a little fellow to convalesce in. Mrs. Stuart seems willing to hand him over."

"You're weakening," said Loring, triumphantly.

"Well, I am. Oh, bring him along, bring him along! That is, if Miss Ridgeman will stand by, and you'll let your Serena and her husband come over and do the housework. I'm not going to leave Annie here when I leave; she's heading for a breakup, or I'm much mistaken."

Loring and Miss Ridgeman exchanged glances of mutual pleasure and congratulation, and the nurse, evidently heartened by her employer's reference to her, came forward and offered him the tumbler; it contained a thick, yellowish fluid from which Bartram winced away in disgust.

"What's that?" he inquired.

"Only your malted milk, Mr. Bartram."

"Take it out of my sight, for goodness' sake! I'll consider a drink of rye whisky."

"Doctor Loring—"

"Bother Doctor Loring. I won't have that stuff."

"Oh, yes, you will, old boy; no whisky for you, this morning; that caffeine I shot into you is all the stimulant you need for a while. Down with it, now; you haven't eaten a mouthful of solid food for—days, is it, Miss Ridgeman?" asked Loring.

"Not much food, Doctor."

"Down with it."

Bartram took the glass, frowned at it, and emptied it. Miss Ridgeman removed it, and herself, from the room. Mr. George Bartram, who had been sitting as if dumfounded, asked: "What's all this about the gypsy?"

"Oh—Loring thinks I might take him in."

"Take him in?" George Bartram stared at Loring.

"Yes. Adopt him, you know."

"One of my prescriptions." Loring looked down at his patient with a smile, patted him on the shoulder, and said in a low voice, "Good for you."

"Adopt that kid?" George Bartram's face was a mask of incredulity.

Mrs. Bartram, who had seemed almost as greatly taken aback as her husband showed himself to be, intervened:

"What a perfectly lovely idea, Carroll! Perfectly lovely. But do you know all about him? They are so careful in the hospitals, and nurseries, and places; they never let people adopt children if they don't know the inheritance. It might be so bad." She, also, glanced with surprise and reproof at Loring, who answered cheerfully:

"I think it's much more sporting to take them sight unseen, as you might say. If he turns out a horse thief or a nitwit, Carroll can turn the psychiatrists on him. Whatever happens to him, he'll be the dickens of a lot better off than he'd be in a Boston slum."

"Well, I think it's just lovely. Don't you think it's lovely, George?"

The warning note in his wife's voice was not unheeded by her husband. He said: "Certainly, certainly," and looked bewildered.

"And now to the real business in hand." Bartram turned to a small table at his elbow, and lifted therefrom a good-sized leather box, which he placed on Mrs. Bartram's lap. "Here you are, Adèle; I hereby appoint you guardian of this in behalf of your daughter, Irma Bartram, and I hope you'll get some fun out of it while Irma's growing up. It's a solemn transfer of property, you know. Very informal, but we have a good many witnesses to the transaction, and one of them is a detective."

"It's Mother's old jewel box." George Bartram bent forward, interested.

"Of course it is; and it represents Julia's estate." Bartram spoke quietly. "It's a way we have in the Bartram family, Gamadge; unbreakable tradition. The jewelry goes to the oldest girl. My mother willed it to Julia, as you know, George. And now, of course, you're the oldest girl, Irma; go and take a look at your property."

"But, Carroll, see here. It belongs to you, now." George Bartram spoke hesitantly, while Irma scrambled down from his knees.

"By law, perhaps; but morally, no. What do you think Mother would have said about it? Trouble is," continued his brother, watching Irma as she hung over the open box, which Mrs. Bartram had just succeeded in freeing from its complicated fastenings, "trouble is, the stuff has so little market value. I don't believe there's anything in that collection, except Mother's old solitaire ring, that a modern jeweler would look at."

Mrs. Bartram lifted the lid of the box, gasped, and exclaimed "Carroll!" in a voice of wonder and delight. "Carroll!" she repeated, almost in a shriek. "George! Come here and look at these!"

"I don't have to look at them." George Bartram got out of his chair, however, and leaned over his wife and daughter. "Many's the time we've seen 'em—haven't we, old boy? Mother thought they were worth a fortune, didn't she? Remember how we used to tease her when she got that wall safe put in?"

"Yes; and you drew a picture of a burglar opening it with a shoehorn, and fainting when he saw what was in it."

Mitchell, who had also advanced to peer over George Bartram's shoulder, remarked that things like that probably cost plenty to buy, though.

"And they're back in fashion!" Mrs. Bartram held up an impressive-looking necklace of turquoise and filigree. "A whole set of turquoise; coral; garnets; gold bracelets; ever so many earrings, and a rope of seed pearls. Oh, Irma!"

Irma, greatly interested and pleased, grasped a large cameo brooch, was instantly pricked by its formidable pin, and dropped it on the floor.

"That's what you get for snatching things. No, darling, it doesn't hurt; see, here's a little gold bead chain that you can wear now!"

She fastened it on Irma's neck, while Gamadge picked up the hideous brooch and restored it to the jewel case.

"There aren't many as bad as that," said Carroll Bartram. "I'm glad of it, for Irma's sake. Don't miss the secret compartment, Adèle."

The secret compartment, however, proved disappointing; it contained a couple of daguerreotypes, some bits of broken coral, a red Chinese tassel, a watch chain made of hair, and two old keys.

"I could have told you," said George Bartram. "Those are sentimental keepsakes. I hope you'll throw that hair thing away; it gives me the creeps."

"Well, I only hope you'll wear the things yourself, Adèle; if Irma agrees, of course." Her brother-in-law looked at her with amusement, but he spoke affectionately. "Lord knows, you deserve more than this junk. You've been a brick, these last few days."

"Irma would have something to say to me if I lost any of them!" She fastened a short string of huge coral beads about her neck, and fingered it lovingly. "Carroll, I don't know how to thank you for these! Irma will, when she's old enough. Now come on, darling, and let's show them to Miss Ridgeman and Annie."

"And Ad'laide," said Irma, skipping off.

"She just loves that funny Adelaide. Aren't children queer?" Mrs. Bartram closed the lid of the jewel box, and hurried out, all smiles. This time Carroll Bartram managed to rise, and remained standing; one elbow on the mantelshelf, his head bent, and his eyes fixed on the embers in the fireplace.

"That's off my mind," he said. "I'm glad your good, kind little wife likes the things, George."

George Bartram cleared his throat. "It was mighty nice of you to dig 'em out, old man. I never should have thought of 'em."

"Why should you? They're not very important. Well, let's get on with it." He did not lift his head, and his fingers tapped the ledge of the chimney piece nervously. "Anything to tell us, Mitchell? Any ideas, Mr. Gamadge?"

Gamadge said: "We seem to be wandering in a fog, Mr. Bartram, unless we decide to adopt the gypsy theory, and write the thing off as a tragic accident."

"But will those poor devils of gypsies get into trouble if we do that?"

"Not serious trouble, unless we find evidence against 'em," said Mitchell. "Of course we couldn't let 'em come back here, or any place within fifty miles of Oakport. The community wouldn't stand for it."

"That seems so brutally unfair."

"And the tribe might make some kind of a fuss about it; the men, I mean."

"They hate trouble," remarked Loring. "They wouldn't fuss much."

"We don't exactly want to take advantage of that."

"We don't want to take any advantage of them at all," said Bartram. "If it happened through one of their children, it's a thing that wouldn't happen again in a thousand years; I don't believe it ever happened before—not in this part of the world."

"Well, if you don't like the gypsy theory, we can consider Tommy Ormiston's evidence about a lady in a car. A harmless lunatic—"

Loring interrupted. "As a professional man, I can't let you assume that all lunatics are necessarily well-intentioned; especially if they go about distributing poison."

"Even a layman doesn't assume that, Doctor; but the point is that this second theory deals with a person without sane motive. Leaving it aside for the moment, we turn to theory number three—that a sane person had a definite reason for distributing the berries. Can you supply me with a reasonable motive which would embrace the Beasleys, the Bartrams, the Ormistons, and perhaps the gypsies? Or do I understand that there's some doubt about little Elias having had any atropine?"

"I'll stake my professional reputation he hadn't," declared Loring. "Between you and me, Cogswell's diagnosis was a pure case of wishful thinking; he wants to pin this business on the gypsies, and get rid of it."

"Well, how about the three other families?"

"Fantastic."

"Then we're faced with the assumption that only one family was the real object of the attack; somebody had something to gain, or a grudge to work off. The other poisonings were carried out to confuse the issue, and keep investigation off the right trail."

There was a silence. Then George Bartram exploded:

"That's the craziest thing I ever heard." He glanced about at the others. "Carroll—Loring. Isn't that the craziest thing you ever heard of?"

"No, George, it isn't." Loring turned narrow eyes on him. "It's logic. Mr. Gamadge is simply going over all the possibilities. Do face it intelligently."

"I know what you think about my intelligence, Bob; but I say there never was any such plan as that carried out except in a dime novel."

"I must lend you some of my criminological treatises, George. Well, Gamadge, as you were saying?"

"As I was saying, we ought to take that special motive into consideration. The motive of gain, say, or the motive of revenge."

"I don't believe anybody has a grudge against either of the Beasleys," said Mitchell. "Everybody around here knows all about the Beasleys; good stock, both of 'em. I spent a lot of time since Tuesday on the Beasleys; if they have an enemy in the world they don't know it."

"And you couldn't find out any reason why they should have an enemy without knowing it?"

"I don't believe they have."

"Well, the Ormistons; what about them?"

Loring said, with an amused look: "I should think Bert Ormiston must have hundreds of enemies—that is, if he's anything like what he was as a youth. But whether they are the sort who would go to such appalling extremes to express their disapprobation, I hardly know."

"You don't take the idea seriously?"

"I really can't. Not where Ormiston is concerned. Take his work seriously, by all means, if you happen to like that sort of thing; but not poor old Bert Ormiston himself."

"Well, then; have *you* an enemy, Mr. Bartram?"

Bartram looked up, straightened, put his hands in the pockets of his dark-gray flannel coat, and gazed past Gamadge towards the bay at the end of the room. "No," he said, "not one."

George Bartram suddenly grinned. "Unless you want to except Ormiston," he said, with a glance at Loring. Carroll Bartram frowned.

"He can't exactly love you, though, can he, old boy? Not if he ever looks in the glass," persisted George.

"Nonsense." His brother looked annoyed.

"You might let us in on the joke," suggested Mitchell.

"What do you say, Carroll? Shall I?"

"You'll have to, now, you ass." Carroll Bartram turned away with a disgusted look, and sat down again on the davenport.

"I talk too much; always did; you mustn't make too much of the story," said George Bartram, uneasily. "Ormiston may have forgotten all about it."

"Don't be too sure of that." Loring also had a faint smile on his lips.

"You go ahead and tell it, Bob. You know more about it than I do. I was only a kid." The younger Bartram grinned again, unsubdued.

"Well..." Loring glanced at his patient, who sat lighting a cigarette and looking bored. "It all happened years ago, when the four of us were at school. Dear old Prep, you know; Newcome's. It's a great favorite with Bostonians, the kind that like to keep their precious boys near home. I wasn't in the charmed circle, of course, being merely the son of a poor Oakport G.P.; but I played with the young Bartrams every summer, and old Mr. Bartram was fond of my father. He made it possible for me to go to that excellent, if rather old-fashioned, school; and I am still grateful."

"Cut that." Carroll Bartram moved impatiently.

"Although," continued Loring, with a smile at Gamadge, "I have never yet been allowed fully to express my gratitude. Well; Ormiston was in our class, Carroll's and mine; and a precocious, gifted, conceited, generally objectionable young pup he was. Not at all in the Newcome tradition. I can see now what he must have gone through; but then I simply joined with the other young barbarians in boycotting him. He retaliated—amply retaliated—by making the most diabolical caricatures of us all. Really diabolical. I don't believe anybody who ever saw a caricature of himself by Ormiston, even at that early period of his genius, felt quite as cocky about himself as he had felt before."

"I can well believe it," said Gamadge.

"You've seen his later things; just try to imagine them inspired by personal rage and resentment! Well, Carroll didn't like his; so he sought out the lumbering Ormiston, who was twice his size but permanently out of training, and broke his nose."

"Really broke it?" Gamadge was politely interested.

"Really and truly broke it—in fair fight, of course. Just one of those things. He smashed it flat, and flat it has remained ever since. I may say that there was a most horrible row. The parents came down, goodness knows what all. We tried to explain what the awful provocation was, but nobody would take us seriously; and Carroll was in disgrace for some time."

Bartram said, smiling a little, "Father told them I ought to be expelled. I wasn't, for some reason."

"Of course you weren't; old Newcome wasn't quite a fool. He knew that accidents will happen. Old Mr. Bartram begged old Ormiston to let him have Bert sent somewhere for plastic surgery, but Bert flatly refused. He went through the rest of the term—our last—as an interesting mutilé; enjoying it, I have no doubt, tremendously."

George Bartram said, "I was a lower-form boy, but even kids like me knew what a crazy idiot Ormiston was. He had all kinds of notions. Why, he was a vegetarian!" George Bartram's tone expressed a kind of horror. "At his age!"

"He's a Social Perfectionist, now," said Gamadge.

"No!" Loring was delighted. "Is he really? I haven't seen him for years; don't know how he's turned out, personally. Old Mr. Bartram, with his usual kindness, kept in touch with him. The Ormistons were always hard up; Mr. Bartram persuaded Bert to accept the money for his session at the Beaux Arts, saw him from time to time afterwards, and I dare say lent him plenty of cash."

"Have you seen much of him since those days, Mr. Bartram?" asked Mitchell, upon whom the story of the broken nose seemed to have made an impression.

"Almost nothing. We used to run into each other in Boston, sometimes, but he's in New York now. I never see him up here."

"You wouldn't say he still had a definite grudge?"

"Goodness knows; I hope not. It can't be a serious one."

"What do you think, Doctor Loring? Would a fellow like that—a neurotic, perhaps—would he let a thing like that smolder along till it finally flared up? Of course I know he'd have to be definitely crazy to do anything like this, with one of his own children involved—"

"I'm no psychologist; can't tell you. Never see the fellow. Shouldn't think it likely—he has an outlet in his work, and plenty of adulation. He's quite the fashion, just now."

"He behaved pretty cool about that boy of his; Sheriff couldn't get over it."

"Oh, he's a tremendous poseur, you know; it's hard to say what such people are really feeling. He may have been putting up a front. Ormiston's reactions to anything wouldn't be ordinary; he'd see to that."

"His wife seems like a nice lady; but very calm and placid."

"She'd have to be placid to stand living with him. I have met her; wrapped up in her children."

Mitchell looked thoughtful, but said nothing. It was Gamadge who remarked: "Mitchell said she stayed with the older ones when the little boy was lost, while the rest of the family—except Ormiston, I believe—rushed about searching. I don't quite know why, but that struck me as odd."

"Well," said Loring, "of course it's very lonely up there, with all the other places empty; and Ormiston wouldn't be any good as a guardian; he might forget all about the children. I suppose she simply didn't dare leave them."

"She's a calm sort of lady," reiterated Mitchell, in a dogged kind of way. "Took the whole business very quietly. Well, you never know. We'll have to pay them a call. You can't help us then, Mr. Bartram? No mystery, nothing at all in your family history that might throw any light on this?"

"We're probably the stodgiest family on record."

"And the only mystery there is," said George Bartram, "doesn't interest anybody but Carroll and myself. You can say what you like, old man; but it is a mystery, and I always thought so."

Carroll Bartram had not spoken, but he had made a wry face, and looked at Loring with a weary half-smile. "Still worrying about that, are you, George?" he asked.

"No, I'm not worrying about it; but it would come in mighty handy now; I can tell you that!"

"What would, if you don't mind me asking?" inquired Mitchell.

"Family business; I talk too much." George Bartram grinned. "You don't want to hear about it."

"If it's a mystery, I certainly do."

"Well, it's just that we never could make out where Father's money went to. His cash, I mean. The cash we thought he must have had when he died."

"Cash?"

"I mean securities. The business was in good shape, and there was enough to buy Mother a comfortable annuity; but we thought there would be more."

"How much more, Mr. Bartram?"

"Well, at least four hundred thousand dollars."

CHAPTER NINE

Four Hundred Thousand Dollars

"FOUR HUNDRED THOUSAND!" Mitchell sat up in his chair.

"About that. It can't have been much less."

Carroll Bartram rose from his corner of the davenport, and walked off to the bay window at the other end of the room. "I don't believe I can sit through it," he said. "You'll excuse me, George; but I thought we stopped crying about that mythical nest egg ten years ago."

"Yes, but Carroll, it wasn't mythical," protested his brother. "Father had the securities—he'd been investing for ages. They were in his box, and nobody else had a key. He must have sold out—must have; we even traced some of the sales back to him."

"I know." Carroll Bartram turned wearily from his contemplation of the green world beyond the window, and sat down at a radio placed on the left of the bay. He turned it on; a chatter of war news burst upon the air, but was quickly subdued to a murmur. George Bartram, his thoughts suddenly wrenched back to the present, looked wistfully at the radio, one ear cocked to listen.

"Isn't it the damnedest thing?" he complained. "I almost wish now that I'd stuck it out. I don't believe it'll spread to the neutrals. My job wasn't the kind you can drop and pick up again. That Dutchman Bloomveldt has been waiting for it for five years. Fine for Bloomveldt—stepped right into my shoes; try and get that job or any other job away from him!"

"I guess you're better off in your own country, now, George," said Loring, not unsympathetically.

"That's what they all said. I don't know."

"That four hundred thousand, Mr. Bartram," insisted Mitchell.

"Oh yes. Well, it was this way: Father died in 1927, and he left the mills to Carroll and myself, and everything else to Mother. Just what we expected; but we thought she'd be well fixed—better than that; rich woman, from some peoples' point of view. We got the surprise of our lives. During the last two years of his life, the old man had sold out four hundred thousand dollars' worth of bonds, and there wasn't a thing to show for it. Mind you, his lawyers and his business associates and everybody else who could get their noses into it started right out to check up on it; and I may say they didn't leave many stones unturned. There was enough to buy that annuity for mother, which kept her going the way she always had gone—the old house in Boston, her old servants, and her old limousine; but she couldn't have done it without the annuity."

"Darned nice of you two to buy it," said Mitchell.

"Only thing we could do; we didn't hesitate. Besides, things were different then; we didn't either of us think we were going to need her money. I sold out to Carroll—always meant to—and went into this partnership—Treves Incorporated. Carroll ran the old business. Then the crash came, and were we glad we'd bought that annuity just in time! But it didn't leave us any margin. I took the European end of the business—gave me a better income. Never got the time to come back—not till now.

"Well, nobody could ever find out what Father bought with that money, or what he did with it. Mother didn't know, and she wouldn't discuss it; she thought he was perfect—said that if he spent it, he must have spent it wisely." George Bartram smacked his hand down hard on the arm of his chair. "Gad! I wonder whether she'd have been so cool about it if there hadn't been enough left to keep her comfortable!"

"Gently, gently," suggested Loring.

"All right; but I get wild when I think of it."

Loring, with his half-closed eyes wrinkling at the corners, turned to Mitchell. "You must understand," he said, "that the usual explanations won't work in Mr. Bartram's case. They really won't; I mean it. I'm healthily agnostic where the perfectibility of human nature is concerned, but you can take it from me that old Mr. Bartram wasn't leading a double life—not in any sense at all. The executors wanted Mrs. Bartram to get her money, and they didn't take anything for granted, or handle the situation with gloves, I can tell you."

"Father and Mother went to Europe every summer," said George Bartram. "We got to the point where we wondered if he'd been playing the races, or taking fliers at Monte Carlo."

"I didn't get to that point," murmured Carroll, without turning.

"Mother swore there wasn't anything of the sort; they were always together, you know. I don't believe they were separated for more than seven hours at a time since they were married—and that means business hours."

Mitchell said: "You'll excuse the question; did anybody think of blackmail?"

"Everybody thought of blackmail, except the family, and persons like myself, who knew old Mr. Bartram," replied Loring. "But that led nowhere."

Gamadge inquired, with mild interest, "Did he collect anything?"

"What kind of thing?" asked George Bartram, puzzled.

"Any kind of thing. People will pay a good deal for a book, a manuscript, a letter; I know that from my own experience. They will pay an extraordinary sum for a Chinese pot, a coin, a watch, a fan—if they're collectors, of course."

"I never heard that he collected anything. Last time he was in Paris, in 1927, he bought a lot of pictures; job lot. He said they were a bargain. He didn't pay much for 'em."

"Did he understand pictures?" Gamadge looked up at the landscape over the mantelshelf. "That's a nice Kensett."

"Oh, that's always been there; he didn't buy that. No, I don't think he cared for pictures at all. These were some that a Frenchman wanted to sell—one of those aristocrats you hear about, trying to get rid of family stuff. Ormiston introduced them."

"Mr. Ormiston introduced your father to this Frenchman?"

"Yes. Ormiston and his wife were living in Paris then. Father always looked them up when he went to France."

"And Ormiston engineered this deal?"

"So I understood."

"What became of these pictures?"

"I don't know. They were in our attic in Boston. I understood Father bought them out of charity. What became of those pictures Father bought in Paris, Carroll?"

Carroll Bartram answered without turning his head: "Mother let Ormiston have them for what they cost Dad. She said she had his receipted bills for them."

"She didn't have them appraised, I suppose?" asked Gamadge.

"No, the customs people appraised them when Dad paid the duty."

"Why did Ormiston want them?"

"He said he'd clean them up, scrape about six coats of old varnish off some of 'em, and make a couple of hundred on the turnover; that's what he told Mother, anyway. I suppose he knew how to market such things."

"And Mr. Ormiston was already familiar with them, and

knew their history; at least I presume he was, if he managed the original deal."

George Bartram said: "There was some kind of joke about one of them. What was that joke about the little old dark picture, Carroll?"

Bartram turned off the radio, got up, and lounged slowly back to the group around the fire. "How did you get on the picture subject, anyhow?" he asked, eying his brother with the wry amusement that George Bartram seemed often to provoke in him.

"I don't know how we got on it. Mr. Gamadge wondered if Father sank his money in some hobby."

"The mill was his hobby."

"I wondered whether your father had been put on to a good thing in pictures," said Gamadge.

"There's no trace of anything like that. How would they get by the customs?"

"Well, there are all sorts of games; pictures have been known to be painted over, faked in some way. The collector then 'discovers' them elsewhere."

"Father wouldn't do a thing like that!" The younger Bartram was indignant.

"Not if it was just a question of doing the customs? It's very odd, you know, what otherwise strictly honorable people will do when it's only a matter of paying duty."

George Bartram scowled. At last he said: "*Mother* wouldn't stand for it. She was great on civic responsibility. Remember the time we rode free on the train, Carroll, and she made us go back and make full confession and restitution to the conductor?"

"Yes." Carroll Bartram smiled. "I suppose Father might not have told her a thing about it."

"But Ormiston knew, and bought 'em off her for nothing!" George Bartram's face turned dark-red.

Loring said, laughing, "We haven't an atom of proof against your father, George."

"No; but—what was that little picture they joked about, Carroll?"

"Don't ask me." The elder Bartram, using the glass of the Kensett as a mirror, readjusted his smoke-gray tie. "Dutch school," he said; "which is all Dutch to me. It wasn't signed."

"They used to say it was by somebody—who was it? Somebody good."

"Began with a V; I know enough," he added, smiling, "to know it wasn't Van Dyck."

"Or Vermeer." Gamadge also smiled.

"That's the fellow—Vermeer." Bartram looked round in surprise at the inarticulate sound made by Gamadge, and at Loring's wild crow of mirth, instantly subdued.

"Wake me up, somebody," implored the doctor, wagging his head until a lock of fairish hair fell over his eyes.

"What's the matter?" inquired Bartram, mildly. "I seem to have dropped a bomb."

"Oh, nothing's the matter, old man; only, a Vermeer is at present what George would call a wanted article."

"Somewhat in demand, just at present," agreed Gamadge, solemnly.

"A bit scarce. Why, you poor benighted heathen," said Loring, addressing the brothers almost violently, "don't you really know that Vermeer of Delft is not only the height of the fashion, but that his few and jealously counted pictures are valuable beyond your wildest dreams?"

"Oh? Why?" asked Carroll Bartram, politely.

"Because a lot of his things were scattered and burned up or lost, you innocent, and a lot of them were ascribed to other painters. Then he was rediscovered—when, Gamadge?"

"About seventy-five years ago the craze began, I think."

"And since then hordes of people have been hunting around in all the holes and corners of Europe, trying to find Vermeers, signed or not. I thought they were all placed, now."

"There are supposed to be still a few in existence, waiting to be found," said Gamadge. "Your father really must have been joking, Mr. Bartram; there isn't much chance of a Vermeer falling into his hands like that."

"How much would one be worth?" asked George Bartram, whose flush had not entirely subsided.

"I hardly know. What do you think, Loring?"

"Well, before 1929 I'm sure a Vermeer would have brought at least a hundred thousand, in the open market."

"What!" George Bartram started as if he had been stung.

"Just forget it, George, old boy," advised Loring, with a grin. "Drop the whole thing. We have no proof that your father ever bought a decent picture in his life. If he did, and Ormiston got it from your mother for a song, he won't tell."

"But couldn't we make him produce the things, or find out what he did with 'em?"

"If he sold a picture for a hundred thousand dollars," said Mitchell, "he wouldn't be so hard up as he is now."

"Is he hard up?" inquired Loring.

"They tell me so. I oughtn't to have mentioned it. When did you say your father sold the bonds, Mr. Bartram?"

"Between the summer of 1925 and the summer of 1927; wasn't it, Carroll?"

"If you say so; I don't remember."

"Sold 'em for cash?" asked Mitchell.

"Well, not quite like that," said Carroll Bartram. "The proceeds of the sales were duly deposited in the bank, and he drew out the cash himself, in amounts running from a thousand to ten thousand dollars."

"He might have transferred it to another bank—under another name."

"So he might."

"Funny he didn't say anything to your mother."

"He may have intended to. He died suddenly, you know; of heart failure. Shock to us all."

"Well, it certainly does look as if he heard of some investment while he was in Europe in 1925; realized on his securities in the next two years; and bought whatever he did buy, in 1927."

"There are long odds against the possibility of cheating those fellows at the customs," said Gamadge.

"Long odds against old Mr. Bartram cheating anybody, too," said Loring.

"Well, we must certainly interview Mr. Ormiston. I'll let you know," said Gamadge, as he rose, "how the gentleman reacts to the words Varnish, Value and Vermeer."

George Bartram shook hands, forcing a smile; he was undoubtedly shaken to the depths of his soul by this exasperating hypothesis. Carroll Bartram had for some minutes been looking exhausted. He shook hands silently with Gamadge, and sank back on the davenport.

Loring went to the front door with the two visitors. "Look here," he said, "what about lunch at my place? It will save you the trip to Burnsides and back, and we'll have a chance for a real talk. Impossible to discuss things freely in there." He jerked his head backwards. "Now, don't be afraid of taking potluck with me; I run a bachelor doctor's establishment; no fixed hours, plenty of food in the cupboard, and a good plain cook who loves company."

"What say, Mr. Gamadge?" Mitchell was evidently pleased with the invitation.

"I'm entirely in your hands."

"Good!" said Loring. "You don't know my house, do you? I'll just get my car—it's in the back lane."

"We'll join you there. I'll get you to let me telephone Mrs. Burnside, and ask her to save that tinker mackerel for supper." Mitchell and Gamadge started down the steps, and Loring disappeared into the house.

Mrs. George Bartram, Irma Bartram and Miss Adelaide Gibbons were picking flowers from the borders along the flagged walk. Mrs. Bartram still wore the coral necklace, and Irma the gold beads; Irma had also somehow managed to persuade someone to pin the enormous cameo brooch to her sweater, whereon it reposed, blandly incongruous. Miss Gibbons, gaunt, freckled, and unprofessionally clothed in a short red-and-white silk dress and patent-leather pumps, wore long gold filigree earrings, from which half the tassels were missing.

"Long stems, Irma," admonished Mrs. Bartram, glancing rather helplessly at the other two, who were tearing marigolds from their stalks and casting them into a flat basket, without much regard for the niceties of the task, but with great rapidity.

Miss Gibbons smiled up amiably at the two men.

"Pickin' a bouquet for dinner," she said, "and look at all the help we got here. Never you mind, Irm, we can float the short ones in a dish, like my mon does with pansies. See what Irm gave me out of her box of joolery. Ain't they pretty?"

"Short stems, Irma," repeated Mrs. Bartram, a little stiffly.

Irma, as usual, said nothing, but the look she bestowed on Gamadge was blissful; she was being horribly spoiled, she knew not for what reason; and she had found an affinity.

CHAPTER TEN

Casebook of a Country G.P.

GAMADGE SETTLED HIMSELF into his seat in Mitchell's car and got out a pencil and a badly smudged Torquemada puzzle. He buried himself in it so effectively that Mitchell gave up trying to talk to him.

They drove east to the limits of the Bartram property, turned left, again followed the white picket fence, turned left again, and found themselves in a narrow lane, between the Bartram grounds and the woods. Loring awaited them in front of a garage which contained two cars, one of them George Bartram's bargain in Cadillacs. Loring's own well-worn two-seater looked as if a garage seldom sheltered it.

"Have you been in this way?" he asked Gamadge, indicating the Bartram gate.

"No. I won't get out, thanks." Gamadge looked towards the summerhouse, of which the wire netting shimmered among shrubs.

Loring preceded them along back roads to a cheerful frame house, standing on a quiet corner among old maples. A pleasant, gray-haired woman received them hospitably.

"I have a big dish of fish chowder all ready," she said. "How's Carroll Bartram? I hope he's bearin' up."

"He is, better than I thought he would. Serena, this is Mr. Mitchell; state detective. You watch your step. And here's Mr. Gamadge, from New York. This is my housekeeper, Mrs. Turnbull. She'll show you the way to the office washroom, while I go and get out something worthy of the fish chowder. A dry white wine, don't you think? I need something rather special, after this morning's very exacting work."

"I sh'd think you would," said Serena. She led Gamadge and Mitchell through the office on the left of the door, and to a well-equipped lavatory. Mitchell took the liberty of using the office telephone to call Burnsides, and Gamadge stood at the side door, evidently cut through for the benefit of patients, which gave on a sunny lawn with a border of late-blooming flowers.

"'An innocent life, yet far astray'?" He intoned it questioningly. "I shouldn't mind being far astray in a place like this."

"You'd think you were far astray, in winter," said Mitchell. "My heavens, you need snowshoes to get around these back roads. *Nothing* gets through. I bet Loring uses the old cutter, bells and all."

They crossed the hall, hung their hats on a rack which already bulged with masculine outer garments that exuded a leathery, rubbery smell, and joined Loring in a small, square dining room. It was neat and bare, with faded roses on the walls and clean muslin curtains at the windows. Serena brought them huge dishes of fish chowder, followed by a cucumber salad, for which she apologized:

"The doctor will have his greens."

"Yes, and not in chunks, either. I hope those cucumbers are sliced thin, Serena. I see they are; bless you." Loring made a superlative dressing, refilled their glasses with Graves, and asked Serena to toast some more brown bread.

"This Mrs. Turnbull of yours, she's some cook," said Mitchell, and Gamadge remarked that Doctor Loring was probably some cook, too.

"Well—she does the native dishes perfectly; I supply the trimmings, and make out the menus. I'm a gourmet."

"So am I," said Gamadge, "and I can assure you that I never ate a better lunch in my life."

"Glad to hear you say so." Loring served the dessert—home-preserved fruits and spongecake—and they finished the meal in the silence of appreciation. Afterwards they adjourned to a large room at the back of the house, where Serena brought them coffee.

Gamadge sank into an old green rep chair in front of the Franklin stove, and sighed.

"I call this a room!" he said.

"It's the old parlor and sitting room, thrown together."

It ran across the width of the house, with two windows on the south, one on the east, and a fireplace, fitted with the Franklin stove, in the north wall. Green rep, fading to bronze, hung from the windows to the floor, which was covered by an ancient green-and-white carpet. Yellowed engravings in wide mahogany frames hung between latticed bookcases. A broad table in the southeast corner was spread with papers. The wall was a panorama of quiet landscapes, which Mitchell gazed upon admiringly.

"I had the paper made," confessed Loring; "had it copied from scraps I found in the attic. I suppose I was a fool, but I do like things to be in keeping. I can't tell you how I hated having the whale-oil lamp, there, fitted for electricity."

"And he has those curtains up nine tenths of the year," said Mrs. Turnbull, who had come in to take away the coffee cups. "Men are the greatest ones for curtains; lucky they don't mind dust."

She departed, and Loring said: "We're reasonably sure of being let alone for the moment. Have a drop of brandy? To the deuce with those great silly glasses, say I; I like mine in a thimble."

He and Gamadge had their thimblefuls, Mitchell refusing.

"I feel good enough the way I am," he explained, filling his pipe. "This kind of thing is apt to make you forget you're working against time."

"You really must go tomorrow night, Gamadge?" asked Loring. "Too bad. It's a comfort to have a civilized being to talk to, once in an age."

"I should say that Mr. Bartram was highly civilized."

"In the strictly worldly sense, yes; I don't pretend to emulate him, and he, in turn, has no use for—er—*belles lettres*."

"You write, don't you, Doctor?"

"Trifles, nothing you could read. 'Leaves From the Casebook of a Country Doctor'—that sort of thing."

"I imagine I could easily read them."

"They go pretty well, nowadays; seem to be the fashion. I do them to avoid complete atrophy of the brain. Mine, you know, is the saddest of all cases," and he smiled, not at all sadly. "My character was ruined early, and forever."

"How was that?" asked Gamadge, also smiling.

"Well, I graduated rather well from medical school, lots of promise; but a friend of mine had a rich father, with arthritis, who owned a yacht. He signed me on as traveling body physician, and I went all over creation with him, in the most luxurious manner. When he died, I had acquired the tastes of a multimillionaire, some skill at bridge and poker, a smattering of European languages, and a knack for mixing salad dressings. I had lost all desire to fight my way up in my profession, and I was completely out of touch with it."

"But he must have paid you pretty well for your services. Didn't he leave you anything in his will?" Mitchell was interested.

"Yes, to both questions; but like a good many other people in those dear old days, I went on the market. The fall of 1929 saw me back here in Oakport, figuring on how to pay the taxes and keep the old roof mended."

"Didn't the feller's son help you out?"

"Unfortunately, he also had gone on the market; or stayed on it, rather. He didn't bear up as well as I did; shot himself. But the Bartram family stood by, I can tell you. The mills were having one of their periodical slumps, but Carroll tided me over, just the same. I started practice on that, and on my father's reputation, and here I am; perfectly happy."

"It takes experience to teach you what you can be satisfied with," said Mitchell.

"It does. I hope poor old George won't have to learn the lesson; he wouldn't react favorably."

Mitchell thought for a moment, seemed to decide against whatever he had contemplated saying, and relapsed into silence. Gamadge said:

"I should think you might find the Bartrams' Annie a subject for inclusion in that casebook."

"Annie? Why? Senility isn't particularly interesting."

"It seems to be taking a curious form with her. She's convinced there is an evil influence—supernatural, I gather—working in this vicinity. Why does she insist that there's a curse on the place?"

Loring seemed to take this seriously. He said after a pause for thought: "I believe her mind has been tending in that direction ever since that bad time we all had, seven years ago last May. It really was a bad time, you know—very bad. Ironical, too. When this last calamity arrived, I suppose she considered it a sort of fulfillment of doom. I'll get her out of here as soon as I can; Monday, if possible. If she's in for a general breakup she may as well have it in the old country, where she wants to be. Her son's there, you know."

"I heard that he was."

"Yes. She's never been right—what I call right—since the troubles in Ireland. But about the trouble at Bartram's—back in 1932, that was. About a year after old Mr. Bartram died, Carroll got married to a perfectly charming girl, just the type for him; Caroline Hardwick. George had escaped to Holland by that time; I say escaped, because the Boston atmosphere never did suit poor George. He got out of it as soon as he could, and you saw this morning what sort of type *he* prefers. Nice little woman; but of course not in Caroline Bartram's class at all.

"In the winter of 1932 old Mrs. Bartram had a slight stroke, and when she was able to move she wanted to come up here to the old place. As it happened, Carroll and his wife were more than willing to come too; Julia was on the way, and Carrie was none too strong. They settled in—cold, stormy weather it was, for May. Annie came along as resident cook, and they got outside local help for the rest of the work. I engaged Miss Ridgeman to look after Carrie, and keep an eye on the old lady; regular battleship of the old school, she was; wouldn't have a nurse, didn't need help going up and down stairs, all the rest of it. She was the sort you can't control until you get them helpless in bed.

"Miss Ridgeman came on that train that gets in at about seven thirty. She was unpacking in her room, when suddenly she heard the most fearful thumping in the hall. Old Mrs. Bartram had had her second stroke, and fallen downstairs; and Carrie Bartram had seen it happen. When Miss Ridgeman got there Carrie was half out of her wits, trying to lift the old lady, who weighed a ton. Bartram got hold of me, and I grabbed Serena Turnbull. Among us, we got old Mrs. Bartram to bed in a room on the ground floor—'parlor bedroom', you know.

"By that time Carrie was in a bad way. We got her up to bed, Serena standing by downstairs. Julia was born that night, and early next morning Carrie died. I said something about irony, didn't I? Carrie Bartram died; but old Mrs. Bartram did not. We fully expected her to; the man I got from Boston didn't give her a week; but she came around like a hardy perennial, moved back to Boston in a month, and remained in her old house there, bedridden, half-paralyzed, but perfectly chipper otherwise, until last June. Is that irony, or am I misusing the word?"

"No, I don't think you are."

"Carroll Bartram doesn't expose his feelings to the public gaze, but he goes under—pretty deep. It was young Julia that saved him from a crash then; I think that little gypsy may just possibly do the same for him now. You know something?" and Loring looked very alert and artful. "I believe I'll smuggle the kid in tomorrow."

"Good for you. But the George Bartrams won't like it," said Mitchell, archly.

"I don't care whether they like it or not. Miss Ridgeman can put him on the top floor, out of their way. They're going Monday, anyhow."

"Annie will lament over him," said Gamadge. "She doesn't consider the place safe for children."

"I'm not at all sure that she'll need to know he's there. She can't climb stairs. I'll get her off on Monday, too. Leave it to Miss Ridgeman. She's so thankful to do anything for Bartram, she'll deal with the whole boiling of 'em; Annie, the Georges and all. Carroll was inclined to blame her, at first; but I made him see how confoundedly ungrateful that would be. He owes her a good deal, and she's heartbroken."

"Have you any opinion to offer us on this nightshade business, Doctor?" asked Gamadge. "I understand you don't much care for the gypsy theory."

"I have an open mind on the subject."

Mitchell looked surprised. "I thought you were dead against it," he protested.

"My dear man! If Carroll Bartram is to take in this little—what do they call him?—this little Elias, he mustn't have it dinned into him that the boy may have unintentionally killed his own child."

"You have no theories on the subject of these poisonings, then?" persisted Gamadge.

"I'm inclined to think it may have been the work of an irresponsible. I can let you see my casebooks, if you like," he said, smiling quizzically at Mitchell. "You'll find enough oddities in them to set you off suspecting half the county. That's what I wanted to speak to you about; I'm going to get a man up, man who knows his subject, to give my doubtfuls the once-over. I don't want you policemen sending all the dim-wits in the neighborhood out of what poor sense remains to them."

"You think they're harmless, do you, Doctor?"

"Yes, I do; but I'm not qualified to dogmatize. I shouldn't in the least recognize the symptoms, if some hitherto well-meaning eccentric took it into his or her head that the time had come to impersonate the angel of death."

"We'll wait for your report before we start on your case-books. Do you take any stock in that idea of a grudge?" asked Mitchell.

"I boggle at it; all that kind of thing seems pure insanity to me. Ormiston, for instance—he's an exhibitionist, but I doubt if he's insane."

"Do you think he could be a swindler on a big scale?"

"The Vermeer!" Loring threw back his head to laugh. "I'm sure I don't know; but if he is, I doubt if you'll catch him at it."

"Well, we'll go up there and have a talk with him. That money old Mr. Bartram had, and then didn't have; there might be a lead, there. What do you say, Mr. Gamadge?"

"We shouldn't be justified in ignoring the possibility; but it's all a long time ago. We may not turn up anything."

"Well, best of luck." Loring stood waving to them until Mitchell had turned the car, and driven off to the northeast.

"I didn't like to say anything about George Bartram," said Mitchell, relieved to observe that Gamadge had not again brought out the Torquemada puzzle. "I wanted to; but I have a kind of a feeling that Loring wouldn't keep a thing like that to himself. He'd tell Carroll Bartram."

"Tell him what?"

"Well, tell him we knew George had time to go back, after he left his wife and little girl at Ford's Center, Tuesday morning, and hand around that nightshade."

"It would be worth telling him, if he would tell us what George Bartram's motive could have been. I myself can see no motive whatever, unless he means to exterminate his brother, too; not to mention little Elias, now that Carroll Bartram thinks of adopting the boy."

"You make it sound silly, but people have done such things."

"I don't make it sound silly; I'm saying that George Bartram had nothing to gain—unless he's a mass murderer."

"Carroll Bartram might marry again, and have half a dozen children."

"He may, if he lives long enough."

Mitchell glanced sharply at Gamadge, and said after a moment: "I don't know if you're serious."

"Perfectly serious, but it doesn't do to be too serious. 'Laugh or go mad'; isn't that the phrase? Well, well; here we are, again; on the dear old Tucon road."

"What do you think the doc would do," persisted Mitchell, "if I spoke to him about George Bartram?"

"Anything most likely to shield his friend Carroll Bartram from danger, trouble or anxiety."

"Even if that meant withholding evidence—against a murderer?"

"Doctor Loring is no moralist."

"He wouldn't even give the gypsies away, I don't think. I got an impression that he won't give away his patients, even if some of 'em are loony enough to poison a whole community with nightshade berries."

"His point was that you can't tell whether they *are* loony enough."

"I wish he felt like helping us. He's smart. But he won't even say what he really thinks about Ormiston."

"No. We'll have to get on as best we can without Doctor Loring."

To Mitchell's disgust, Gamadge again buried himself in his Torquemada puzzle.

CHAPTER ELEVEN

Curious Personality of an Artist

THEY DROVE THROUGH the settlement of Tucon, where shuttered windows and an absence of human life were evidence to the fact that its colony of artists and craftsmen had retired for the winter. Half a mile farther on the road took an eastward turn, and led them through a belt of dense woods to a wild and rocky shore. They drove northward, Gamadge lifting his eyes from his squares and smudges to gaze at a cold, dark-blue, white-capped ocean.

"Every month here seems to have its own smell," he said. "This September one is the best of all; but I say that about each of them. Here comes a young fellow who appears to be making the most of a short holiday from the city. He'll be sorry."

The young man in question, who was driving a coupé with the top down, had indeed acquired a violent sunburn. He wore a pepper-and-salt suit, his felt hat was on the seat beside him, and his steel-rimmed spectacles flashed in the sun as he turned his head to look at the passers-by. The look was a sharp one, from sharp close-set eyes.

"Didn't somebody say something, some time this morning, about a feller with spectacles and a suit like that?" Mitchell threw a glance over his shoulder, and again met the young man's interested gaze.

"The George Bartrams saw him at the cemetery, talking to Mrs. Ormiston."

"Oh, yes. I remember. He'll know us if he sees us again."

They approached Harper's Rocks, a string of weathered cottages perched on the rising cliff. "How unutterably empty and forlorn a summer colony does look when it closes up," said Gamadge.

"Yes, it does. That's the trail through the woods to the Beasley road."

Gamadge turned his head, and had a glimpse of a dark opening among trees. Mitchell drove on for a few yards, coming to a stop at the foot of a steep, grassy slope, where three conveyances were already parked; a big one which was much in need of a wash, a small two-seater, and the piano-like trailer of which Mitchell had spoken. A shingled cottage topped the rise. Halfway up the slope was a sand pile under a stunted pine.

They climbed with some difficulty, the path being little more than a beaten track. Gamadge paused beside the disorderly little mound of sand, in which a tin pail and shovel lay partly buried.

"I don't like people who leave little boys forgotten on sand piles," he said.

"Tom was not a favorite child;
Only six, and running wild."

Mitchell stopped, and looked back at him. "What's that you say?"

"I'm taking a high moral tone, and blaming people; that's what mankind invariably does, if it dares; they love to blame people when a misadventure happens; they particularly love to blame parents.

"Let's be thankful; someone gave
Tommy Ormiston a grave."

Mitchell asked: "What's the matter with you, anyway? The boy's all right."

"I was thinking of the might-have-been; or 'ben', as the poet Whittier seems to wish us to pronounce it."

Mitchell silently climbed the path, *Maud Muller*, Mr. Ormiston and the Bartram family lot churning in his brain. He and Gamadge mounted to a porch which extended around the house, and on the south side of which a lady and two children sat playing Chinese checkers.

"How do, Mrs. Ormiston," said Mitchell. "This is Mr. Gamadge; I telephoned about him."

Mrs. Ormiston had the placidity that Gamadge had been prepared for, but he had not expected to find her so handsome. She was large and olive-skinned, with a coiled mass of thick, dark hair, and brown, bovine eyes. And she dressed for comfort; her costume being a blue knitted dress faded almost to gray, brown woollen stockings, and brown canvas tennis shoes.

"How do you do?" she asked, with a pleasant smile at the two men. "My husband is expecting you. Run away and find Dave, children; and remember, you're not to go off the place without him."

The children, a stout girl of twelve and a delicate-looking boy of ten, demurred.

"We always went everywhere by ourselves till Tommy got lost," protested the girl; and the boy, flung pleadingly against his mother's knees, complained: "Do we have to be with grown people all the rest of our lives, just because he picked some poison berries? It isn't fair."

"I know it isn't, darling; but you be a good boy, and do as I say."

They disappeared around the house, and Mrs. Ormiston said: "I suppose I'm silly, but I'm nervous after what happened."

"I can't blame you, ma'am. Where's the little feller?" Mitchell glanced about him, as if he expected to see Tommy emerge from under the table.

"He's up the road with Millie Strangways. She's painting on the rocks."

"How is he?"

"Perfectly all right, thank goodness. I do blame myself so for what happened."

"Did I understand that you were in the cellar that morning, Mrs. Ormiston?" asked Gamadge.

"Yes; or in the back yard. I had so much to do. I thought Millie or David Breck had Tommy. You know how things are on moving day; or perhaps you don't," and she smiled at them.

A tall, redheaded, homely young man in shirt and slacks, with a hatchet in his hand, came around the east corner of the house and stood on the turf below, looking up at them.

"The kids want to bathe again," he said. "Do I take them down, or do I go on chopping firewood?"

"Oh dear. I really do think Millie might—"

"She's got young Tom to look after."

"I'll take the children. It's so cold at night, we just must keep the fire up. This is Davidson Breck—Mr. Mitchell, and Mr. Gamadge. Oh, I forgot; you know Mr. Mitchell, don't you, Dave? I'll just speak to Mr. Ormiston, and then I'll take the children—Oh dear. I ought to drive in and get some things for supper. I think I'll take them with me; only they fuss so."

She went along the veranda, and turned the southeast corner of it. Mr. Breck watched her go, a gloomy expression on his freckled and intelligent face. Gamadge said, poising himself on the porch rail and lighting a cigarette: "I'm supposed to be making a few inquiries."

"I know you are." Breck eyed him without much favor.

"You were engaged indoors on Tuesday morning, I believe?"

"I believe so, too. Some people seem to think I'm to blame for what happened to the poor kid, but let me tell you that if it hadn't been for Millie Strangways and myself he'd have been lost or killed half a dozen times this summer."

"I understood that it was your job to look after him."

"It was my job to look after 'em all, with special reference to Sidney, the other boy. He's delicate; needs an operation on his neck, or something. He's the only one that never did get mislaid."

"But the girl is better able to take care of herself than a six-year-old is."

"She could take care of the whole family, I think, if she had to. She probably will have to," said Breck, with a slight scowl.

"You must all have had a bad time on Tuesday morning. How did you manage with the search?"

"Oh. Yes, it was pretty awful. Millie turned up from the beach, heard Tom was missing, and left in her car, with Ormiston swearing his head off. She spent hours driving up and down and through the woods by herself—must have covered miles. She'd get out every now and then and search on foot. She never came back until after he was found—completely exhausted, she was. But she sat up all night with him."

"You weren't with her?"

"No. I chased around in the other car, and got mixed up with the Beasley search party. That took me out Bailtown way. I kept coming back here to report to Mrs. Ormiston. She stayed and hung on to the other two children, and Ormiston simply packed his sketching kit and got out of it all; along the beaches. Brought back quite a good picture, too."

"Quite detached from mundane affairs, isn't he?"

"Not so you'd notice it. Well, he's an artist—a real one; I suppose they have just so much energy to use outside their work, and when that's gone, they can't bother."

"Well, thanks, Mr. Breck. I won't keep you from the wood pile."

"Very kind of you." He hurried off, and a short, clumsily built but muscular-looking man came around the corner of the porch. Tow-colored hair stood up in an untidy crest above a wide forehead; light, greenish eyes were set flatly in a flat, pasty face, on which the slightly flattened nose was barely a disfigurement. He wore an undershirt, a pair of corduroy trousers, and white tennis shoes; and he held in the fingers of his right hand a piece of red artist's chalk.

He stopped, looked the arrivals over, remarked with great coolness: "I'll see Gamadge," and turned away. He was lumbering off down the porch when Gamadge's amiable voice halted him:

"Can't be done, Mr. Ormiston. This is official."

"Official? What does that mean?" Ormiston glanced back over his shoulder.

"I'm here to assist Mr. Mitchell; police investigation. I can't interview witnesses privately."

Ormiston stared. "What am I witness of?" he inquired, belligerently. "I've talked to the state police and the sheriff till I'm sick of the sight of them. Oh well—come along, then, both of you."

He lurched off around the corner. Gamadge, looking after him with considerable amusement, asked: "Will he punch my nose? If he does, you'll have to carry me out; he looks hefty."

"It's all talk. He's a show-off."

"Forward, then—into the lion's jaws. He looks rather like a lion—man-eater."

They turned the corner of the porch, and a strong wind blew in their faces, making them clutch their hats. The house was practically flush with the high cliff, at the foot of which big waves were rolling and flinging up plumes of spray. Ormiston stood within an open door.

"Come in," he said. "Everything's packed; nothing to paint with, and nothing to see."

They entered a large, high studio, walled and ceiled with native pine, a great window almost filling the north end of it.

A stone fireplace faced the door, jugs and tins stood on a long trestle table, and an easel in the middle of the room held a big square of rough gray cardboard.

"Sit down," said Ormiston, "and smoke, if you can find anything to smoke with. I don't indulge, myself; fearful habit."

Mitchell lowered himself upon a camp chair, and equably lighted his pipe. Gamadge sat on a corner of the table. Ormiston stood with his back to his easel, chalk in hand.

"I rather wanted to meet you, Gamadge," he said. "You're an able man; but your work's not creative—none of it."

"Precious little work looks creative in comparison with such as yours," replied Gamadge, swinging a leg. "'Ormiston's mighty line', you know. You can afford to make allowances for the less gifted."

"Where art is concerned, I never make allowances. And this side line of yours, or hobby, or whatever you call it; this police work—criminology. Futile."

"But constructive."

"Destructive, you mean."

"Not at all. To hear of a particularly mean and ugly crime, to fear that a conceited scoundrel is going to get away with it, and to build up a case against him—that's construction."

"Build up a case! Browbeat witnesses, you mean. Nine tenths of all cases are solved, as they call it, by that; and by paying for information."

"I can construct a simple little case for you, here and now; without having browbeaten any witnesses, or tried to extract any information."

"What case?" demanded Ormiston, looking fiercely at him.

"Why, the case against your being Tommy's father, and Mrs. Ormiston his mother; and the case in favor of Miss Millie Strangways being his maternal parent—though I don't absolutely insist on that. I'd bet on it, though."

Ormiston stood for some moments with his legs planted wide, staring at Gamadge. Presently he said: "I was afraid my wife would give the show away; the poor girl has a heart of gold, but she can't play a part. Not that she isn't fond of the boy; she is. Young Sidney's on her mind just now—that's the trouble."

"Well, however I did manage to catch on," said Gamadge, "I caught on. That's not the important point; the thing is, it gives us a new line on the nightshade case."

"I don't know what you're talking about."

"Why, up to now, we have had to confine ourselves to wondering who can have had a grudge against you, or the Bartrams, or the Beasleys. At present we are able to extend our researches to Miss Strangways. Plenty of people must know that Tommy is hers."

Ormiston looked very much discomposed. "There isn't a nicer girl living," he said, "and I don't want her bothered. Grudges! What rot." He turned to face his easel, made a free, circular motion in the air with his piece of red chalk, and then seemed to transfer the gesture to the gray surface before him, as lightly and surely as if some delicate mechanism had controlled his hand. But there was nothing mechanical about the flowing line that resulted, or about the other lines that followed without pause or forethought. He stepped aside, indicated the sketch of a girl's head that stood out against the rough background with uncompromising reality, and said: "There! Know who that is?"

"Yes, I do," replied Gamadge. "It's Martha, the gypsy."

"Excuse the representational quality—I wanted it to be a photograph. Look at that face; look at that expression—or lack of expression. That's gypsy, for you. Vacant, mindless, unteachable. I've done two oils of her this summer—if there were anything in her head I should have had it out, I can tell you. There isn't. Those people merely exist, like the stupider animals. There's no stupidity they're incapable of; and the only thing they know how to do is to evade the results, by flat denial. A few years ago I used to draw her sister Georgina—or her aunt, or whatever she is; they never seem sure about their family relationships. I cannot make out what they think they gain by these small deceptions, unless lying is the breath of life to them. Georgina looked just like Martha, then. The boy William—he's quite capable of poisoning whole communities, merely from pure inability to reflect."

"You credit them with these poisonings, then."

"Well, yes; I do. They're always about, all summer; trying to sell their rubbish, tell fortunes, beg old clothes. You'll never prove anything. What I want to say is, let that poor girl Millie Strangways alone. Her name isn't Strangways—it's Walworth; Mrs. Lawrence F. Walworth. Does that tell you anything?"

Mitchell said: "My soul and body." Gamadge slowly drew forth a package of cigarettes, lighted one, placed the match carefully on the edge of a Mexican tile that lay beside him, and spoke as if under the spell of memory:

"He would have been electrocuted five years ago, if he hadn't died in prison."

"Yes! For poisoning a whole family with arsenic. For their money. His aunt and uncle died; his cousin—their only child—got over it, physically. But they had to put her in a sanatorium, and she only came out, cured, a few months ago. That's Tommy Walworth's inheritance. Do you wonder his mother gave him up?"

Mitchell said: "They could have gone some place else, under another name."

"She hadn't a penny; not by the time that trial was over. Besides, the girl has one obsession—I wonder she hasn't more. She wants the boy completely separated from Walworth, not only in name but in everything else. I believe it would kill her if she thought he would ever know anything about it. We were fond of her—she was a pupil of mine, and a friend of my wife's. She's a promising water colorist, but of course she doesn't make any money at it, yet. We took the boy when he was a mere infant, five years ago. In the summers she comes up here to be with him. Least we can do."

"Cooks, doesn't she?" suggested Mitchell.

"If she didn't, we couldn't afford to have her. You may have heard that times are hard for the arts," replied Ormiston. "I think it may turn out to be a very interesting experiment—bringing the boy up, watching him develop. I'm keen about it. Whatever happens ought to prove something or other."

"Heredity is such a complicated affair, though," murmured Gamadge. "You may be in for a disappointment, Mr. Ormiston."

"Disappointment? Not at all. I'm prepared to have him grow up a social menace."

"But he may grow up a respectable citizen, and probably will. No fun in that."

Ormiston glanced at him suspiciously. "Are you indulging in sarcasm?" he inquired. "Hanged if I see why. I say it's interesting."

"You must have been brought up on Wilkie Collins. I never met anything like it since I read *The Legacy Of Cain.* And the mother being on the premises gives it a touch of *East Lynne.* I'm afraid I suspect you of getting a little innocent entertainment out of this harrowing situation, Mr. Ormiston."

Ormiston received this with surprising mildness. He worked for a time on the head of Martha Stanley, and then said abruptly: "At least we're keeping Mildred's secret, or trying to. The reason I told you all this was because I didn't want you to go stumbling around, setting the newspapers on her, upsetting her plans for the boy. If you do, I won't answer for the consequences. She's had enough."

"She needn't have any more, so far as we're concerned," said Mitchell, annoyed. "I bet we can keep her secrets better than you have, anyway."

Gamadge intervened. "Talking of secrets; was there any secret about that picture deal you arranged for old Mr. Bartram, in 1925 or 1927, Mr. Ormiston?"

"Picture deal?" Ormiston, busy at his sketch, did not turn; he continued to elaborate the pattern of Martha's bandanna, as he asked: "What picture deal?"

"Some pictures the old gentleman bought in Paris of an impoverished French nobleman, or somebody."

"Oh, I remember. The only secret about it was that poor old Buissonville didn't want the business talked about."

"What were the pictures?"

Ormiston turned, and said angrily: "What is all this? Do the Bartrams want to buy them back again? I shall be delighted. They are still in my studio in New York, waiting until I have time to bother with them—if that time ever comes. It would be exactly like George Bartram to hear about my having them, and begin lying awake worrying for fear lest I should have got 'em too cheap. Is he in this country again, by the way? He would be. Where peril is, George Bartram is not. Lord! When I think of that decent old gentleman, and what he got for sons—a moneygrubber and a playboy!"

Gamadge waited until this outburst had subsided, and then said, gently: "I should like to know what the pictures were. An interesting point came up while I was at the Bartrams' this morning—"

"I cannot imagine an interesting point coming up at the Bartrams', this morning or at any other time. Duller dogs than those brothers never lived. George, of course, is a clod; Carroll's a crashing philistine, with the brain and vision of one of his own silkworms. And I don't say that," he concluded, rubbing his nose, "because he deprived me of my fatal beauty. I forgave him a long time ago, when the old man sent me to Paris. I'll tell you something: If it wasn't for Bob Loring, those two Bartrams would have perished of their own inanity long since."

"I rather wondered why old Mr. Bartram cared to acquire these pictures."

"Merely because of the goodness of his heart. Buissonville needed the money, and he had these daubs—one of 'em was quite a nice little seventeenth century Dutch interior, though; the last of the family collection, and not worth much; painter unknown. I advised him to pay the six hundred Buissonville wanted, for the sake of that one, and take the others so as not to hurt the old fellow's feelings. They were horrid things by his son-in-law—who couldn't paint at all. Barbizon school, at its fuzziest and worst."

"And you took them off Mrs. Bartram's hands for six hundred dollars?"

"Plus duties, which weren't much. The old lady was delighted."

"Bartram seemed to think there was some joke or other about the Dutch picture."

"Now I come to think of it, there was. Old Mr. Bartram and I used to say that we were going to put it on the market as a lost Vermeer, and see if we couldn't fool some of those Boston critics that thought my work so repulsive. Of course I put him up to it; he didn't know Vermeer from Vanderdecken. We half thought we'd stage a show for a few people, ask their advice and opinion, see what came of it. But it was sailing too close to the wind for the dear old boy; he was afraid some pompous ass might take the joke seriously."

"Has Buissonville—that his name?"

"Charles de Buissonville. Yes."

"Has he any more pictures to sell?"

"He's dead."

"Oh. I'm fond of a bargain myself. Nothing I like better than hunting up lost Vermeers in dealers' attics."

"You can't have mine. Old Mr. Bartram said he was going to leave it to me in his will—Make my fortune, you know. But he didn't, of course; people never do. He died suddenly, you know."

"Wasn't any of his stuff appraised?"

"Bless you, there was never any question of that. All his property except the mills went to Mrs. Bartram. There wasn't as much property as they thought—again, there never is; so the brothers purchased an annuity for the old lady. How they must be suffering over that now! I saw her will in the paper, last June; a few thousands between the boys, and the jewelry to young—" His face changed. "That was tough," he said. "What happened to young Julia, I mean. Is Bartram badly knocked up?"

"Rather badly, I should say."

"I keep forgetting; but still, that catastrophe doesn't alter the fact that he was an oaf. Probably is still."

Gamadge laughed. "'Oaf' is the last word I should apply to him. Well, we shall have to see Miss Strangways, but I assure you that we shan't distress her more than can be helped. Something must be done to clear up this nightshade mystery, if possible."

"Oh, let it alone. You'll never find out anything."

"Would you say that if one of your own children had had the poison, Mr. Ormiston?" Mitchell, who had risen, walked to the doorway behind Gamadge, but stopped there to survey the artist with some displeasure.

"Yes, I should. What does Bob Loring say about it, by the way? He's a man of sense—or used to be."

"Very much what you say," Gamadge told him.

"You see! Save your constructive work for something more important," Ormiston advised him. "If we weren't on the branch, I'd ask you to come again and see my summer work."

"Thanks very much. We may come again, anyway."

CHAPTER TWELVE

Odd Behavior of a Murderer's Cousin

"YOU CERTAINLY PUT YOUR finger on what's been worrying me since Tuesday," said Mitchell, as they drove past the cliff dwellings of Harper's Rocks.

"You would have put your finger on it yourself, sooner or later."

"I'm not any too sure; but I did think she was pretty calm about the boy."

"And pretty nervous about the other two. Do you suppose that Breck fellow knows? I think he must. He's up here as Miss Strangways' friend, or I miss my guess."

"What makes you think that?"

"I don't believe his type would choose this way of working out a vacation unless he had some private reason for doing it. He looks competent and wiry."

"Lots of young fellows, starting out in life and hard up—"

"His kind doesn't go in for baby tending. And it doesn't take orders from such as Ormiston. A disciple might; Breck isn't that."

The car turned left, and began to round a blunt promontory; no human habitation was in sight; low rocks and pebbly sand separated the road from the ocean. A young woman sat on a log of driftwood, her drawing board propped up in front of her by means of a stick. A large box of water colors and a tin of water stood on the flat rock beside her, in front of which a yellow-haired little boy sat playing in the sand. As the car stopped, he pointed at it and said something. Miss Strangways turned, glanced at them, and then went on with her painting.

Mitchell and Gamadge got out and picked their way among the boulders. As they approached she looked over her shoulder again, and went on looking.

"Just a word, ma'am," said Mitchell. "This is my friend Mr. Gamadge. We wanted to ask you something."

Miss Strangways got up, placed the water-color board on the rock, and stared at them. Gamadge studied the oval, rather thin face, with its slate-blue eyes, wide forehead, and firm, large mouth. Her straight yellow hair, not much darker than Tommy's, was braided and worn flat against the back of her head. She had on a painter's gray linen overall, which nearly concealed her red-and-white cotton dress. He made up his mind.

"I'm sorry to interrupt your work," he said; "I wanted to speak to you about your boy."

Miss Strangways justified his first impression of her. She neither screamed nor fainted, nor did she burst into tears; but she turned pale under a healthy coat of tan.

"Mr. Ormiston told you," she said.

"No, he didn't. I guessed it."

"And then he told you the whole story."

"Yes."

She looked at Tommy, whose attention was engrossed by his building operations, and said with a kind of quiet desperation: "It will all come out. I knew it would. I don't think I can stand the publicity."

Mitchell protested: "I don't know why you think there has to be any. If we don't have to, we won't say a thing; and we probably won't have to."

"You don't understand. I was trying to make up my mind. Now it's been made up for me."

Gamadge was looking at her painting, which was not a sketch of rock, sea and sand, but a bold and original study of seagulls, in flight against gray clouds. He said: "You won't have to leave Tommy in other people's care for long, Miss Strangways. Not at this rate. This is a lovely thing." He added: "I suppose the Ormistons will let you have him back when you're ready to take him?"

"Yes. They've been awfully good to me."

"I hope so. You look just a trifle underweight. I believe that you've been cooking for seven people, including two men?"

She answered his smile with a faint answering twitch of the lips. "It isn't so bad," she said. "David Breck helps a lot, and so does Mrs. Ormiston, when she has time."

"Squash me if I'm impertinent; I have a feeling that Mr. Breck is here on your account."

"He's an old friend of mine. He would come; I begged him not to waste his summer." She looked a little distressed, and Gamadge said quickly: "Don't you worry. Young men of his type spend their summers as they prefer; and here he comes now, on the run."

Mr. Breck, in fact, was rounding the bend in the road at a fast trot. When he saw the group among the rocks he slowed, and finished the distance walking. Miss Strangways greeted him with a fair imitation of composure: "It's all right, Dave. You're in plenty of time."

He cast a stern and unfriendly eye at the two men. "In time for what?"

"They know all about everything, and I didn't tell them."

"Ormiston, I suppose. That fool's always bursting with it."

"No; this gentleman says he guessed it. I knew somebody would, sooner or later."

Breck addressed Mitchell with some heat: "See here; if you set the newspapers on this girl, it'll kill her. I mean that. She nearly died of it before—she was sick for months. If she hadn't been, do you suppose she'd have let Tom go?"

"I might have." Miss Strangways emptied her tin, and replaced tubes of water color in her box. "I still think he'll be better off without me."

"You think everybody will be better off without you. See here, Mr.—Gamadge, is it? Can't you persuade these people, state police, whoever it is that's making this investigation, to keep Miss Strangways out of it? If the papers get on her trail again they'll be the death of her, I tell you."

Gamadge replied mildly: "I don't see why you are both so sure her identity will have to come out."

Breck stared, and Miss Strangways explained, quickly: "They don't know about Evelyn, yet."

"Then why bring it up? No reason why they should. Let it go, Mil."

"No. I've made up my mind." She faced Mitchell, and said calmly: "We're talking about Evelyn Walworth. You know who she is."

"Yes, I do." Mitchell spoke bluntly. "She was the one that got over the arsenic poisoning, and she was the principal witness at the trial."

"Against her cousin Lawrence," said Breck, excitedly. "And you know the kind of witness she made. Her own lawyer couldn't keep her from turning her evidence into an accusation of Millie, here. She practically asked them to acquit that devil, and put Millie in his place. If she hadn't been obviously demented, they might have done something about it, by Jove! As it was—"

"As it was," said Mitchell, "nobody paid any attention to her."

"Oh, didn't they! Do you remember the newspapers? Did you hear the talk?"

"There's always talk, when there's a murder trial."

"There wouldn't have been enough to bother anybody, if it hadn't been for this malicious old creature. She never liked Millie; jealous of her. Wouldn't believe a word against her darling Lawrence."

Millie Strangways frowned, and shook her head. "Nonsense, Dave. She was fond of him; that's what drove her out of her wits. You must see that she was only trying to persuade herself he couldn't have killed her father and mother, or wanted to kill her. She wasn't sane, and I don't wonder."

Breck ignored this. "And now," he went on, addressing Gamadge and Mitchell with a kind of frenzy, "Millie Strangways wants to forget all about it, and let this woman see her, and see Tom."

"She has a right to see me, if she wants to, Dave. Perhaps you'd better take Tommy home."

"Do you mean," asked Mitchell, interested, "that she's in the neighborhood?"

"Yes; she's been at Robson's all summer. I didn't know it, but she seems to stay there regularly, in a boardinghouse called The Bayberries."

"Robson's! That's only a couple of miles down the shore, below Oakport."

"She's at Ford's Center now; she's staying at the Pegram House. I got a letter this morning. She said she was driving up this afternoon, and hoped I'd see her. I thought it was only decent. The doctor wrote me, two years ago, and said she was cured."

A great light seemed to have burst upon Mitchell. "Look here; is she a kind of a tall, thin, funny-looking woman, dresses in black, drives a little Ford coupé?"

"It sounds like her. She was always rather—eccentric."

"Lady in the car, all right!" Mitchell cast a triumphant glance at Gamadge. "You think she means to let bygones be bygones, do you, Miss Strangways?"

That young woman looked uncertain, and rather distressed. "She's sane again, you know. I did think of Tommy's 'lady in a car', but it seems so improbable."

"Oh, does it?" Breck smiled. "Tell them about her mania, old dear."

"Well—it developed into religious mania, and she got the idea that she was to save Lawrence's soul. She thought it could only be done by a sacrifice."

"What kind of a sacrifice?" demanded Mitchell, suspiciously.

"Tommy's death." Miss Strangways spoke in a low voice.

"For heaven's sake! And you were going to let her see him? You must be crazy, yourself!" scolded Mitchell.

"Miss Strangways is not crazy," said Gamadge. "She is behaving very well. In the first place, Miss Walworth has been pronounced cured by reputable physicians."

"They're supposed to be tops," admitted Breck, grudgingly.

"Supposed to be tops. In the second place, Miss Strangways is very sorry for her, recognizing her as a fellow victim and a martyr. In the third place, the poor lady was out of her head when she made the threats and tried to cause trouble. In the fourth place, Mr. Breck was to be present at the interview; or why should he have come running?"

"Well." Mitchell reflected. "With all of us here, I guess it's safe enough for her to see the boy. If he recognizes her as the lady in the car, he might close the case here and now. We could go after evidence—"

Miss Strangways interrupted him wildly. "I can't do it. I thought I could, but I can't. They say she's cured, but she may not be; she wrote me that she'd had a sign."

Gamadge made a wry face, and shook his head. "I think you're right not to risk it, Miss Strangways; she might give your boy a bad scare. If she thinks she's had a sign, she may make some kind of occult demonstration that would frighten a philosopher; Tommy's far too young to be dubbed Knight Companion of the Rosy Cross, or something. You'd better cart him off home, Breck. We'll stand by."

Breck walked down to the sandy spot where the chubby boy was piling up shells, and swung him to a shoulder. From that eminence he stared at the strangers out of slate-blue eyes like his mother's, until he and his protector were out of sight. Mitchell watched them go with a frown.

"I think we're making a mistake," he said, and repeated it: "I think we're making a mistake. Of course you never know, with children that age; they'll say anything."

"Poor Mitchell had a terrible lesson this morning in the vagaries of infant witnesses," said Gamadge, smiling. "He's thinking of Miss Irma Bartram. Tommy might very well recognize the lady in the car; but afterwards he might recognize half a dozen other ladies in cars, and by that time his nerves would be shot. No, Mitchell; if you don't mind, we'll leave him out of it."

"I can't see any harm in just letting him take a look at her."

"We'll take a look at her first."

"He's nervous now, when you keep asking him questions," said Miss Strangways. "If you go on, he cries."

"Of course he does."

"But she may be a danger to the community. We ought to try to find out any way we can," insisted Mitchell.

"We'll find out, somehow. The child's word isn't worth a cent to you, Mitchell; you can't use it, and it might do Miss Evelyn Walworth a grave injustice. No; if Miss Walworth has had a sign, I refuse to introduce her to the party concerned. If you insist, I withdraw from the case." He favored Mitchell with a flinty stare.

Miss Strangways looked at him as Andromeda might have looked at Perseus, and Mitchell remarked mildly: "Don't get so mad."

"You haven't seen me mad yet."

Mitchell said: "The boy's word is all the evidence we have."

"Perhaps Miss Walworth will provide us with more. Here she is now, unless I'm greatly mistaken."

A small car approached from the west, its slightly drunken progress, heralded by the strains of *Bess, You Is My Woman, Now*, played on an excellent radio, and sung in a bleating tenor voice. A metal rod, stiffly rising in front of the coupé, glittered in the sunlight.

"She loves radio," murmured Miss Strangways.

George Gershwin's complicated melody ceased as the car drew abreast of them. The elderly lady who had been so early on the road that morning, peered from a window. She then opened the door, alighted, cleared her long black skirt from the step, and came up to them, beaming. Her black cloth-topped shoes tripped daintily through the dust.

Gamadge removed his hat, and Mitchell removed his. Miss Walworth threw back her chiffon veil with a black-gloved hand, and advanced upon Millie Strangways, who allowed herself to be embraced and kissed.

"Dear, dear Mildred! After these many years! And how well you look!" Miss Walworth released her cousin-by-marriage, and stepped back to get a better view of her. "This was indeed worth waiting for. I don't see our little Tommy."

"He's having his nap, Cousin Evelyn."

"Quite recovered, I hope? You can imagine my feelings, when I saw about his accident in the papers. Please forgive these funereal garments; very hastily assembled, I am afraid! I went to the Bartram funeral, this morning. So sad; but we won't talk of sad things now; this occasion is a joyful one." Miss Walworth turned, smiled at Mitchell, and went happily on: "This is Mr. Mitchell; oh, no indeed! I require no introduction to Mr. Mitchell, Mildred, I assure you. We are fellow guests at the Pegram House, and as he is a local celebrity, he has been pointed out to me any number of times. But perhaps," and she surveyed Gamadge archly, her head on one side, "perhaps Mr. Mitchell will be surprised to learn that I need no introduction to Mr. Henry Gamadge."

"That so, ma'am?" Mitchell was indeed surprised, and showed it.

"That is so, and I will tell you why. You remember meeting me on the road, early this morning? I had been calling on my friends the gypsies. I greatly value the few relics of romance left to us."

Gamadge unobtrusively winced.

"And I love to have my fortune told; one needn't actually believe in a thing to enjoy it, need one? As for the hour, all hours are opportune to me. Why should four A.M. seem less respectable to some people, than four P.M.? It is often more beautiful."

"A question that applies to other things besides the hours of the day and night," suggested Gamadge, gravely.

Miss Walworth tittered. "Delightful wit," she said. "I quite expected it. You see, I recognized Mr. Mitchell this morning, and I wondered who his distinguished-looking friend from New York might be; you had obviously just come in on the through train, Mr. Gamadge."

"Cleverly deduced."

"We know who would have declared it elementary! But I immediately undertook a piece of detection that I flatter myself was worthy of you, and of Mr. Mitchell also. I turned my car, and I followed you at a discreet distance until you turned into the drive at Burnsides."

"No!"

"I did; but of course I didn't pursue you to the very door. I stopped there on my way up here this afternoon, and quite openly got your name from Mrs. Burnside. I was quite delighted, Mr. Gamadge, to find that I knew all about you."

"I can hardly believe it, Miss Walworth."

"But I did, though! Your little volume—*Technique of a Book Forger*—it was in the library of my nursing home. I have been ill, Mr. Gamadge."

"I'm very sorry to hear it."

"But I am quite well again, now. So interesting to meet you; we are fellow authors."

"Are we, really?"

"I put out a little book of poems, when I was young. *Rainbows*. You wouldn't have come across it."

"Excellent title."

"But I never ventured again."

"We all have at least one book in us, Miss Walworth."

"But sad, don't you think so, when there is only one? However; this is the sort of thing that makes summer so pleasant; one meets people one wouldn't otherwise meet at all. Life is very quiet at Robson's, though. Such a dear little resort, so simple and unpretentious. And I have my own suite at The Bayberries—an outside staircase. I must have complete freedom, wherever I am. I suppose it is the result of having been so shut away from the world in my nursing home. A mild claustrophobia," said Miss Walworth, laughing.

"How did you find out that Miss Strangways and Tommy were so near you, ma'am?" asked Mitchell, who had been watching Miss Evelyn Walworth, and listening to her, in baffled wonder.

"Oh, I found out where they were two summers ago, and planted myself near *them*!" Miss Walworth rolled her eyes in his direction. "It was quite easy to trace them, you know. When I left my nursing home, my first thought was for Mildred. I went to an agency, and I engaged a man; a very civil man. He found Mildred and Tommy without any trouble at all. To my horror, I discovered that she was in what amounted to domestic service."

"But you waited two years, almost, before you did anything about it."

"Well, yes; I must explain." Miss Walworth's face became serious. "You must understand that before I was so ill, I had been misled; tragically misled; and I had behaved very badly. During my retreat from the world—a rest cure of the soul, Mr. Mitchell—I had a really wonderful experience. A revelation."

There was a silence, broken by Mitchell's voice. He asked, in an expressionless tone: "What sort of a revelation, ma'am?"

"Incommunicable, Mr. Mitchell," said Miss Walworth, brightly. "However, my one idea, as a result of it, was to make up to Mildred for my previous attitude and behavior. So I came to Robson's, and for two summers I have waited for a sign. It came, at last."

There was another pause, and again Mitchell broke it: "What sort of a sign?"

"Why, dear little Tommy's accident, of course. I knew that the time had come to withdraw Mildred and Tommy from these most unsuitable surroundings, and to offer her a competence and a home. Mildred, my dear child; you know that I live alone in that big Boston house, and that I have plenty of money. I have fitted up the top floor into a charming self-contained flat, with all the modern conveniences. You and Tommy will be completely independent, and you will have service from my own staff. There is a large north studio. I shall make you an adequate allowance until you are earning an income of your own, and wish me to discontinue it. Now and then you may feel like coming down and sitting with me beside my radio; that is all I shall ask of you, and it will be quite sufficient. The obligation will be mine. Now, don't attempt to make up your mind yet; you can reach me until Monday at the Pegram House—where the cooking, I assure you, is frightful—and after that at the old address. You know it well."

"Cousin Evelyn—"

"Not a word until you have thought it over! Goodbye for the present, my dear child. You are young still; too young to need a revelation. You can forgive and forget without that."

She embraced Miss Strangways, bowed ceremoniously to Mitchell and to Gamadge, and climbed into her coupé. It disappeared around the corner of the road, accompanied by a stentorian announcement that we must expect a change in the weather late tomorrow afternoon: southeast winds, and rain.

The three looked at one another in silence. Mitchell finally asked: "Is she completely crazy, or just flighty, or as sly as they come?"

"She did sound so kind, at the last. But oh," said Miss Strangways, "that awful house! Dark, and dreary, and old."

"Where two ruthless murders were committed by your husband," thought Gamadge, "and where the survivor of them may be slowly going mad." He said aloud: "The top floor sounds cheerful, but I hope you won't accept her invitation until you've taken advice."

"I won't. Only—" Her eyes strayed from the blue and dancing ocean to the line of rocks; and thence, across the road, to the dark woods. "It's queer—*she* doesn't frighten me so much; but I want to get away from this place."

Mitchell considered this, frowning. "Could young Breck stake you for a while?"

"He says he can; he's been wanting to for ever so long, but I wouldn't let him."

"Let him now. Look at it as a business proposition, borrow the money, and take the kid away from here. If the Ormistons complain, or try to make any trouble for you, I'll settle them; your boy has been in jeopardy of his life. He isn't legally adopted, is he?"

"No. They wouldn't make trouble; they've been awfully kind. I don't know what I should have done if it weren't for the Ormistons."

"That's all very well, but you can't do their work and look after the boy, too; and Breck can't, either. I say, take him and get out."

"David Breck wanted to give me a one-man show in New York, this fall. I ought to get my pictures ready for it. Aren't the Ormistons leaving on Monday?"

"You cut loose from the Ormistons. Tell 'em the whole business has been such a shock to you, you want to look after the boy yourself from now on. Ormiston is a regular sieve; if he knows where you are, he'll let it out to somebody. I'd rather nobody but Breck had your address for some time to come. Where would you go?"

"There's a very nice woman who'd share her apartment with me, and take care of Tommy when I had to be out. I'll give you her number; she's near Gramercy Park."

Gamadge asked: "May we drive you back to Harper's Rocks?"

"No, thanks, I see Dave coming."

"When will you pack up and leave?" persisted Mitchell.

"Tomorrow afternoon?"

"That's right. You'll drive your car, I suppose."

"Yes. It seems hard on Mrs. Ormiston—"

"Forget that. Write your New York address down here."

She scrawled it on a leaf of his notebook, and then stood watching them, her paintbox under her arm, while they drove westward, straight into the glare of the declining sun.

CHAPTER THIRTEEN

"The Finest Child in Maine"

"AND WHY DID YOU engineer that elopement?" Gamadge turned an amused eye on Mitchell, who replied shortly:

"Don't you ask me that. If you'd let the boy stay and take a look at the Walworth woman, perhaps we could have done something about her. Now she's wandering around loose—"

"Not entirely so, I trust?"

"I'll put a man on her trail as soon as I can get hold of a telephone."

"Two men, I hope; don't forget that four A.M. is as respectable an hour—"

"Oh, heck take it."

"I wondered whether you weren't beginning to worry about the moral qualities of the Ormistons, also."

Mitchell said with cold conviction: "So far as I'm concerned, the case is closed. Walworth may be crazy, or shamming crazy and as sane as we are, but she gave those children that night-shade. She had two good reasons for doing it—religious mania, or plain revenge, or both; she had opportunity; and she's flighty enough to take risks. We have no evidence against her, or rather the lawyers would say we hadn't. I don't want to run up against medical experts. We won't get a thing out of them that will put her behind bars. I'll see Loring, and find out whether he thinks there's a chance of getting her back into her sanatorium before she commits any more murders. Perhaps William Stanley is old enough so you'll think it's proper to have him look at her and say how she stopped him and took his picture and gave him candy; I suppose she'd run out of nightshade berries by the time she got around to him."

"How very inaccurate you are, Mitchell. The lady who *started* to take William's picture was a stranger to him; he and his tribe have met Miss Walworth; she says so herself."

"That's so. I forgot that."

"There's another benevolent tourist going about the countryside; Miss Walworth has a rival. You haven't answered my other query: Don't you like the idea of Miss Strangways keeping on with the Ormistons?"

"No, I don't; but I can't exactly tell you why. You put something funny into my head, with that poetry of yours."

"But I improvised that when I still thought Tommy might be the child of unnatural parents."

"I know; just the same, I don't like the setup there. Ormiston may find himself in trouble about those pictures, before we get through with him; we'll have to follow up that lead about the Bartram money. And if there's an investigation, somebody will rake up the Strangways girl's past. I say, leave her out of it. If she borrows young Breck's money, and can't pay, she may decide to marry him."

Gamadge, vastly entertained, contemplated Mitchell's wooden profile with affection. "One good thing, there isn't much Walworth apparent in Tom," he said. "Ormiston's experiment would have been a dud."

Mitchell made a sound of disgust. They turned south, passed sand dunes, then pastures, and arrived in front of a big red barn. Gamadge left the car. He walked up the ancient ramp, in the crevices of which the hayseed of summer still clung, and stood in the wide doorway, peering into stillness and gloom. Six kittens suddenly rushed from all directions, and flung themselves upon his shoes; he bent to stroke each head, and to allow six pairs of forepaws to embrace his finger. Then he straightened, and looked at the nail from which hung five bright-colored ribbons and five tiny bells.

"Whitey," he said, addressing a pearl-colored creature which lay on its back, biting one of his shoestrings, "I think I have something of yours. See you later."

He left the barn, wandered around to the back of it, and slowly climbed to the top of a rise; thence he looked down at the subtle red and yellow of the marsh, and its blue canals; their water as calm and as blue as the cobalt sky. He turned, and went back to the car.

The farmhouse stood back from the road on a small hill of its own, among tall maples. They went up a gravel path bordered with tiger lilies and petunias, and turned, at the porch steps, to remark that lilac bushes cut off their view of Mitchell's car.

"And you can't see the barn at all," he said.

"No. Or much more than a glimpse of the road."

"Those elms on the right cut off that hill behind the barn."

"So they do."

"I kind of hate to bother Mrs. Beasley again." Mitchell rang, and the door was opened part way by an alert-looking, black-haired girl of fourteen.

"Mother can't see no strangers," she said, resolutely.

"We ain't strangers," Mitchell reminded her. "At least I ain't. You've seen me before, Claribel; and this is a friend of mine come all the way from New York—"

"To borrow a kitten," finished Gamadge.

This statement not only caused Claribel to stare, but drew poor Mrs. Beasley herself from her seclusion. She appeared behind the girl, and looked wonderingly at Gamadge; a dignified and straight-backed figure, with dark hair like her daughter's, and fine dark eyes.

Gamadge said: "Do please forgive us for coming in on you like this, Mrs. Beasley, without an invitation. That little girl down at the Bartrams', George Bartram's little girl, you know; she had to leave her cat behind in Europe, when they came over. She misses it. She's a nice little thing, and she's a little lonely down there. I thought you might spare her one of your kittens. The white one, as a matter of fact. She wants a white one."

Mrs. Beasley said, opening the door wide, "Claribel, go get a small peach basket, and a piece of cheesecloth."

Claribel disappeared along a narrow hall. Mrs. Beasley continued: "Won't you come in while she's catching the kitten?" She motioned them into a room on the right, and they all sat down in cool dusk, smelling of geraniums and mildew. Gamadge and Mrs. Beasley contemplated each other in silence. At last he inquired:

"Do you have the gypsies up here much in the summertime, Mrs. Beasley?"

"No, they don't bother. We don't buy from them."

"They don't pass along the road often, then?"

"No. We brought the children up to be kind of afraid of gypsies."

"Many other people drop in on you here? It's not really out of the beaten track, is it? I mean, lots of people must come through, from Portland and Bailtown."

"They don't, much. There's a better route above here."

"Then you don't get tourists looking for drinks of water, people with car trouble, that kind of thing."

"No. Our house ain't very close to the road."

"There's a lady with a little car; fond of children, likes old-fashioned places. I wondered if she'd called on you this last week. I happen to know her, slightly. She—"

Mrs. Beasley interrupted him, with a slight show of animation:

"You mean Miss Humphrey?"

"Er..." Gamadge, completely stumped, wondered whether to say yes, or to say no. Miss Walworth's foibles might include the use of an alias. Mrs. Beasley saved him the trouble of making up his mind:

"The lady photographer. She come on Labor Day, late afternoon."

"Oh. The lady photographer. No, I don't think—" Gamadge cast a side glance at Mitchell, whose face was squarer and blanker than he had ever seen it before, and said quickly: "I did hear something about a lady photographer."

"She come for Sairy's picture. She was takin' pictures of six- to eight-year-old children for the competition."

"Really!"

"Yes. She was takin' for the whole county."

"What competition, Mrs. Beasley?"

"For a magazine—*Health In The Home*, she said it was. She said the competition was for the finest child in Maine."

"How very interesting."

"The child that got the most votes in a county got a prize; and the one that got the most votes of all, got a hundred dollars. This Miss Humphrey—cute little camera she had. First she wanted me to give her a picture of Sairy, or tell her where to get one; but I didn't have any except a snapshot, that wasn't good. So she took the photograph herself. She promised me one, if Sairy got a prize."

"And the children were all to be of a certain age, Mrs. Beasley?"

"Six to eight. But she was willin' to take younger ones, if she thought they'd take a good picture."

"This was on Monday, you say."

"Yes, about four thirty."

"When are the pictures to come out?"

"She couldn't say. Beasley thinks it's a scheme to make us subscribe to the magazine."

"I don't believe it is. A good picture, you know, would cost more than the average subscription."

"I'll tell Beasley that." Mrs. Beasley's tragic face had lightened a little.

"I wonder if she's the woman I've seen about here. How does she dress? I suppose she'd be smart and up-to-date; most of these people are."

Mrs. Beasley's eye held a glint of amusement. "She was pretty smart, any way you look at it. But she was painted too thick, and her hair was dyed—I never see such a yeller. There was curls of it stickin' out, under her hat. She wore one of those short veils, with embroidery on it."

"Very smart indeed. Young woman, was she, Mrs. Beasley?"

"No, I wouldn't call her young. She was spry enough. She looked quite nice, I must say, and she talked real pleasant. Claribel can tell you just how she looked."

"Was she driving herself?"

"I don't know. You can't see the road good from here, and I didn't go down to the gate."

Claribel came in, carrying a basket covered with cheesecloth; something bounced obscurely within, and Gamadge inspected it with sympathy.

"Poor Whitey!" he murmured. "We'd better get back with you as soon as possible. You seem very frantic. They always are frantic, aren't they, in circumstances such as these?" He took the basket, and rose. "You remember that photographer woman, Claribel?"

"Miss Humphrey. Yes, I do," said Claribel, eagerly.

"Your mother says you know just how she was dressed."

"She had on a long coat, down to the edge of her dress, with big black and white checks on it. She had a little white hat with a black nose veil, pearl earrings, quite big ones, and a diamond pin in the neck of her shirtwaist. It was a white silk shirtwaist, and she had black and white pumps without any toes, and flesh-colored silk stockings. There was a bug embroidered on her veil, right over one eye."

"Bug, was there?"

"Dragonfly or something. A big one."

"Was *she* big?"

"Kind of tall."

"Thin?"

"Kind of big."

"I'd call her a big woman," said Mrs. Beasley.

"Would you know her again, Claribel?" asked Gamadge.

"I'd know her if she was dressed the same."

"Not much view of her face, was there?"

"Only her mouth."

"With the lipstick on it," said Mrs. Beasley, dryly. "Claribel's just livin' to get some on her own mouth, like her sisters have. They're comin' tomorrow, and all their husbands and children, and the boys are comin', and their wives. We don't hardly know where we'll put 'em. Jennie's comin' all the way from St. Paul."

"That's pretty nice, Mrs. Beasley."

"I guess it is."

"You must be cooking like mad. We'll leave you to it." He moved towards the door, but turned to ask: "Did Miss Humphrey take any pictures of the place? Get you to show her around?"

"No, she was in an awful hurry. Wouldn't let me change Sairy's dress, or crimp her hair."

"Well, I'm greatly obliged for the cat. If they aren't too rushed getting off—they're going on Monday—they'll probably drive up and thank you themselves."

Gamadge went down to the car, Mitchell lingering to use the telephone. Then they were once more on the road, and driving back towards Harper's Rocks; no word having been exchanged as to this return upon their tracks. Gamadge said at last:

"Another lady in a car. There will be half a dozen, before we get through with them. I forgot, though; if the case is closed, as you say, Miss Humphrey is Miss Walworth in disguise. I should love to see her in a blond wig, an inch of make-up, a nose veil, and pumps."

"That contest may be on the level."

"There may even be a magazine called *Health In The Home*, but we don't think so, or we should not be rushing back to ask the Ormistons and the Bartrams whether they also had a visit from Miss Humphrey, the lady photographer."

"I wish people didn't withhold information; I asked the Beasleys fifty times if there had been strangers around."

"Only you didn't make any inquiries about Monday."

"And why the dickens should this woman go around Monday, or any other time, taking pictures?"

"Somebody had to spy out the land; these poisonings were timed, as I keep telling you."

"That was a good disguise."

"Yes. Those veils don't merely conceal most of the features—they distort them. I wonder if Miss Walworth has an effective alibi for Monday afternoon."

"I bet she hasn't any alibi for any time; her with her outside staircase."

"When did she arrive at the Pegram House?"

"Tuesday—suppertime."

The whole length of the north road was deserted except for sandpipers, screaming and whirling gulls, and a curious seal, whose head bobbed in the still waters beyond the surf. As they rounded the eastern bend Mitchell said: "The George Bartrams could have made it. They could have driven right down here Monday afternoon, and got back to Haverley for supper."

"You can build Mrs. Bartram up into Miss Humphrey, I suppose; but I hardly think that George Bartram will trim down to her."

"No, and the gypsies won't fit. I'd laugh if she was a real canvasser, after all."

"I shouldn't; I should fall insensible."

Mitchell swooped down on the Ormiston cottage with a scattering of pebbles, and was out of the car before Gamadge had untangled his legs and deposited Whitey's basket on the seat. He reached the foot of the path when Mitchell had charged up the first half of the slope. Mrs. Ormiston, sitting beside the sand pile in the attitude of the Thinker, Tommy's shovel in her hand, looked up, surprised.

"Just a question, ma'am," said Mitchell, panting. "Do you know if a Miss Humphrey called here Monday, any time, taking photographs of children?"

"Why, yes; she came in the afternoon. I was here alone with Tommy; the others were all at the ball game."

"What time, do you remember?"

"It couldn't have been much after half past four."

"Take a picture of the boy, did she?"

"I'm afraid she got a snapshot. I was annoyed; Millie..." she paused, and Mitchell said:

"We know Miss Strangways is his mother. I don't think that photograph will be published, Mrs. Ormiston."

Gamadge, standing in the road, asked: "Did you get a good look at the woman, Mrs. Ormiston?"

"No, I didn't. She was rather big, and wore loud clothes. That's all I can tell you; I was on the porch, and Tom was down here. She had a veil on, and a long checked coat."

Gamadge followed Mitchell back to the car, and they drove furiously down the shore road, and into Oakport. The Bartram house slept among its trees, green shutters closed against the blinding dazzle of the sunset. This time it was Gamadge who got out first, and went up the flagged walk, basket in hand. Miss Ridgeman was watering the flowers along the borders. He said:

"Here's Irma's cat, Miss Ridgeman. Name of Whitey. To be returned, if necessary, to the Beasley farm. I hope Mrs. Bartram will see her way to letting Irma keep it, though."

"It's awfully good of you, Mr. Gamadge." Miss Ridgeman took the basket, and peered through the cheesecloth at the mewing prisoner within.

"I have an uncomfortable suspicion that the burden of its existence is going to fall upon you."

"Annie likes cats."

"Thank goodness for that. Er—Irma is young; she won't absolutely maul the animal, I suppose?"

"We'll see that she doesn't."

"Look here, Miss Ridgeman; did a woman come around on Monday, asking to take a picture of the little girl? Woman in a black-and-white checked coat, white hat, nose veil? Name of Humphrey?"

Miss Ridgeman, looking startled, said: "Why, yes; she did. She said something about a magazine contest. Of course I didn't allow it. What—"

"How did she impress you?"

"I didn't like the look of her at all. She was a loud, common sort of person, made up like a chorus girl. I wouldn't have let her take a picture of Julia for anything."

"Did she ask for one, before she offered to take one, herself?"

"Yes. We hadn't any. Mr. Bartram was going to—I wish he had, now."

"What time did she come here?"

Miss Ridgeman considered the question. "Late in the afternoon."

"Can you put it nearer than that? Anybody else get a look at her?"

"No; we were in the summerhouse, and she walked right in the back gate."

"See her car?"

"I'm afraid not. Is it important? What had she to do with—"

"We're just checking up on strangers. Thanks, Miss Ridgeman."

On their way out of Oakport Mitchell stopped at headquarters and was gone for some time. When he came out, he looked slightly less glum.

"Walworth hasn't come back to the Pegram House yet," he said. "I've started the Humphrey investigation, and the inquiry about that contest and that magazine. I want to know where

George Bartram spent Sunday night, but I have to go careful, there."

He got into the car, and started it.

"Yes," said Gamadge. "Care is indicated."

"I could make a lot of trouble for myself. I wouldn't so much mind that, because it's all in the day's work; but I can't fit Mrs. Bartram into the picture. I just can't do it."

"Mitchell, beware; you know what happens if you follow that line of reasoning."

"I can't help it. I want to tackle William Stanley about his friend in a car."

"Leave William until tomorrow; I'll get Pottle to show him that little bicycle—on approval. William isn't the right age, Mitchell; if Miss Humphrey bothered with him, she was only broadening the field of inquiry."

His voice had acquired a dryness that Mitchell recognized. The detective watched him out of the corner of a squinting and puzzled eye, and finally asked: "You beginning to see any glimmer of sense in this mix-up?"

"Just a glimmer."

"That's more than I see." There was a pause, during which Gamadge looked out of the car window at the quiet evening landscape, and Mitchell kept looking at him. At last the latter said: "How about passing along your information? I could use it."

"No, you couldn't. I want facts."

"Well, we'll get 'em for you, if they can be got."

"I don't think you can get them for me, without giving the show away before we have any proof of what happened."

"Good gosh; you talk as if you really had a line on this business."

"I have," said Gamadge, calmly. Mitchell nearly sent the car into the ditch. He righted it, and made the turn that led them down the highway to Burnsides. Then he said, sharply:

"If you know what it's all about, hand over what you've got. We can't take any chances."

"You'd clap me into Miss Walworth's nursing home. I'll tell you this, Mitchell; I'll have to convince you that what I think is true, convince you absolutely, before you'll lift a finger to get the proofs we want. I can't do that tonight, but I'll give you my conclusions, unless I've given them up and thrown them out of the window, some time tomorrow morning."

Mitchell, grumbling, drove on to Burnsides. Mr. Burnside came out on the porch.

"Young feller to see you," he said, addressing Mitchell. "Young feller in steel spectacles."

CHAPTER FOURTEEN

Young Man in Steel Spectacles

THE DRUGSTORE HAD supplied the young man with something for his sunburn; it glistened on his nose as he rose to greet them, dabbing meanwhile at his ear with a silk handkerchief. He had light hair, light eyes, and a narrow face; perhaps a slightly foxy one, the foxiness being mitigated by humor.

"My name is Schenck, Mr. Mitchell," he said. "The sheriff sent me over to see you. Here's my card." He glanced politely at Gamadge, and added: "I'm afraid my business is confidential."

"This gentleman is assisting me." Mitchell accepted the card, without looking at it. "And nothing's confidential to the police unless they decide it is."

"Well—the sheriff said you would be discreet."

"I can't seem to hear Enos James saying any such thing. He may have said I don't talk more than I need to." Mitchell looked at the card, his eyebrows went up, and he handed it to Gamadge. It said:

ROBERT C. SCHENCK
Investigator
THE REAL ECONOMY INSURANCE CO.
NEW YORK CITY

The young man put his handkerchief in his pocket and stood in an easy attitude, while Gamadge read the card and returned it to Mitchell.

"Sit down, Mr. Schenck," said the latter. "I'll be glad to hear what your business is. It must be important, for you to come all the way from New York on it; or perhaps this is just one of your regular trips."

"I don't make regular trips—not on my job."

"I guess you don't. Well, if you want privacy and discretion, I'd better look see where the Burnsides are. This place ain't built to tell secrets in." He went to the dining-room door, and came back, after closing it, to report that Mr. and Mrs. Burnside, together with the help, were laying the table for supper.

"They set a good table, too, I understand," said the young man, taking a chair in front of the fire, between Mitchell and Gamadge. He spoke rather wistfully. "I'm staying at the Pegram House. I didn't think my expense account would stand Burnsides. Pretty expensive, isn't it?" And he looked about him in some surprise at the big, bare room, carpeted with drugget and devoid of amenities.

"These places are luxury spots," replied Mitchell, getting his pipe out, "though you wouldn't think so, to look at 'em. Well, here we are, all set. What can we do for you?"

Mr. Schenck hesitated, warmed his hands for a few moments before the blaze, and at last decided to talk:

"Everybody knows that old life insurance motto—'Shut up and pay up.' The last thing we want is to give policy holders the idea that there'll be any trouble collecting."

"I'm paying premiums on considerable insurance," said Mitchell. "I don't expect Mrs. Mitchell to have to fight for her money, when I pass out."

"Naturally not. We never make unnecessary inquiries even. When this nightshade case broke, for instance; we would have delivered the goods—on your say-so, of course—without asking any questions."

Mitchell, glancing quickly at Gamadge's impassive profile, said: "I don't know what you're talking about."

"No, of course not. Could I have this gentleman's name?"

Mitchell's introduction was brief; it consisted, in fact, of the word "Gamadge," irritably pronounced.

Mr. Schenck returned Gamadge's bow, and got out a cigarette. "Five years ago last spring," he said, "Mrs. Albert Ormiston came into our downtown office and took out a policy on the life of Thomas Strangways Ormiston, aged one year and seventeen days. Two years ago she came in and took out a policy on the life of Mildred Strangways; Mrs. Strangways having just been passed as a good risk by our medical officer."

Mitchell coughed. Gamadge continued to gaze into the flames.

"A very nice lady, Mrs. Ormiston seems to be," said Mr. Schenck, his eyes behind their glittering lenses turning from one face to the other. "The office was favorably impressed. I met her this morning for the first time; at the Bartram funeral. The sheriff was just going when I called, and he took me with him in his car. I hired one later for my own use—when I discovered how much ground there was to be covered. More than I expected."

"You were saying," Mitchell reminded him, "that your office..."

"Yes. Mrs. Ormiston was very frank on both occasions. Very frank. Explained fully that the child was Mrs. Strangways son, and had been unofficially adopted by her husband and herself from charitable motives. We investigated, of course. Sad story, isn't it?"

Gamadge, who thought this almost a miracle of understatement, spoke for the first time: "Mrs. Strangways, or Walworth, was a party to the arrangement?"

"She fully concurred in it; but she is not a beneficiary on the child's policy. Mrs. Ormiston explained that her husband was not cognizant of her step; that he was reserved in matters of finance, and would object seriously to having it known that they were in modest circumstances. Mrs. Ormiston accounted for her wish to insure the child in this way: If, while under her care, he had an illness and died, there would be considerable outlay. Her own son was in delicate health, and she would not feel justified in diverting the money from him to the Strangways boy. She proposed to pay the premiums out of her house-keeping allowance, and such sums as she earned, from time to time, by making hooked rugs."

Gamadge asked: "Miss Strangways was not well enough, five years ago, to pass your physical examination?"

"No. She was suffering from anemia and general disability, and she was twenty pounds underweight. When we finally agreed to insure her, she was a very good life. The boy was always strong and healthy."

"And she approved of the arrangement for Tommy."

"Fully. Told us herself that she wished to protect Mrs. Ormiston's interests in every possible way, and that she was under heavy obligations to her."

"Is Mrs. Ormiston insured, herself?"

"Yes. In favor of her own children. Well; the sums involved were not large, especially in the case of the little boy. We don't insure children for large amounts, you know; we don't much like to insure such young children, at all. The rates have been getting lower and lower, you know—to discourage interested parties from—er—cashing in on the decease of minors."

"Very delicately put," said Gamadge.

"It's a delicate subject. However, when we are convinced of the *bona fides* of the parties, and after full investigation, we do insure a child of one year or upwards; a hundred dollars at first, and a hundred more with each successive year. If the Strangways-Ormiston boy had died, we should now owe Mrs. Ormiston in the neighborhood of seven hundred dollars."

"I see." Gamadge stretched his legs out, leaned back in his chair, and closed his eyes. "But now you don't have to pay."

"No," agreed Mr. Schenck, his glasses shining. "Not this time."

"You think somebody's out after the boy's life?" Mitchell inquired, studying him with interest.

"We have no idea what to think. My company hopes very much that you will see your way to co-operating. The point is: shall we be reasonably safe in renewing the policy on the boy's life, and on the life of his mother? Or have you information which leads you to think that it would be a mistake on our part? It would be a great favor, and we should hope to be of service to you in the future. We often are, you know."

"You insurance people certainly are." Mitchell looked at him uneasily. "How did you get the idea that the business might not have been an accident, or some kind of a mistake?"

"We can't find that the case is closed, or that you've got after the gypsies. And none of you up here has taken steps, so far as we can find out, to put the blame on anybody. The whole thing seems to have been left in the air."

"Pending investigation," said Mitchell, sharply.

"Exactly. We thought you might be willing to tell us where your investigation seems to be leading you."

"And whether," said Gamadge, turning his head to smile faintly at Mr. Schenck, "it seems to be leading anybody to the conclusion that Mrs. Albert Ormiston poisoned, or attempted to poison, three children for a little less than seven hundred dollars."

"Well, Mr. Gamadge," replied Schenck, responding to the smile with a still fainter one, "you'd be surprised. I'll give you a few factors which you might take into consideration: First, Mr. Ormiston is in a terrific jam; I find that he owes money in New York, that he owes to every tradesman in Oakport, that he may lose his cottage at Harper's Rocks for back taxes, and that he's selling personal property. Second, we have only Mrs. Ormiston's word for it that he doesn't know about her taking out those policies. Third, that Sidney Ormiston is in immediate need of an expensive operation. And finally, that nobody up there at the Rocks saw Mrs. Ormiston at all from eleven A.M. on Tuesday until Breck came back with the news of Tommy Strangways' disappearance. As for killing three children, I understand the little Bartram girl died, you might say, accidentally, and that nobody knows whether the little Beasley girl wouldn't have got over it, if she'd been found."

"Really, Mr. Schenck," said Gamadge, sitting up and regarding the young man with admiration, "you don't seem to have been wasting your time! Mitchell, let's co-operate."

Mitchell hesitated, and Mr. Schenck continued, blandly:

"And on Wednesday we got in touch with the company that insures Ormiston himself against fire. I've got a copy of their inventory in my pocket. He's been selling curios and stuff out of his studio."

"Mr. Schenck, you're a walking wonder. How on earth did you think of all that?" asked Gamadge.

"Just routine investigation. He sold in June."

"When old Mrs. Bartram died, and couldn't check up on what he got for some old pictures, say. This is interesting, Mr. Schenck; I won't deny it. Real interesting," exclaimed Mitchell. "How in the world did you get the Solidarity to give you this information?"

"When it's a question of the *bona fides* of policyholders, the various companies are glad to—er—to—"

"Co-operate," suggested Gamadge, gravely.

"That's the word I wanted."

"Mitchell, *we* really must co-operate. We want to see that inventory."

Mitchell said: "All right; don't advise your company to renew till I give you the word, or until you see something official in the papers. We don't know much—at least I don't," he amended, casting an irritated glance at Gamadge, "but we know enough to say that in confidence."

Mr. Schenck, looking gratified, drew a typewritten sheet of paper out of his wallet, and Gamadge got out of his chair to read it over Mitchell's shoulder:

"Antique Ghiordes rug; clair-de-lune vases; Japanese lacquer screen, eighteenth century; brocades, Venetian; Japanese prints, *curious*; jade cups. I wonder if he got anything like these prices? They're appraised pretty high, all these things."

"We contacted the dealer that bought them, but he hasn't come across with the figures yet. Dealers don't always—"

"Co-operate. You're right, they don't. Here we are, Mitchell; 'Six modern French paintings, Barbizon School, $350; Nymphs dancing, attributed to Coypel the elder, $650.' But not a sign of a Dutchman, master or pupil. He didn't sell it, or have it appraised, either. How long do you plan to stay on, Mr. Schenck?"

"I thought if I could get my information, I'd go back on the ten o'clock tomorrow night. Might as well stay through Sunday, anyhow."

"Good. We'll entrain together. I hope you and Mitchell will have supper with me here this evening; it ought to be ready pretty soon, by the smell."

Mr. Schenck, inhaling the heavenly odors wafted to them from the kitchen, said that he'd be delighted to stay, only he had to get back to the Pegram House right afterwards and write up his report, so it would catch the night mail.

"You sit and write it up in the lobby, there," Mitchell adjured him. "Then you can keep an eye on a Miss Walworth, guest of the hotel. I have one man on the job, but she flits around so, she might get away from him. If you watched the front, till I got back myself—"

"I could put her car out of commission for you; just till tomorrow, you know," suggested Mr. Schenck.

"You could, could you?" Mitchell went to the telephone, and called the Pegram House. "That you, Hoskins? I'm staying here at Burnsides for supper. If—what! Not showed up yet? Where in time is she?"

"Leave Hoskins to it," said Gamadge. "His mistakes are worth other people's bull's-eyes."

Mitchell came back to the fire. "I don't know but what I'll take you up on that proposition, Schenck; if she ever does get back to the Pegram House, I mean to say. You wouldn't damage the car, I suppose?"

"No, just fix it so she couldn't very well light out again tonight. Who is she?" Schenck gazed at him alertly.

"Never you mind who she is. I want her anchored in the hotel till tomorrow. It's practically impossible to keep all these folks in line; I'd need a regiment. Mind telling me what Mrs. Ormiston said to you today?"

"Not at all. This morning I just made a date to see her this afternoon. She was nervous about her husband finding out about the insurance, so we arranged for her to meet me in the road, just beyond Harper's, and bring the boy. She told me the gypsies were to blame, and that everybody thought so. I gave her some talk about the company wanting information for their records; she took it as cool as you please. All she wanted, so she said, was to keep Ormiston out of it. Young Tommy looked to me like a pretty healthy specimen; but when I asked him who gave him the berries, he started to bawl."

"Hostile witness," said Gamadge. "They ruin a case."

"Well, it's a queer sort of show, if you ask me."

"We don't have to ask you," Mitchell told him.

Mr. Schenck went upstairs for a wash before supper. Gamadge, eyeing Mitchell rather warily, went over to the desk and picked up the telephone. He called his own number in New York, and then extracted an object from his pocket which Mitchell recognized with a grin.

"Going to use the code," he remarked, while Gamadge laid the little green book on the desk, and riffled its pages with his free hand.

"Yes. Our friend upstairs is deeply interested in our proceedings, as well he may be; and, as you said, Burnsides isn't built for privacy." The call came through, and Gamadge opened the conversation.

"Harold?... I'm fine. Burnsides is a great place, wonderful food, centrally located between Ford's Center and Oakport... Yes, I've had quite a day, so far. All ready with the code?... Here goes, then. Simcox... Yes, I said Simcox... Of course it's here—right in the book.... No such word in the code? Nonsense... It doesn't mean anything? Neither do half the other words. I know you say they all mean something, but—What's that? I can't read my own writing? Certainly I can. If you can't, that's nothing to me. Here it is, S-I-M-C-O-X... What?... *Smilax?* Oh. Wait a minute. Well, Smilax, then."

He cast an injured glance at the grinning Mitchell, and went laboriously on:

"The next word is Toves, and the next, Pandion. I know what you've been reading; keep it up. Sad old poems are just what you need. Yes; Toves and Pandion. That'll do for the present. Sure you understand?... Good. Report to me here as early as you please, tomorrow morning; by telephone, naturally. Have you money to go on with? Good. Till tomorrow, then."

He hung up. Mitchell said, climbing the stairs in his wake, "I bet you told him to get a picture expert, and go burgle Ormiston's studio."

"Wish I'd thought of it."

Mitchell made a quick toilet in Gamadge's private bathroom, while his host finished unpacking by dumping the contents of his bag on top of the Burnsides' fumed oak dresser. Afterwards, rocking gently, and with his own notebook on his knee, he made penciled scrawls which only he could read. Gamadge splashed water, and then rubbed his head and neck furiously with a Turkish towel.

"Worst muddle I ever saw," said Mitchell. "Was that stuff about the life insurance some of the facts you were waiting for?"

"I won't know until tomorrow morning."

"You're the most obstinate feller living. Let's see what we got today. Gypsies. Little boy could have brought that red bell down to Bartrams'; but they don't seem to have any more motive than they had before; less, because old Mrs. Bartram was a friend of theirs and gave Mrs. Stuart old clothes and knickknacks. Was that gold chain any good?"

"No," replied Gamadge, from the bathroom door. "The gilt was wearing off it."

"Bartrams, Mr. and Mrs. George. Motive, if any, the Bartram property. Opportunity, lots—if we admit Mrs. Bartram as an accomplice, which I don't." Mitchell doggedly made a note. Gamadge said:

"For the second time, beware!"

"You beware of not taking character into consideration. Have I left anything out about the Bartrams?"

"Their return from Europe was unpremeditated and hurried."

"But they had lots of time on that boat to think about the financial situation. Irma could have brought that red bell into the Bartram property."

"She's too old to be allowed to witness such a scheme being carried out under her nose."

"She might have been sound asleep in the car all the time."

"Both times. Well..."

"I know there's plenty the matter with the idea. Ormistons, Mr. and Mrs. Motive, money."

"Not quite seven hundred dollars."

"They need it bad, and Ormiston has another motive—Carroll Bartram busted his nose."

"And he is suffering from delayed shock," murmured Gamadge, busy at his nails.

"If he cheated them out of old Mr. Bartram's four hundred thousand, that'll prove how far he'll go for money."

"Where's the four hundred thousand, that he has to murder somebody, or try to, for seven hundred more?"

"He hasn't been able to market the picture, or pictures. Ormiston is a selfish, ruthless type, doesn't care for a thing but his painting and drawing. That was great, wasn't it, the way he drew that head of Martha in three or four strokes, without even thinking about it?"

"Great; that's the word for him, when he's at his best."

"Mrs. Ormiston is the type that would see everybody else in the world blown to smithereens, if it would do her children any good."

"I don't see people as types; never could."

"You've got to cut a few corners, or you'd never get anywhere; not in a police investigation. Both Ormistons need money right now. I don't know how they'd get hold of the red bell, but perhaps they had Tommy with them on Tuesday, and he had it from Sarah Beasley."

"Very ingenious."

"Evelyn Walworth: and she's still my best bet. Two good motives, single or together—religious mania and revenge. Women like that, lonesome, unbalanced, they get to brooding. I can see her carrying that red bell around—just what she'd do. Probably had all the opportunity she needed. I wish she'd get back to the Pegram House; I don't like the idea of her driving around, thinking up crazy things to occupy her mind."

"There was nothing very crazy about the way she tracked us down, Mitchell. She enjoyed my nice little book, too."

"Miss Humphrey, the unknown quantity. She could be just about anybody, except a big man. She's a fake, because a real canvasser wouldn't go visiting summer cottages and family mansions; Miss Ridgeman saw through her right off. A real canvasser would stick to the natives. Well, I guess that's all. You wouldn't condescend to add anything, would you?"

"I would." Gamadge finished brushing his hair, and put on his tie. "It seems very odd to me that Miss Humphrey should have used a complicated device like picture taking to learn the habits and customs of those families."

"Well, I don't know." Mitchell looked down at his notes. "You think I better put that in?"

"As you please."

A gong sounded belowstairs, and Gamadge put on his coat and stood at the door. Mitchell, grumbling, preceded him down to the lobby, where Mr. Schenck awaited them, looking ravenous.

CHAPTER FIFTEEN

Action

MR. ROBERT SCHENCK had departed. He was full of tinker mackerel, succotash and creamed potatoes, and he had some of Mrs. Burnside's own special sunburn lotion on his peeling nose. He had given Mitchell a solemn promise to do nothing worse to Miss Walworth's car, if it ever did return to the Pegram House, than to flatten a tire.

"That'll hold her, until one of us can camp on her trail," said Mitchell. "Gosh darn it, where is the woman?"

Mr. Schenck said she was probably at the movies, since there was a revival of "Snow White" at the Center. He drove off into a chill, clear evening, and Mitchell applied himself to the telephone. Gamadge sat before the fire, one leg over the arm of his chair, a glass of his own whisky on a table beside him, and the New York paper—whence all mention of the nightshade poisonings had vanished—on the floor where he had allowed it to fall.

"There's no such paper as *Health In The Home*, and no such contest," Mitchell informed him. "The Stony Ridge

House in Haverley says the George Bartrams got there about six on Monday evening, all tuckered out, and the little girl was asleep in the car. She never woke up when they carried her in. Bartram drove out again in about half an hour."

"But did he get down to the short cut Tuesday, around eight?" murmured Gamadge, sleepily.

"I was wondering when you'd begin talking about the short cut."

"No use talking about it until we have some data. I suppose you'll have to try and find out where all the rest of 'em were, about then on Tuesday."

"Including Walworth?"

"Automobile tools are so heavy, some of them; and even state policemen are not on their guard when motorists ask them to look at a tire, say."

Mitchell set his jaw. "What in time did he see?"

"Perhaps I'll make a guess—tomorrow."

"Ain't you putting things off rather late?" Mitchell stood with his elbows on the high desk, consulting his notes; Gamadge drowsed. The telephone, when it rang, gave the usual impression of mortal urgency. Mitchell picked up the receiver:

"Hello, Mrs. Ormiston?...Miss Strangway's *gone?*...What do you mean, lost?...Before supper? Where's Breck?...He oughtn't to be hunting in the woods, he ought to have called state police headquarters. Nobody there?...Where's Mr. Ormiston?...At the movies?...I'll be up—no time at all."

When he reached the car Gamadge was already under the wheel, and the engine was running. Mitchell fell into the seat beside him, and slammed the door while they shot away from the porch steps.

"Take the short cut," said Mitchell, "and stop a minute at headquarters. I want to get hold of Bowles, if I can. My heavens. Mrs. Ormiston telephoned from Beasley's. It's tough, their not having their own telephone."

"I gather that she's left the three children alone in the house."

"She couldn't help it. Breck, the fool, is searching the woods; lost his head, I suppose. Miss Strangways put Tommy to bed, and then went out for a stroll. That's the last any of them saw of her. Ormiston took her car and went to the movies, right after supper. Mrs. Ormiston is nearly crazy. They thought she'd come home, gone upstairs."

"And fell into a panic when they found she hadn't?"

"Yes. Do you think Walworth happened along and took her for a ride?"

"I don't think anything." Gamadge turned into the short cut. He had observed the road with some care that morning, and now drove on the extreme right of it, one wheel following the rank grass that bordered it. Even when they entered the woods, he did not slow down. Mitchell, bounding in his seat, gasped: "I knew something would happen to the girl! But with Breck there..."

They were rushing towards the spot where Trainor had been killed, their lights two thin beams amid pitch darkness. Mitchell saw the slender huddle of clothing in the road, the pale hair scattered on black earth; he shouted, and his shout changed to a yell as Gamadge pressed his foot down.

"For God's sake—don't you see?"

Gamadge's voice came sharp in his ear: "Take your hand off the wheel. Don't you know an ambush when you see one? Keep your head in the car."

The jolt, when it came, was hideous. Mitchell, peering wildly through the back window, saw sticks and straws flying, a yellow wig tossed aside. He stuttered, a hand on the door: "Let me out of this."

"Use your wits. We were meant to get out."

"My Lord, was that how Trainor got his? A dummy!"

"For goodness' sake take your hand off the door, and sit back. We don't know where the fellow is. I hope there's no wire."

"He'll clear that dummy away. Humphrey's wig—I bet that was Humphrey's wig."

"Very likely."

"Whoever it was will be through to the upper road and away, before we—"

"Can't help it. We were supposed to get out, one at a time—in the car lights. The party may have a rifle."

"Why didn't he shoot at our tires?"

"We'd have stayed in the car, and you'd have held the siege with your gun till somebody came along. I know you're still dying to walk back and shoot it out, but that's suicide. Too much cover."

The car emerged into starlight, and Gamadge slowed. Mitchell asked, almost tearfully, "Why try it on *us*, the darned fool?"

"We're The Men Who Knew Too Much. You've seen about it in the movies."

"We don't know a thing. Or at least I don't, and you're only guessing, so far."

"Somebody doesn't care for our guesses."

"How'd you know enough to drive over that thing, for the land's sake?"

"I was half expecting something."

"I don't know how you did it! That crunch when we went over—I feel funny."

Gamadge produced his flask, and Mitchell, who loathed whisky, unscrewed the top, and drank.

Gamadge said: "I didn't believe Mrs. Ormiston would leave her children to go and telephone at the Beasleys, and I didn't believe Breck would desert her while he hunted in those woods. If you had been watching for a trap that dummy wouldn't have deceived you for a minute."

He stopped in front of headquarters. The extreme rage of Officer Bowles, a large and beetle-browed young man, when informed by the still confused Mitchell that he had been out of the office, took some abating; it changed to stupefaction when Mitchell explained.

"Of course the whole thing was a put-up job," he finished, "but I can't get it out of my head, even now, that there may be something wrong up at Harper's Rocks. I want you to ride up there as fast as you can. Find out who's home and who ain't, get a full report on where they are and what they're supposed to be doing, and make 'em show you the little feller—Tommy. See with your own eyes if he's safe and sound. Then go over to Beasley's and report from there. I'll be here, or at Bartram's. Wait a minute."

He called the Beasley farm. Claribel's voice came tinkling volubly over the telephone. No, nobody'd been there using the phone; yes, somebody could come and use it; they wouldn't be in bed. Her oldest sister and her oldest sister's husband had come already, and they were all helping Pop fix extra beds for the menfolks in the big hayloft. Mom had made ten huckleberry pies; and how was the kitty?

Mitchell said the kitty was fine, and slammed down the receiver. "Where's Pottle?" he demanded.

"Just gone home."

"Get him for me; and when you do get him, tell him to hurry. He's to ride along to that place on the short cut where Trainor was killed—right opposite the wood trail. Tell him to look around and see if he can find any traces of that dummy, or of a car parked in the woods, or anything else. We'll be there before long, and have a word with him."

Gamadge asked diffidently whether somebody could be posted on the upper road, where the wood trail came out.

"Certainly, if you think it'll do any good. He might find car tracks, at that. Or footprints."

Bowles got Pottle on the telephone.

"Just starting for the movies, with his girl," he said. "There's a picture at Ford's Center for tonight only—revival of 'Snow White.' He's a little sore."

"Too bad about him."

"Wants to know if he can bring the girl along with him to the short cut. It's that Luvy Wells he's so gone on," explained Bowles, "and he's afraid somebody else will take her to the picture if he don't."

"He's the damnedest state cop I ever heard of. Certainly he can take her into the short cut, if he don't mind her head getting blown off, or something. Does he know he may have a fight on his hands in there?"

"Oh, no, he won't. For goodness' sake!" expostulated Gamadge. "This isn't a war; and it's the fellow's time off."

"No state policeman has time off, in an emergency."

"This isn't an emergency."

"You tell him if he says one thing to this girl about this business, I'll have him fired. Court-martialed."

Bowles conversed with his colleague, said it was all O.K., and went out to bestride his motorcycle. Mitchell seized the telephone. After a minute's rapid talk, he said: "The call to Burnsides' was sent from Picken's drugstore. Pay telephone. Come on."

Still nursing the finest case of jitters that Gamadge had ever seen, he left headquarters at a run, and cast himself into his car. Gamadge had hardly got aboard before they were off.

Picken's clerk was busy; several couples were having a Saturday night carouse of sodas and sundaes at the counter, and customers were buying candy, cigarettes and papers. However, Mitchell and Gamadge were finally ushered into the prescription cubicle in the rear, and the clerk listened to Mitchell, and shook a bullet-head.

"I don't notice folks using the booth," said the clerk. "I only noticed one stranger this evening. Lady. No, I didn't pay any attention to what she had on. Black and white checked coat."

"Yellow hair?"

"I didn't see her hair. Her hat was pulled down. Lots of make-up. Veil."

"Tall woman? Medium? Short? Fat or skinny?"

"I couldn't tell you. Ordinary size."

"Shoes?"

"How would I notice her shoes? She wore pumps, I think."

"Di'mond pin?"

"Her coat was buttoned right up to her ears."

"Gloves?"

"Thick drivin' gloves, white with black seams. Say, I don't specially notice folks that don't buy nothing. What is this?"

"I think you notice a good deal. Here, gimme a can of tobacco."

Mitchell pointed out his brand, seized the can, rammed it into his pocket, and rushed out, Gamadge at his heels.

"And that's that," he panted, starting the car. "I never came up against such a thing in my life. Perhaps *you* expected Humphrey to turn up at the other end of that telephone call."

"You haven't said whether the voice sounded like Mrs. Ormiston's," said Gamadge, mildly.

"It sounded like a woman in a hurry, scared to death and gaspin'. That's what it sounded like."

He relapsed into a bleak silence, which he maintained until they had reached the cheerfully lighted doorway of the Bartram house. Miss Ridgeman let them in, looking frightened.

"I heard you drive up, and I saw you hurrying up the walk," she said. "Is anything the matter?"

"Oh, no; everything's as nice as pie," said Mitchell. "Who's home?"

"We're all home except Mr. George. He went to the movies."

"'Snow White', of course." Mitchell's sarcasm increased, and Miss Ridgeman, bewildered, replied yes, that's what he was going to see.

"Well, don't disturb the others. Just get hold of Loring for me, will you?"

Miss Ridgeman went to the telephone behind the stairs, and returned in half a minute to say that Doctor Loring would be over.

"Where can I see him for a short talk, before we join the family?"

"In the dining room." She indicated the door on the right, and asked again: "Is there any more trouble? Mr. Bartram's asleep, in there. I don't want—"

"We may not have to bother him at all."

"Mrs. Bartram at home?" asked Gamadge.

"She's listening to the radio."

"If the radio doesn't disturb Mr. Bartram, I shan't." The white kitten came bounding along the hall to meet him. He picked it up and went into the living room.

Carroll Bartram lay on the davenport, eyes closed, head comfortably pillowed, Boston newspapers drifting about him. Mrs. George Bartram sat at the other end of the room beside the radio, which discoursed the music of Mozart. Gamadge drew up a chair.

"Good evening, Mrs. Bartram," he said.

She looked up, pleased; rather Irma-like, this evening, Gamadge thought, with her fair hair fluffed out, and her short-sleeved blue dress spreading about her.

"Why, good evening, Mr. Gamadge! We must talk low, and not wake poor Carroll. George is at the movies; he always wanted to see 'Snow White'."

"Mitchell came over to talk business, and he brought me along. You like chamber music, Mrs. Bartram."

"Yes, I do. Mr. Gamadge, I love this place! It's the loveliest place I was ever in."

"Lovelier than Ohio?" asked Gamadge, smiling. "Lovelier than The Hague?"

"Yes; it's so cool, and the sun is so bright."

"That's a rare combination, I agree."

"Nothing could spoil Oakport for me—not for long. I do hope Carroll won't decide to shut it up, or sell it. I do so hope that Irma can be here sometimes."

"The house and grounds don't seem melancholy to you, any more?"

"If some of those evergreens were cut down, and the bushes pruned, it would be perfect. And of course I should have that awful playhouse taken away."

"You don't like the summerhouse?"

"I hate it, and so does Irma. I took her there this afternoon, and she almost kicked a hole in the netting. We never shut her up anywhere—she won't stand it."

"Let her kick it to pieces; then little Elias won't have to play in it."

"That's something else I've changed my mind about; I agree with Miss Ridgeman—the little boy will be splendid for Carroll. At first I didn't like the idea—his being a gypsy, you know; but I really think Carroll may find him more interesting, just because of that. I don't think the average man cares much for an ordinary child, do you?"

Whitey had gone to sleep on Gamadge's arm. He asked: "May I inquire what your immediate plans are, Mrs. Bartram?"

"Oh, dear! I ought to be in New York this minute, looking for a little apartment for us to live in while George finds out what's going to happen to the business."

"Why don't you go tomorrow?"

"Tomorrow? Sunday?" She looked surprised, but rather eager.

"Yes. Take Irma and leave on the midmorning train. You could get ready in time, couldn't you?"

"Of course; but I ought not to leave Carroll."

"Your husband can stand by, and Miss Ridgeman is here. You'd be in New York all ready to start apartment hunting on Monday morning. I can give you the name of a very comfortable family hotel."

"I wish I could, there's so much to do. George and Carroll could follow day after tomorrow with Annie."

"Certainly they could. You've done your share, up here."

"I'll speak to George about it. They'll have Adelaide, too. She's so funny, Mr. Gamadge; she was coming in here this afternoon, to listen to the radio, while we were all here! Carroll just laughed."

"His family has known Adelaides for a couple of centuries; you must get used to them, too, Mrs. Bartram."

"Irma loves her. I'll ask George about it tomorrow, as soon as he comes in."

"And there's something you can do for me," said Gamadge, feeling in his pocket and producing the wad of red ribbon and the red bell. "This is Whitey's, and I promised it to Irma. I have an idea she remembers such things, and I shouldn't like to let her down. Will you tie this on the cat tomorrow morning, and tell Irma I kept my promise?"

"Of course I will."

"I'm afraid it's rather dirty."

"Perhaps I can find another ribbon for it."

"I think we'd better stick to this one."

"Children do notice when a thing's been changed, don't they?" Mrs. Bartram took the bell, and put it carefully in her bag.

The door opened, and George Bartram came in breezily.

"Well, people! Hello, Gamadge! What brings you here?" He kissed his wife, shook hands with Gamadge, and caused his brother to wake suddenly, looking bewildered. "Let me at that radio—the news bulletin ought to be on." He twiddled a knob, and went on talking at the top of his voice, while an announcer bellowed war news. "Some picture, that 'Snow White'! Prettiest thing I ever saw. You see it, Gamadge? Great, isn't it? You'll have to take Irma, Dell."

"I told you, dear, Irma and I saw it in Rotterdam, that time."

"I know, but they had those Dutch titles."

Carroll Bartram said drowsily: "That you, Gamadge? What's up?"

"Mitchell wanted a word or two with you and Loring. He's in the dining room. Don't disturb yourself."

"Adèle, why don't you get us all some whisky? I'm a rotten host."

"Lead me to it!" But George Bartram did not wait to be led; he barged out of the room, followed by his wife. When he returned, a few minutes later, his face was no longer smiling. Mitchell and Loring came with him, the latter very grave.

Mrs. Bartram had brought ice and glasses on a tray. Her husband poured Gamadge's drink, and came over, carrying it and his own.

"I think that idea of yours is a good one," he said heavily. "About Dell and Irma getting out of here tomorrow. I'll telephone for their tickets, and I'll get them off before noon."

"Hope you don't think me officious. It was just a suggestion."

"Mighty good one. This place isn't fit for a dog to live in, from what I hear. Mitchell says you were shot at, coming over tonight."

"Not quite."

"And that dummy! Look here; what do you two know that's so important? Mitchell swears he doesn't know a thing."

"Nor do I—yet."

"Are you sure the dummy wasn't a kid's trick? Mitchell said you didn't stop and investigate."

"No, I thought we'd better try to live a little longer."

"By heaven, in your place I'd have got out of that car! I swear I would. I can't believe the fellow meant business. What did he think would happen, when you two were found there in the road?"

"I don't suppose that bothered him; if it was a him."

"Some crank! A case like this always brings dozens of them out of their holes."

Mitchell and Loring had been conferring with Carroll Bartram, who had got himself into a sitting position, and was gulping whisky.

"Take it easy," begged Loring. "Some crank, as George says."

Mrs. Bartram, hovering on the outskirts of the group, looked terrified. "Oh, this is dreadful!" she was saying, almost in tears. "Oh, Miss Ridgeman," as the nurse came in, "have you heard? You'd better come away tomorrow with me and Irma."

"I'll stay right here." Miss Ridgeman's square, homely face was grim. "This crazy person won't attack us, Mrs. Bartram."

"How do you know he won't? I wouldn't let Irma stay for anything!"

Carroll Bartram asked, almost with violence: "What criminal idiot is doing these things, Loring? Are you trying to find out?"

"Easy, old man; you're getting your psychopathology mixed. Mitchell wants me to look over one subject—if he can catch her, that is."

"Her?" cried Mrs. Bartram.

"Her. I'll investigate some others for him. Meanwhile, let's decide that it was nothing but an attempt to scare our friends here; and a very successful attempt it seems to have been."

"Very," admitted Gamadge, in a cheerful voice.

Mitchell said that he still couldn't get over the crunch when they hit the dummy. "I don't know how Gamadge did it."

Gamadge rose, placing Whitey carefully on the floor. "Quite unpleasant," he said. "A sixth sense comes into action when it's a question of preserving one's life."

"I'd have sworn it was little Miss Strangways. Ugliest thing I ever had anything to do with. That yellow wig." Mitchell shook his head. "No kid's trick there, Mr. Bartram."

"Want an escort to Burnsides?" asked Loring. "George and I will oblige; Carroll can supply us with a couple of duck guns."

"No, thanks. We have some reserves," said Mitchell.

"I wish you wouldn't go tomorrow, Gamadge, just when things seem to be getting hot. This appears to be your show, now." Loring watched him, critically. "Mitchell doesn't seem to know why the attack was made. You must have been giving yourself away, somehow."

"I really haven't. Mitchell knows as much as I do, and more besides."

"Whoever engineered the thing knows all about the Ormistons."

"And all about the Beasleys."

George Bartram, lowering and uncertain, accompanied them to the door. "Must you quit tomorrow night?" he asked.

"I must."

Mitchell and Gamadge drove to headquarters in silence. When they arrived there it was exactly nine thirty. "Seems like midnight," said Mitchell, going to answer the telephone, which began to ring as they went in. It was Bowles.

"They're all fine, up here," he said. "I saw the kid—fast asleep in Miss Strangways' room. Nobody'd been off the place except Ormiston, and he came in just before I left. He'd been—"

"To see 'Snow White'," growled Mitchell.

"That's just where he was! Mrs. Ormiston was in the studio all evening since right after supper, laying out a hooked rug."

"Anybody see her there?"

"No. Breck and Miss Strangways were playin' rummy in the sittin' room. They were hard at it when I came."

"You come on down and relieve Pottle in the short cut, so he can go to the movie. I wouldn't like to have him miss it," said Mitchell, with sarcasm. "Such state police I never saw in my born days."

Mitchell then telephoned to the Pegram House, and got Schenck. That young man informed him that Miss Walworth, to whom he referred as Her Nibs, had come in half an hour before, told the clerk that she had sat through two performances of "Snow White", and gone upstairs.

"You and Hoskins beat it out and go over that car."

"We did."

"No! That's the first sensible thing I've listened to since suppertime."

"We found a—er—cannon in one of the pockets, wadded down under a bunch of those paper handkerchiefs. I took some of 'em—to put Mrs. Burnside's lotion on with."

"Cannon!"

"Big old .45, loaded. And the neatest little Leica camera I ever saw."

"That's nice. What did you do with 'em?"

"Left 'em there. Hoskins is sitting on the car step."

"I'll be over." Mitchell, in a kind of waking dream, replaced the receiver and hurried out to the car. He was still commenting on Miss Walworth's idiosyncrasies to Gamadge when they reached the middle of the short cut. Pottle was keeping guard over a few twigs and some straw, scattered among the ruts in the road; and Pottle's young lady, in a rakish hat and a pink marabou cape, dozed in his sidecar. They were told to wait for Bowles.

Miss Luvy Wells, shuddering slightly in her airy best clothes, remarked that they would be in time for the second show. Mitchell drove away as if afraid that she might mention the name of it.

"If that girl hadn't been along, I would have got Pottle to follow us," he said, boring doggedly along between the dark regiments of trees.

"The bolt is shot for tonight, I think," replied Gamadge.

"You better borrow my gun."

"I'm ever so much obliged, but I think not. Don't worry about me."

"See you tomorrow."

"Yes. I'm going to turn in as soon as I can get ready. I feel like sleeping ten hours. Can't believe it's still Saturday."

"Sleep twelve, if you want to; there's nothing to get up early for, far as I know."

"You never can tell."

Burnsides looked very much isolated, and very dark. Mitchell watched Gamadge enter with his key, and then actually got out of the car, turned the corner of the house, and waited until he saw a light spring up in Gamadge's bedroom. Afterwards he drove as fast as he dared to the Center, wondering uneasily what it was that he and Gamadge knew.

CHAPTER SIXTEEN

Storm Signals

AT TEN O'CLOCK the next morning Mr. Schenck found Gamadge basking in the sun on Burnsides' front steps, the Boston Sunday papers strewn around him. He was affable, but he did not seem talkative.

"Well," began Schenck, "Mitchell went over Miss Walworth's car. It's all tracked up with leaves and dirt, and there are pine cones in the rumble. She says she likes to get out and ramble in the woods."

"I dare say she does." Gamadge had laid the papers aside, and was leaning back against a post, cigarette in mouth. It waggled as he spoke.

"The gun was dripping with oil; it was fully loaded. Mitchell took the shells out, and took away the rest of the ammunition, and put the gun back."

"He'd better."

"Yes, I bet she'd have the law on him at the drop of a hat. While she was at breakfast Hoskins searched her room. I don't know what for. He didn't find anything compromising, so far as I can make out."

"He and Mitchell seem to be heading for trouble."

"Unless you can call this compromising," continued Schenck. He took a piece of paper out of his pocket and offered it to Gamadge, who glanced at the other's expressionless face, and unfolded it.

"That's only a copy, of course," explained Schenck. "They put back the original."

Gamadge read:

ADEPTS PREPARE
For the third coming of Ithuriel
Who will descend upon the terrestrial globe
On Sunday, April 7th, 1940
In the Great Purple

"There's a lot more," said Schenck. "I only copied the title."

"Oh. Where is Miss Walworth now?"

"She drove off a little while ago, with Hoskins right behind her. He mended her flat tire. He was telling me about you. He says when you get in a case, funny things happen. I said you impressed me as a quiet, easygoing type; very cool, but—"

"But slow."

"Hoskins said if I stuck with you I'd feel as if I was sitting in that cave behind Niagara Falls, with the Great Cataract roaring past me; and then I'd feel as if I was going over in a barrel."

"*In* the barrel, you notice."

"Hoskins said that I'd end up swimming around the whirlpool, hanging on to what was left of the barrel."

"He had a shocking experience last summer, but that wasn't my fault."

"Pottle rode in while we were at breakfast. He says Mr. Ormiston went to the movies last night in Miss Strangways' little car. He says both it and the Ormiston bus are a mess; twigs and sand, but no straw—whatever he meant by that.

Samples of all the different kinds of soil between here and Kittery. Bits of flowers. The Ormiston car has fishing tackle under the back seat, and a dead starfish in one pocket of it."

"I've seen family cars in the summer."

"I came here by way of the shore, and Oakport. The troops seem to have been called out; policemen on their bikes every few yards. I began to think Hoskins was right."

"He isn't right very often, I'm sorry to say."

Mr. Burnside came to the front door and said that a young feller had been on the telephone for Mr. Gamadge.

"He said not to disturb you, and the message is 'Nix'."

"Nix?"

"Nix."

"Thanks very much, Mr. Burnside."

Mitchell's car drove in, and Mitchell got out of it. Gamadge rose.

"Excuse us, will you?" he asked Schenck. "I have a confidential report for Mitchell."

That gentleman's face brightened. "You have?"

"Just came."

"Nix," muttered Schenck, as the two went into the house.

Mr. Burnside, in the dining room, heard voices in Gamadge's room. Then he heard Gamadge's voice, talking steadily, and suddenly a crash, as if someone had leaped to his feet, overturning a chair. There was a loud exclamation or expletive, and then both voices alternated for a few minutes more. Finally Gamadge's door banged, and Mitchell pounded down the stairs and out of the front door. He was driving furiously away before Gamadge sauntered back to the porch steps.

"What's all this?" demanded Schenck, gazing after the car, and then at Gamadge.

"Mitchell has some urgent business."

"Because somebody told you 'Nix'?"

"Partly for that reason. Here comes company."

Miss Strangways' two-seater turned into the drive from the north. It contained Miss Strangways herself, Mr. Davidson

Breck, and Tommy, the latter wedged tightly between them. Breck got out.

"We're off," he said. "I wonder if Mrs. Burnside will put us up some lunch?" He went into the house, and the other men descended to the car. Miss Strangways' face had color in it, which made it seem less thin than before; and it was shaded by a becoming, if incredibly aged, red straw hat. She was smiling cheerfully. Tommy sucked a piece of barley sugar, and stared at Mr. Schenck's shining nose.

"Nice day for a drive," said Gamadge. "Squalls, this afternoon, though. You don't mind squalls, do you, Tom?"

"No, and we have our rubber coats, and all our bags and boxes, and my shovel and pail."

The rumble, in fact, seemed to be bursting open and exuding luggage. Schenck said: "Moving?" He seemed to approve of Miss Strangways' appearance, in spite of the threadbare condition of her clothes.

"All the way to New York."

Breck, returning, supplemented this: "We're swimming out into still water. There's been the dickens of a shindy up at the Rocks."

"I don't think we ought to talk about it, Dave."

"Why not? First time I ever saw Ormiston act naturally. It's a good old-fashioned row. We thought we'd move out before they calmed down enough to make any objections."

"I wouldn't have thought Mrs. Ormiston could fight with anybody," remarked Schenck.

"Neither would I," replied Mr. Breck. "It was refreshing."

"Dave, I wish you wouldn't—"

Mrs. Burnside waddled out, a good-sized pasteboard box in her hands. Breck paid for it, thanked her, and squeezed into the driver's seat.

"I telephoned to Mr. Mitchell from Beasleys'," said Miss Strangways.

"That's right." Gamadge shook hands. "Best of luck."

"He'll let me know about—about Cousin Evelyn."

"Did he tell you that she was submerged in the Great Purple?"

"I can't imagine what it all means."

"You sometimes see elderly ladies reading all about it in busses. Good-bye, Tom."

"Dave and Millie and I are going to have supper tonight in Boston."

"You'd better get going; I see something that looks like the Ormiston sedan approaching from the north."

Breck started the car with a jerk, and only just in time. They had scarcely disappeared down the highway when Mrs. Ormiston drove in, her children squabbling happily on the back seat. She looked flushed and angry.

"I stopped because I saw you here, Mr. Schenck," she said. "Perhaps you can tell me what all this means."

Schenck, with a glance towards Gamadge, politely said that he would be glad to, if he could.

"Mr. Gamadge," she went on, her large brown eyes turning balefully in his direction, "is it a fact that the state police will not allow me to leave this county?"

"Not to my knowledge, Mrs. Ormiston. Who in the world told you so?"

"My husband informs me that I am watched, and that I shall be arrested if I try to leave. I shall drive down to Robson's, and if I am stopped, I shall—I shall—"

"Why does he think you will be stopped?"

"It was Bert who wanted to tear off before the Bartram funeral. I wouldn't stir. I have nothing to hide. There has been a policeman up at the Rocks, last night and again this morning."

"To protect you all, I suppose."

"Then why did he go to everybody and try to find out if I really was in the studio last night, starting my hooked rug?"

"There's a certain amount of routine..."

"Nobody saw me, of course; not until that policeman came and made such a racket with his motorcycle that he woke Sidney. My husband was at the movies—he left right after supper. Millie and Davidson Breck were together in the living room. I often spend whole evenings in the studio, when Bert is out of it. I happen to belong to a guild of needleworkers. I have my own work to do, I can assure you."

"Why does your husband think that the police are after you, Mrs. Ormiston?" repeated Gamadge, patiently.

"He thinks I shouldn't have insured Tommy. Mr. Schenck will tell you it was a perfectly legitimate business transaction."

"He has told me so."

"If anything had happened to Tommy, somebody would have had to pay the bills. Now Millie and Dave have left, scared away, I suppose, by that policeman; and there is nobody to do the work."

"I dare say the Beasleys can help out. Mrs. Ormiston, why go off like this, tire yourself and the children out, get caught in the storm this afternoon?"

"I won't have my children involved in a police investigation. I shall leave them with friends, and come back this evening."

She drove away, and Schenck whistled gently. "Will they let her go?"

"They'll send word along the route. I suppose one of those fellows has seen her."

"Don't you think we ought to—"

"No. Easy enough to pick that outfit up, if they want it."

Officer Pottle walked up the drive, pushing his motorcycle, on which young William Stanley sat astride, his bare legs dangling. Bliss transformed his dark face, and an elflock hung over one eye. Pottle said: "Witness with information for you, Mr. Gamadge. He's seen that bicycle, and his folks want him to have it."

"Testimony worth it?" Gamadge helped William to descend, and sat down on the steps. William, looking rather hunted, slid around one of the rail posts.

"I don't know; he wouldn't say a word to me. His grandma sent him. The little bike is standing in the middle of the camp, and it looks quite nice. I shined it up a trifle."

"*You* ought to be rewarded. What did you want to tell me, William?"

William, who looked as if the last thing he wanted was to tell anybody anything, said in a mumbling voice: "That woman in the car."

"Oh. Yes. What about her?"

"I was on the road. She stopped, and she took out her little camera. And then she looked ahead of her, and she saw Aunt Georgina just outside our camp. And she said, scared-like: 'You're a gypsy.'"

"Scared-like?"

"Yes. She said: 'You're a gypsy, ain't you?' I said yes, I was. So she turned her car, and she drove right away."

"I see." Gamadge's eyes screwed up as he looked into William's. "What about the candy?"

"She handed me that out of the car window when she asked to take my picture."

"Oh. She was scared, you say? Not just surprised, or disappointed, or anything like that?"

"No, she was scared. She had a pink face. It looked funny."

"Funny? How?"

"Pink spots stood out on it."

"Veil, had she?"

"Yes. Gold hair."

"Notice her hat, or her coat, or her dress?"

"Pin on her collar."

"Bright pin?"

William nodded. "It was Monday."

"Thank you ever so much, William. You couldn't tell me what time it was?"

"Right before supper."

"They eat early," explained Pottle. "Half past five or so."

Gamadge looked earnestly at William, and William looked at him. Pottle said: "His folks hadn't heard anything about this woman, till he mentioned her to you yesterday morning. They kind of discouraged him from talking then, because they thought she might have something to do with the nightshade, and they don't want any part of that. Now, for some reason, they don't think she *was* mixed up in the nightshade case."

"Why not, I wonder?"

"I suppose they think it was somebody else." Gamadge took seven dollars from his wallet. "Here you are, Pottle. The bicycle is William's."

"Worth the money, was it?" Pottle folded the bills, looking curiously at Gamadge, who replied: "Well worth it."

Pottle swung William across the saddle of his machine, and they moved off. Schenck remarked: "I begin to hear the roar of the mighty cataract."

"You must have good ears. Who's this coming? It's Ormiston, the abandoned and deserted. Hiking."

Mr. Ormiston, burdened with a knapsack and carrying a stick, came up the drive, scowling. He acknowledged Gamadge's greeting with a short nod, and Schenck's introduction to him with a glare. "You're the insurance fellow, are you?" he asked. "Where's my wife?"

"Off for Robson's," said Gamadge. "Lovely morning for a walk, Mr. Ormiston."

"How else can I get about, with both cars gone?"

"You look hot. Have a drink."

"If you mean alcohol, I never touch it." Ormiston laid his painting kit aside, and lolled against the rail. "My place is a madhouse, this morning. Or it was. It's empty at present. Everybody cleared out for the day—or forever, so far as I know. I thought I might as well get a sketch, somewhere. Nice Japanese effect of pines just below here; I noticed it one morning."

Gamadge said: "Why so annoyed at Mr. Schenck—and for the matter of that, at Mrs. Ormiston?"

Ormiston's flat, lowering face reddened. "Women are the very devil. My wife—I couldn't believe it when she finally told me. She insured that kid's life. Insured Millie Strangways' life, too. There's going to be a most unholy scandal when it gets out;

but what does she care? And what does she care if everybody knows we happen to be hard up at the moment? It's purely temporary. I have a big commission, and several other irons in the fire; and Millie Strangways will be able to support her own kid before long."

"She could support him now, if she decided to accept an offer that was made her in my presence."

"Breck's? She won't marry. Has a complex."

"Not Breck's. She has been offered a home for Tommy and herself, and an allowance; by a member of her husband's family."

"Her husband's—who are you talking about?"

"A Miss Evelyn Walworth."

Ormiston's face expressed utter amazement, and something more. Presently he said: "You're joking."

"Certainly not."

"That woman's mad. She was in an asylum."

"Dismissed cured."

"She's here?"

"Free as a bird, in the Pegram House, Ford's Center."

"But they can't live with her! It's a crime. She was a dangerous lunatic. Threatened to kill Millie and the boy."

"She says she doesn't want to, any more. She had a revelation."

"I tell you, Gamadge, she's as mad as a hatter, and that kind never gets over it. Revelation!"

"I suppose she had to have one, if she was to live at all."

"And she wants Millie to live with her in Boston? In that house? It'll have to be stopped. It would be murder to let it go through. Have you seen the woman?"

"Yes. Don't ask me what I think of her mental condition; I'm not competent to judge."

Ormiston turned fiercely on Schenck. "If Millie Strangways and her boy set up housekeeping with that woman," he said, "don't advise your company to renew those policies. You'll lose the money in three months."

Mr. Schenck's lamblike acceptance of Ormiston's bad manners seemed to have been deceptive. He now trained his spectacles on the artist, and remarked composedly: "If Miss Strangways and her son can be removed from the proximity of the beneficiary, my company will certainly feel encouraged to renew."

This Johnsonian sentence had an immediate effect. Ormiston said: "Perhaps I deserved that. I ought not to take it out on you, of course. You're not even an agent; I mean, you're only investigating. See here: what I wanted to tell Gamadge or the detective was this—the policies are not going to be renewed anyway. I'll see to that. I may be financially a bad risk, just now, but I am averse to the sordid."

He shouldered his kit, picked up his stick, and lumbered down the drive; pausing to stare at the strange procession which passed him at the lower entrance, and came on to the porch. It was headed by Officer Pottle on his motorcycle; behind him advanced Miss Walworth's coupé; and an ancient and official Ford car, driven by Deputy Hoskins, brought up the rear. The top of the Ford was down. Hoskins leaned forward over the wheel, his small wiry body tense, and his eyes snapping. He wore, as his custom was, no collar; a lack which seemed to make his neck look thinner, and his prominent nose more predatory. He was smiling, less diffidently than usual.

The cavalcade stopped. Miss Walworth, red of face and a little wild of eye, got out of her car; this time neglecting to clear her skirt, which parted from the crack of the door with a loud rip.

"How do, Mr. Gamadge?" said Hoskins. "Glad to see you again."

"How are you, Hoskins? Good morning, Miss Walworth." Gamadge turned an inquiring eye on Pottle. "No trouble, I hope?"

Pottle opened his mouth, but Miss Walworth spoke first:

"You may well ask, Mr. Gamadge!" She panted, and made flurried efforts to replace wisps of hair under her hat. "I insisted on being brought here to see you. Nobody is more anxious than myself to assist the authorities; but I will not submit to unnecessary coercion. This person," she continued, indicating Hoskins, "who has been most kind and civil throughout, was a witness to the whole affair. He will tell you whether or not I was hustled by this officer."

"Hustled by Officer Pottle?"

"If that is his name."

"But why, Miss Walworth?"

"I do not know. The fact is, Mr. Gamadge, that I am a martyr to hay fever, especially during the post-goldenrod season; therefore, I always carry a supply of paper handkerchiefs with me, in the pocket of the car where I keep my revolver."

The four men gazed at her, fascinated.

"Your revolver, Miss Walworth?" repeated Gamadge, respectfully.

"I always carry one, of course, on my solitary drives. Nobody has more confidence than myself in the ultimate goodness of human nature; but I am not a fool."

"Certainly not."

"I am a fair shot. I was taught to use it by a young cousin of mine, who is—no longer with us. My cousin Lawrence," said Miss Walworth, firmly. "He was an excellent shot himself. Well, to make a long story short, I discovered just as I was passing the gypsy camp that most of my handkerchiefs had unaccountably disappeared."

Mr. Schenck blinked rapidly.

"I cannot imagine what has become of them. I remembered that the gypsies have been selling gaily colored cotton handkerchiefs, and that they are in boxes, and therefore presumably sanitary. I stopped at the camp, where this officer was, or appeared to be, oiling a small bicycle. William came up to me—you know William Stanley?"

"I do, Miss Walworth."

"I always carry a little present or two for such children as I meet on my travels. I got out my bag, and I offered him my little present. The next moment, Mr. Gamadge, there was pandemonium."

"Pandemonium?"

"That is the only word to describe it. Mrs. Stuart rushed up, chattering, simply chattering, in what I suppose was Romany. Georgina sprang at me and grasped me by the arm. William shouted. Even Martha and the baby appeared, and the baby began to cry. This officer hurried up, allowed me no explanations, and hustled me into my car. He said that he was taking me to Ford's Center; but I told him that I had met you, and that you would speak in my behalf. This gentleman happened to be driving along, and I asked him to come too. Really, I hardly knew what might not happen; the officer seemed to have taken leave of his senses."

"I'm very glad you thought of me. What *is* all this, Pottle?"

Pottle silently reached into his pocket, and brought out a paper bag. This he offered to Gamadge, who emptied the contents into his hand. Six glossy jet-black globules lay in his palm, which he gazed at for a moment with repulsion. Schenck, peering at them, felt as if the nightshade case had suddenly taken material form under his eyes.

Gamadge picked up one of the black balls, and suddenly popped it into his mouth. After a moment he removed it, tossed it daintily into the bushes, and said, "I haven't tasted a licorice sucker for twenty years, and I find that my taste for them has vanished. I suppose, Miss Walworth, that you didn't realize how much these things resembled the berries of the deadly nightshade."

"Of course I realized it, Mr. Gamadge."

"You did?"

"Certainly. It occurred to me, when I bought them, how easy it would be for a criminal to poison people with them. I mean, of course, by putting nightshade berries among them, and giving them to children."

Pottle asked, grimly, "Don't you think I'd better take her to the Center, Mr. Gamadge?"

"Mitchell isn't there, and I don't believe the sheriff is, either. Miss Walworth, I won't ask you whether you realized that these ghastly things would scare the gypsies, the natives, and even the state police half out of their senses, because if I did you would probably reply that you realized it perfectly, and didn't give a hang."

"You are joking, Mr. Gamadge; why should a licorice drop frighten anybody? Anybody, of course I mean, who had no sense of guilt upon seeing something that looked like nightshade berries."

"Well, you *have* scared us to death, Miss Walworth; all of us. Please accept that as a fact, and let me dispose of these horrible things. This gentleman is Mr. Hoskins, and he will be glad to escort you to the Pegram House. I hope you'll stay there, as a favor to me, for the rest of the afternoon. This nightshade case is a mystery, you know; although perhaps it isn't one to you. Like Mrs. Stuart, you may have extra-sensory perception."

"I lay claim to no occult powers, Mr. Gamadge," replied Miss Walworth, with dignity.

"Well, you have nerves of steel, at least; but even you must realize that a murderer, in deed if not in intention, is still at large. We'll all feel better if you are not."

"I shall be glad to oblige you and the authorities; but I cannot understand what all the fuss is about."

"Allow me to present Mr. Schenck, of New York; he'll drive back with you, too; and I dare say he'll be delighted to play a game of backgammon with you."

"My Sunday game," said Miss Walworth, all smiles again, "is Anagrams."

"He'll get a box of them at the drugstore; and he can buy you another supply of paper handkerchiefs at the same time. Can't you, Schenck?"

Mr. Schenck, in obedience to Gamadge's compelling eye, said that it would be a pleasure. Upon climbing into his car and taking his position at the tail of the parade, he was tantalized almost beyond endurance to hear Mr. Burnside's loud observation from the doorway:

"That feller was on the line again, Mr. Gamadge, and he says to tell you: 'Absolutely nix.' Dinner's ready."

CHAPTER SEVENTEEN

Storm

A LATE BREAKFAST and a morning of physical inactivity had ill prepared Gamadge for the Burnside Sunday dinner. He ploughed through it under Mrs. Burnside's attentive eye as well as he could, and then declined into a half stupor. Mr. Burnside offered him the use of his extra car, but invisible bonds seemed to keep him within the precincts. He listened to the radio, tried to finish the New York papers, laid out a game of Canfield; but when the Burnsides retired for their Sunday afternoon siesta he succumbed, and followed their example. It would have surprised Mr. Burnside to see him lock the front and back doors, and wedge a chair under the knob of his own, before he turned the key in the lock of it.

His nap was not a success. Anxiety dogged him through a long, confused dream, in which the landscape was green, the skies dark, and none of the people seemed to be more than two feet high. He awoke with difficulty to the sound of wind and rain, and lay for a minute getting his bearings. He decided that

Annie and the Little People accounted for the dream, whatever Freud might say about it.

The room was in twilight, and there was a considerable drip and patter of water somewhere; he could hear it above the howling of the gale. He got off the bed, and discovered that the flapping curtains were soaked, and that the floor beneath the window was a puddle. He shut the window, and did some mopping up with a bath towel, before going downstairs. At the foot of them he paused, to stare across the dim lobby to the glass upper half of the front door. A face was pressed up against it, large, flat and pale. He paused for a moment, and then went and let Mr. Ormiston in.

The artist was dripping. He said: "What's the idea of the barricade?" and came over to the fire. Gamadge poked it into life and heaved a log on it.

"There's a doorbell," he said.

"I didn't want to wake the Burnsides. I suppose they spend Sunday afternoon asleep. So do you, by the look of you." He laid his knapsack on a table, and peeled off his leather coat, which he hung on a chair. "I wondered if Burnside could lend me a car to get home with."

"You can have the one he offered to me. It's in the garage; a black Buick. I'll tell him. No need to rout him out now."

"Thanks." Ormiston put a hand on the chimney ledge, and held out one sodden boot, and then the other, to the warmth. "I got two nice studies of those trees. The gale came up like a cyclone. I stayed under cover till it calmed down, and then I ran for here. No use trying for a ride to Harper's Rocks—you might as well try to thumb yourself to Ultima Thule. How about driving me up, and bringing the car back? Do you good."

"I promised Mitchell I wouldn't go out without a cop."

"You what?"

"Mitchell was going to leave one on the premises, but I said if he'd leave me alone I'd stay in, like a good boy."

Ormiston flung back his head and roared with laughter. "What does he think will happen to *you?*"

"He thinks I might get shot."

"Why, for goodness' sake?"

"I'm supposed to know too much. Like the man in the movies."

"And do you?" Ormiston grinned at him.

"I don't know half enough."

"Haven't been doing any more of that brilliant constructive work of yours?"

"A fair amount; not very brilliant."

"It's absurd. That policeman, last night—is that why he was snooping around up at my place?"

"Yes."

"I don't see why staying at home would save your precious life. You might have a caller." Ormiston glanced about him. "This place is a trap."

"Well, Mitchell thought there wasn't much cover around Burnsides, and Burnside or Mrs. Burnside might look out of a window."

"After you were dead? Consoling thought for you."

"We still think the party or parties are in their right senses."

"Well! Good luck to you. I might as well keep that car—no knowing when my wife will get home, and I promised her I'd call on the Bartrams tonight. She says I'm a boor."

"Oh; she couldn't have meant it."

"She meant it, all right. So I'll run down and condole, after what I suppose I shall have to call supper. You be there?"

"No, I'm taking the ten o'clock."

"Scared right off the map. Well, we'll try and struggle along without your expert assistance."

Gamadge showed a certain alacrity in helping him on with his coat and adjusting the knapsack. He went out with him to the kitchen door, and watched while he backed the Buick out of the garage, and drove away. He was still standing there when Bowles rode up, his sidecar attached to his machine.

"Got it, did you?" Gamadge looked hopefully at the large bundle which the officer dragged out of the sidecar, and carried into the house.

"Yes, sir, we did. How'd you know it would be right near the trail—all of it?"

"Buried?"

"No. Part of it up a tree, the rest stuck behind logs and in bushes."

Gamadge assisted him to carry the big damp roll, which had been wrapped in a rubber sheet, into the dining room. They laid it on a table, and opened it. Gamadge carefully spread out damp garments.

"Had to be there," he said, inspecting the black-and-white coat, the tweed skirt, a rubber mackintosh, a white felt hat. "Humphrey must have been in a devil of a hurry to get rid of the things; knew we'd trace the call to Picken's. We had a full description of these clothes since late afternoon, and everybody knew we had it. Whoever it was that laid that trap for us had to be out of the disguise and out of the woods before we had a chance to get hold of Picken's clerk, and you fellows."

"I suppose she wouldn't risk taking them away with her in her car."

"No, there was no telling what we'd do, or what might happen. Fatal to be caught with the goods. There might have been an accident, collision, anything." Gamadge inspected a green skirt, a green sweater, a blond wig. "These and the raincoat were on the dummy. I suppose you didn't find the gloves or the veil."

"We will, if they're there. This rain makes it harder."

"The things are cheap, and brand-new. You may trace 'em to the stores, but you won't trace 'em to the purchaser, I'm afraid. However, I don't need to tell you how valuable they are."

"Mitchell warned us."

"Get 'em over to the Center as soon as you can, and for heaven's sake don't let anybody talk."

Gamadge helped him roll up the bundle, and put it back in the sidecar. Again he stood watching while Bowles rode away. He went back through the kitchen and dining room to the lobby, and was lighting a cigarette in front of the fire when Doctor Loring, in rubber coat and sou'wester, dashed up the front steps and came in laughing.

"Whew!" he said. "I bet we're in for three days of this. We'll be calling it the line storm by tonight, in the face of science and the calendar. The Bartrams are driving the little gypsy to his new home; and they dropped me here to say good-bye, for us all."

"Good of you. Have a drink." Gamadge got his whisky, and foraged for ice. When he came back Loring was smoking peacefully in front of the fire.

"I had the pleasure of meeting a Mr. Schenck this afternoon," he said. "Over at the Pegram House. I went there to get a look at Mitchell's lady friend the occultist."

"Oh. Like her?"

"With Schenck's help I was able to construct a picture. I'm no psychologist, you know; but she's a borderline case, I think. Very garrulous. Likes to meet people, tell them all about herself—all except the important things. She was glad to hear that I was a fellow author, and she'd read every one of my sketches."

"Did she go into the matter of the revelation?"

"No, she knew I was a doctor, and she kept clear of anything compromising. If Mitchell hadn't warned me, I shouldn't have known a thing about the revelation. Schenck showed me the copy of that prospectus—the descent of Ithuriel, you know. Lots of lonely souls go in for that kind of thing. I shouldn't let it weigh against her, if there were no other evidence. Look here; poor old George. I can tell you why he isn't handing out information about Sunday night. They spent it at an autocamp."

"I see."

"Very nice place, I've often stayed in them; but George seems to think it would be the end of him as a solid citizen if it were to come out. He's not as hard up as all that, you know;

he's merely frightened. His father was the same way, easily panicked about money. I most sincerely hope that you aren't letting ideas about George lead you astray."

"No, indeed."

"Mrs. Ormiston, heaven help her, met me on the road this noon and poured her troubles into my unwilling ear. I like that woman. Did you know that she was a show girl before Ormiston married her, and then an actress in the Charles Street playhouse, and then an artist's model? That's how she met Ormiston. Finally, she was co-proprietress of a Greenwich Village curio shop—'Breton Broderies, Incorporated'. I'm sorry about the French—it isn't mine."

"No! Good for her."

"American womanhood is full of surprises. Take Irma's mother, for instance. Wouldn't you have sworn that that little thing was a product of the middle-Western bourgeoisie, solid tradespeople, with a long tradition of comfortable incomes and cultural advantages, as they'd call them? Well, her father was a bricklayer, and nobody ever could find out what her mother was. Beyond them, the family disintegrates into the realm of myth."

"I knew Irma couldn't be the scion of stodginess."

"Mrs. Bartram was typist on that famous cruise—The House In the Bush, you know."

"I know."

"Fortunately for George, who needed a typist. She worked for him six weeks, and then they were married."

"I shouldn't have thought him so sensible."

"You should have known Carroll's wife. No wonder the brothers never got on. They're antithetical. Well, George will be coming back for me any minute, now. I had a question to ask you, and if you won't answer it, I suppose I must resign myself. But I should like it if we could sleep peacefully in our beds henceforth. Was Bartram's child the intended victim of this—scheme—conspiracy—whatever it was?" He hesitated. "I can see that you might not feel free to tell me. I'd keep it to myself. I'd just like to know that nobody wanted to kill Bartram's child."

"Nobody did, Doctor Loring, so far as I can judge."

"On your word of honor?"

"Certainly on my word of honor. Is there any other kind of word?"

"You take a load off my mind." Loring rose, as George Bartram stamped in.

"Well, Gamadge; too bad you have to travel on a rotten night like this," he said, shaking himself. "You get drenched between the car and the porch. My brother wants me to say he's sorry not to see you again."

"It's very kind of him."

"I got Irma and her mother off this morning, cat and all. Gad, you should have seen Irma carrying the basket; you'd have said she was fifty, instead of five." His red face looked dull and lifeless; the vitality had gone out of it, and out of his voice. He lingered for a minute after Loring had made his dash to the car, irresolute; his hand went into his pocket, and came out again, empty. "I suppose you really do have to go tonight?"

"Do you want me to stay longer, Mr. Bartram?" Gamadge met his shifting eye, and held it.

"It seems too bad for you to quit, just when things seem to be breaking. Last night, I mean, you know."

"Mitchell can handle the rest of it."

"I felt I'd like a talk with you—alone. Perhaps it wouldn't do any good."

"You're the judge of that."

"I don't know. I—"

A hail from Loring made him put out a large hand, shake Gamadge's, and hurry out to the car. Gamadge saw him staring back through the rain-washed window of the Cadillac, like a man who had lost an opportunity, and did not know whether to regret it or not.

The Burnsides came downstairs, lights went on, and the lobby shed its eeriness. Gamadge went up to wash and pack, and when he came down again he was met at the foot of the stairs by a short, dark young man whose hair shone glossily.

"Well, Harold." Gamadge patted him on the shoulder. "How do you like the State of Maine?"

"I haven't seen any of it except stores, and now this hurricane."

"What's the answer?"

"Nix, nix and double nix, except two people that saw them in an automobile."

"Wonderful."

"Soon as I got off the train, and telephoned you—"

"At seven forty-five, confound you."

"I started around Ford's Center. Then I hired a Ford and went to Oakport. I did the beaches. I ended up at Harper's Rocks. The lady there let me wait till her husband got home—not so long ago."

"You've had a day of it. Who are you supposed to be?"

"I'm traveling in writing paper. I brought along some of yours—the kind you get from England."

"Why, you little—did it have my address on it?"

"No, I only brought the plain sheets. I said it was a dollar a hundred, with envelopes."

"You must have made sales, at that price."

"I took orders for about a ton of it. One of those state cops ordered some. They liked getting it C.O.D."

"What did you do about a sample case?"

"I didn't need a sample case. I had the paper in a manila envelope."

"We never do these things right. You should have had a sample case."

"They didn't worry about a sample case when they saw that paper, at a dollar a hundred."

"Your methods are so flamboyant. Go and get ready for supper, and remember we don't know each other."

At seven o'clock Mr. Gamadge and Mr. Bantz sat down to the evening meal in the Burnside dining room. They were civil but distant, as such opposing types would naturally be.

At half past seven the gypsies broke camp, and vanished away as if driven before the wind and rain. An observer, if there had been one, might have seen young William hoist a small bicycle into the rear of the caravan, to the annoyance of his relations.

At eight o'clock Sheriff Enos James, that weather-beaten, kindly but disillusioned man, arrived with State Detective Mitchell at Burnsides. They were closeted in Mr. Gamadge's bedroom for half an hour, where Mr. Bantz also made one of the party; a fact which Mr. and Mrs. Burnside would have been surprised to learn.

At eight thirty, four persons sat over a light refection (cold lobster, potato salad and coffee) at the Turnbulls'. Mrs. Turnbull, free for the evening because her employer, Doctor Loring, was having supper at the Bartrams', had invited Miss Adelaide Gibbons and the Bartrams' Annie to spend the evening, at Miss Gibbons' suggestion. The Turnbulls, particularly Mr. Turnbull, a small, shy man, had not particularly looked forward to the party; but Miss Gibbons, that social genius, had kept them in roars of laughter; even Annie's face wore a demure smile.

"Come on, Mis' Rourke," said Adelaide. "Tell us again what your cousin told the Black and Tan."

At eight thirty-five Mr. George Bartram said he was going to the Center to see a show. He got into his car and drove off; Doctor Loring observed, after he had gone, that he hoped the movies would improve George's spirits, which seemed to be at a low ebb. But perhaps, he added, George was the kind that couldn't exist comfortably without some woman to pet him.

At eight forty-five Mr. Albert Ormiston told his wife that he was going down to Oakport for a look-in on the Bartrams. He then got into the Burnside car, and drove off in the rain. Mrs. Ormiston, who had returned in time for supper, minus her children, retired to the studio and contemplated her hooked rug. She was not exactly nervous at being left alone in the house, but she was not sorry when her husband returned, an hour later.

"George was out," he said, briefly.

"How was Carroll?"

"Dopey and dull. I hate that fellow."

"Don't be silly."

"Loring hangs over him as if he thought somebody was going to do him an injury."

"Somebody has done him an injury. Were they nice to you?"

"Nice to me! They'd better be nice. You going to bed?"

"Yes. Aren't you?"

"No. I'm going to work up something from those notes I took this morning. Tree patterns. Good night."

At half past nine Gamadge and Harold started for the Center in the hired Ford. Mr. Burnside insisted on an early start.

"I don't want to hurry you folks," he said, "but that car of Sloat's you got there has been known to balk a little; and you can't always make up time with the roads like this."

At a quarter to ten Mr. Schenck left the Pegram House. Miss Walworth, who had been waiting at the door to see him off, pressed a little good-bye present into his hand. When he got into the hotel car, he unwrapped the parcel; discovered that it contained a fancy box of chocolates; and threw it out of the window.

"Roar of the mighty cataract," he said to himself, watching the trees bend. "I guess this must be it." But he guessed wrong.

CHAPTER EIGHTEEN

Over the Falls

A TREMENDOUS NOISE and an enveloping cloud of steam ushered the express into the station at Ford's Center. The platform was suddenly crowded with glistening rubber coats and capes, trucks piled with wet luggage rolled towards the baggage car, sodden-looking mailbags were tossed up to men whose caps immediately began to shed water. An elderly lady, who was making the short trip to Providence in a day coach, was hoisted aboard; Gamadge, Harold and Schenck, the only other departing passengers, handed their bags to a porter, and climbed after them.

Gamadge immediately led the way back to the observation platform. When they had reached it, he performed introductions: "Mr. Schenck; my assistant, Harold Bantz."

"Oh. Glad to meet you." Schenck wondered where the young man had popped up from.

"I just ran up this morning," said Harold.

"Oh."

The wheels began to turn. Schenck said: "Quite a few cars parked behind the station, I see. Nobody got off the train, did they?"

"Perhaps we were being seen off," said Gamadge. He stood braced against the end of the car, lighting a cigarette with some difficulty. Schenck, at a loss to know why they were all standing out here in the wet, flattened himself against the other side of the door. The station drifted past, and drifted away. They picked up speed, and Harold's voice rose shouting above the tumult of wheels: "Au reevoir."

"When do you think Mitchell will have some news for me?" shouted Schenck. Gamadge shook his head. "Can't hear."

"When do you think—" but they were rounding a curve, and he swayed against Gamadge. When he regained his balance, Gamadge was holding out a lighter to him. He fumbled beneath his overcoat, got out cigarettes, and managed to light one at the tiny flame. The door behind him opened, and the Pullman conductor came out, smiling.

"Passengers for Greenvale?" he asked. To his amazement, Schenck realized that the motion of the train was lessening. The engine screamed, brakes were applied, and they stopped with a succession of jerks. The conductor unlocked a gate. Gamadge sprang down without waiting for the steps, Harold followed him, and the porter handed down their three bags.

"Lively, please, sir," said the conductor. Schenck hesitated for a split second, and then dropped to a dark platform. The train clanked away, taking, so he wildly thought, safety and sanity with it. He picked up his bag, and went after the others.

Twin lights pierced the wet darkness, and Hoskins' grinning face appeared out of the void; his bag was taken from him, and he found himself tumbling into the back seat of a car, with Harold beside him. They drove away from this ambiguous and, so far as Schenck knew, uncharted spot into a dim whirl of rain and wind-lashed trees.

"Quite a blow," said Harold.

"Quite." Schenck, vague as to his status in the rôle of uninvited guest, felt confusedly that it was not his place to ask questions.

"You're a sport," said Harold. "Decided to come for the ride, did you?"

"After mature deliberation, yes."

This seemed to amuse Harold very much. He said: "Didn't take you long to make up your mind. I was going to hand you back your bag, but Mr. Gamadge said: 'Let him come, if he wants to.'"

"Kind of him."

"Mitchell had them stop for us at that way station."

"So I imagined."

"Mr. Gamadge didn't like to ask you to come back into this business with us."

"Why not? What's it all about?"

"I ain't supposed to say."

They had been traveling along a highway, and Schenck suddenly thought he recognized a landmark. He said: "We're on the road from Ford's Center to Burnsides."

"We're not going to Burnsides."

They passed it, in fact, and drove on northwards, turning left when they reached the intersection to Oakport, instead of right. They were on a rough road, now, and after a time the jolts grew severe. Harold banged his head, said "Ouch", and peered out of the window.

"Where are we?" Schenck also peered from the window on his side. "We're going through gates—big iron gates. What is this place, for Pete's sake?"

The car jolted to a stop. "I wouldn't get out, if I was you," said Harold. "He said to wait in the car."

Schenck let down the window, and put his head out into the rain. When he withdrew it, his face was startled. "It's a cemetery."

"Yes, it is."

"It's the cemetery I was in this morning." Schenck put his head out again. The headlights gleamed palely on a group of men over to the right, on wet umbrellas, and the shaft of a tall monument. "That's the Bartram lot. And that—" he peered through the rain—"that's Mr. George Bartram, standing between the two state police. Sheriff pointed him out to me at the funeral."

George Bartram's white face turned away again, and Schenck could see nothing but a semicircle of backs. He seized the door handle: "I'm going to get out."

Hoskins and Gamadge returned to the car before he had had time to leave his seat. He sat back again, and the car made a lurching turn and bumped off through the gates. The rain was lessening. They had crossed the intersection, and begun the short run to Oakport by way of the upper road, before Schenck leaned forward and spoke:

"Mr. Gamadge?"

"Yes."

"Hope you don't mind my sticking with this delightful party?"

"Not at all. We owe you something. I understand that you've made yourself useful."

"Me?"

"Yes. Sporting of you not to ask a lot of questions. I'm trying to concentrate."

Schenck accepted the hint in silence. They rumbled over Oakport Bridge, rushed through a dark and quiet village, and climbed the gradual and winding ascent that took them to the Bartram house. It was in darkness, except for the living room; a dim light came through the bay window. They went up the flagged walk between storm-beaten rows of flowers, and Schenck, glancing right and left, saw only a dripping wilderness. Gamadge rang. Miss Ridgeman came to the door, and recoiled at the sight of him.

"You went away!"

"I had to come back. Mr. Bartram in?"

"He's gone up to bed. Doctor Loring was just leaving."

"I'd like to see him."

She stood back, her blanched face searching his, and the four streamed into the living room. Loring sat before a dying fire, finishing a highball. At the sight of them he rose, stared, and said blankly: "Back again?"

"Yes."

"Glad to hear it. Hello, Hoskins. Mr. Schenck, is it? And this is the young man who sold an order of note paper to Serena Turnbull. I saw him drive away."

"If you had seen the sample she ordered from, and the price she was paying for it, you might not be here at the moment. I have just come from the cemetery, Doctor Loring. A grave has been opened in the Bartram lot."

Loring continued to look at Gamadge, while he put out his hand, picked up the glass of whisky, and drained it. Then he said: "Really?"

"Sarah Beasley's father has identified her."

"Is poor Beasley capable of identifying anybody—under the conditions you suggest?"

"It's no use, Loring; the whole family is at home at the farm, and if necessary they will identify her too. Don't let us waste time discussing that."

"No. Where, if you don't mind enlightening me, is the body of Julia Bartram, then?"

"Nowhere, as you already know so well. There is no Julia Bartram; there never was a Julia Bartram."

"If you pretend that Carroll Bartram had no child—"

"I pretend no such thing. He had a son, who is now safely upstairs again in his own nursery, after a sojourn with the gypsies. Adelaide Gibbons and Mrs. Turnbull came in by the back way some time ago, and they are taking care of him. George Bartram has assumed full responsibility for his welfare, and will take him to New York tomorrow."

A choking sound made them look around. Miss Ridgeman, livid and trembling, stood in the doorway, holding to one side of it. She whirled, rushed out into the hall, grasped one of the stair posts to steady herself, and screamed, her head thrown back: "Mr. Bartram! They've opened the grave. Do you hear me? They've opened the grave!"

There was a very long silence; no one answered her from upstairs, and at last Loring said coolly: "Not so much noise, Ridgeman. Keep calm, come in here, and sit down. Have a drop of whisky."

She collapsed upon a chair just within the doorway, her shoulders bent, her clasped hands between her knees. Loring poured some whisky into the glass, and took it over to her; but she ignored it and him.

"Oh, all right." He came back to the davenport, and sat down. "Take it like that, if you must; I can't blame you for feeling the shock. It's all up, and we've wasted seven good years on it; but you needn't behave as though somebody could chop your head off for it. Upon my word, I think we'll get off pretty easily. You're a man of the world, Gamadge; sit down, and tell your cohorts to sit down, and let me tell you all about it."

Gamadge sat on a corner of the square table that stood on the left of the fireplace, and Schenck allowed his legs to bend, and his body to sink upon the seat of a convenient chair. Hoskins remained alertly poised near the door, and Harold Bantz, trying to maintain a detached and casual air, leaned beside him, pad and pen in hand.

"The truth is," said Loring, sipping Miss Ridgeman's drink of whisky, "we put ourselves into a spot to oblige a friend, and once in it, we had to stay there. That's all there is to it. We can be had up for conniving at a fraud, but George Bartram won't prosecute—I can bet on that—and I shouldn't be surprised if they let us off with a warning. Bartram's popular, and I'm good in the witness box, and Miss Ridgeman is only a devoted employee, and a woman."

Hoskins, representing the law, suddenly and surprisingly intervened: "You're talkin' before witnesses, Doc, and this young feller here is takin' notes. You want this to be a voluntary confession?"

Loring smiled at him, frankly amused. "Certainly, Willard. Do go and sit down, somewhere, and forget all that legal twaddle you've learned. Neither I nor Miss Ridgeman has anything to conceal—now. Mr. Gamadge seems to have blown us up, somehow, and I want him to hear our side of it. Damn it all, Gamadge, I gave you a good lunch. It ought to have choked you."

"Unscrupulous of me to accept; but I really couldn't refuse. That might have given you food for reflection."

"No holds barred, eh? Well, I'm in no position to complain; but I want you to hear our side of the story—Miss Ridgeman's and mine."

"There's only one side to this story, Loring; you know perfectly well that you will both be held responsible for Sarah Beasley's death."

"It was an accident; a most unfortunate accident. She ought to be alive and well this moment, as the Ormiston child is. Cogswell will tell you himself that she only died because she had an allergy for atropine—my God, he ought to know! He did the post-mortem himself, and ordered the analysis."

"Doctor Cogswell thinks you ought to be lynched, all three of you."

"Because his vanity is hurt by the way we took him in."

"Your imagination has its limits, hasn't it? You actually can't realize the horror and disgust that everybody is going to feel when they hear about your inhuman tampering with these children's lives."

"Now, don't take that tone, Gamadge; I should have thought that you, at least, were no sentimentalist. We didn't use atropine from choice; we used it because it's the drug in nightshade, and we wanted nightshade—for several reasons."

"I know very well why you wanted nightshade; Mitchell and I listed some of your reasons for wanting it, early yesterday morning. We hadn't enough information then to list one of the most important ones, from your point of view; that people don't think of a doctor in connection with poison, if the poison is administered in berry form. But I submit that you did use atropine from choice, and for its own sake; you needed a quick-acting drug, and one that confuses the wits. You could always administer a minute extra dose of it, if the berries hadn't the effect you hoped for. As a matter of fact, *didn't* you administer that minute extra dose, Doctor? And isn't that why Sarah Beasley died?"

"Nonsense. The analysis—"

"No analyst could tell exactly how much atropine may have been present in the berries Sarah Beasley had, and no analyst could gauge the exact amount absorbed by her. Wasn't it that extra hundredth of a grain, say, that probably killed her? It's ghastly stuff to play with. I wonder that you didn't kill the Ormiston boy, too; and I'll be hanged if I think you cared, either of you."

"You exaggerate."

"I don't exaggerate the reaction you are likely to experience from your activities."

"Manslaughter—I'm prepared for a charge of manslaughter; but the verdict won't even be that, I'd be willing to bet on it! Not when people understand that Miss Ridgeman and I went through the whole thing, at great cost to our own feelings, to get Bartram out of a jam."

"That's the defense, is it?" Gamadge smiled crookedly at him.

"Why shouldn't it be the defense? It's true." Loring returned the smile. "Miss Ridgeman is absolutely devoted to Bartram, as you can see for yourself, with half an eye; and he's my best friend."

"And you had nothing to gain by the transaction."

"Nothing. If we seem to have gained by it, I can only protest that money can't pay for such a service as we've rendered. Seven years out of our lives! It's fabulous. As for that poor unfortunate Beasley child, we only meant to borrow her for an hour or two, while the Georges were here. It was all because they came down on us at short notice—we couldn't plan anything better in the time."

"One thing leads to another, though, doesn't it? That affair last night with the dummy, for instance."

Loring's eyes twinkled. "Oh, come now, Gamadge, I thought better of your intelligence. You can't connect the elusive Miss Humphrey with us. Make an attempt on the life of a sympathetic person like yourself? Absurd."

"You'd have had another try at it if we hadn't thrown poor Miss Walworth at you."

"Seriously, Gamadge, why should Bartram and I go for you in that melodramatic fashion? We hadn't the vaguest notion that you had a line on us."

"We had a line on that lost four hundred thousand, though, thanks to George Bartram. And Carroll Bartram knew nothing about your attempt at murder. He was bewildered, when we told him about it last night."

"We were all bewildered. If we had had the faintest inkling of what you were up to, this interview wouldn't be taking place."

"You decided to get rid of Mitchell and myself the moment George Bartram gave us the tip about the four hundred thousand. That tip led us straight to the motive for the whole conspiracy; and, incidentally, it exonerated George himself, since he handed it to us."

"And we thought you were beginning to suspect dear old George!"

"Not after I realized that the fraud must have been directed against him."

"To the deuce with all that. My point is that you can't connect Miss Humphrey with us. A lunatic of a woman, going around taking pictures of children for some nonexistent magazine!"

"Miss Humphrey wasn't taking pictures of children."

For the first time, Loring appeared to be nonplused. He swallowed the dregs of his whisky, lighted a cigarette, and then asked sourly: "What was she doing?"

"She was trying to find out if there were any recognizable photographs of Sarah Beasley available. If there had been, she would have got hold of them all. Her visit to the Ormistons' was camouflage, and she naturally did not visit Miss Ridgeman, since Miss Ridgeman and Miss Humphrey were one."

"Your Mr. Schenck informed me that she also visited the gypsies. Was that camouflage, too?" Loring's smile was a grimace.

"That was a fearful mistake. Miss Humphrey's interview with William Stanley ended abruptly when she realized that he was a gypsy; the last thing any of you wanted was to focus attention on them, since Bartram's boy was in their camp."

"And why should Humphrey want pictures of Sarah Beasley, pray?"

"To destroy them. Atropine is deadly stuff; and if anything went wrong you wanted no pictures of Sarah Beasley in the papers. The George Bartrams might see them; Cogswell might see them, or one of his jury, if you couldn't persuade him out of an inquest; even the Boston funeral people might see them. Of course you *had* to persuade Cogswell out of an inquest, which was the reason why you called him in and let him have his autopsy and his analysis and all the rest of it."

"I don't deny that your exposition is admirable," said Loring, "but I do deny that it is based on fact. You haven't given me one iota of evidence to connect Miss Ridgeman with Miss Humphrey." He added, glancing at the bent figure by the door, "I do wish she'd have a drink; I don't like to see her so disheartened."

"I can do better than that," said Gamadge. "I can connect Miss Humphrey with Miss Ridgeman, and I can connect her with you."

"Me!"

"Yes. You adopted her personality for that very ill-advised attempt in the short cut."

"How, if you please, did you reach that conclusion?"

"Quite simply. After I had conveyed certain information to Mitchell, which I did late this morning, he got a cleaner down from Bailtown; he was introduced into the Bartram garage while you were having Sunday dinner with them, and he thoroughly cleaned your car."

Loring, who now sat back in his corner of the davenport, his bright inquiring eyes turned up to Gamadge's face, said gently, "Did he, indeed?"

"Late this afternoon he performed the same operation on Miss Humphrey's outfit, which was found, together with the dummy outfit, in the woods. From the car and the tweed coat and skirt he collected certain almost invisible objects, hard to remove from rough materials, and extremely hard to see. They were curiously marked cat hairs, Doctor; they had come from the body and tail of a tortoise-shell cat. As I know to my sorrow, it requires special and expert labor to extract them from one's clothes."

After a pause Loring said in a faraway voice: "There are cats and cats."

"Tortoise shells are not the commonest variety. For the life of them, the police haven't been able to find another within a radius of ten miles from the Beasley farm. I suppose Sarah's cat followed the car, when Sarah was borrowed on Tuesday; and, since it mustn't be found on the lower roads, when its mistress was presumably in the marsh, it was taken aboard. I don't know when it was killed, or where it is now."

Loring said: "I think our battery of lawyers will be able to deal with all that."

"Bartram's and Miss Ridgeman's may; yours won't."

"Mine won't?" Loring sat up, slowly.

"No. *You're* facing a charge of murder—in the first degree."

"Why? I only—"

"They may be accessories after the fact, but perhaps they're not."

The whites of Loring's eyes showed, as he said: "I don't know what you're talking about."

"I'm talking about young Trainor. He rode into the short cut with you on Tuesday evening, after he saw you leave Bartram's boy in the gypsy camp. You thought you knew his hours; but he had the gypsies on his mind, and he had altered them. I don't know what story you told him; perhaps the same one that you told them; but you couldn't swear *him* to secrecy. Completely at your mercy, wasn't he, that big young man? Stopped at your request, I suppose, and bent down to look at your lamps or your tire. He was so off his guard that you had plenty of time to bring that piece of iron, or whatever it was, down on his skull. You had to get him and his machine over to the rock, but you smoothed the traces away as well as you could. They left too wide a path across the ruts, and you didn't like to disturb the dead leaves too much."

Loring pulled himself together. "Conjecture won't do here," he said, "and you don't seem to have even circumstantial evidence."

"We have better evidence than that. The gypsies saw Trainor ride into the cut with you at a little after eight; two people saw you come out of it alone; and one of them was a state policeman, leaving headquarters."

Loring burst into a high, gasping laugh. "The gypsies!"

"You were sure they wouldn't give you away about the little boy, and you were right. They haven't, even yet. When they make a promise like that, they keep it. They were glad to harbor him for a few days, until Bartram should pretend to be persuaded into adopting him; I suppose you told them that his cruel and irresponsible parents mustn't know where he was, and that he'd been ill, and needed treatment. What did you give him, by the way, to keep him just not quite awake?"

"Let me tell you that I was taking no chances with Bartram's boy! I gave him a hypodermic three times a day—half a grain of luminal, plus an eighth of codeine; and an infernal nuisance it was. Bartram had me nearly crazy, worrying me about him."

"You kept Bartram pretty well drugged, too, didn't you?"

"Had to; stimulants in the daytime, sedatives at night. He came through it all better than we had expected him to."

"And the gypsies didn't know they were going to be involved in the nightshade case. They never connected little Elias with the case at all. So far as they knew, there was no little *boy* missing. They took your word for the whole thing, and they gave you their solemn word they wouldn't say you'd brought him. Wonderful to be able to do a favor for a Bartram, wonderful to be able to oblige Doctor Robert Loring, whose position gave him power almost of life and death over such as they. They're terrified of you."

"I'm sure I don't see why they should be."

"Extra-sensory perception, no doubt. Unfortunately for you, there was another matter that you would have been very glad to ask them to keep quiet about; but you simply didn't dare. Even your exalted powers were not strong enough to count on, when it was a question of murder—the murder of one of their friends. These state policemen aren't Cossacks in the eyes of the gypsies; they are protectors and allies. You couldn't ask them not to say that you had ridden into the short cut with Trainor. So when Mitchell and the sheriff went down to see them this afternoon, and told them the whole story—that was the advantage, you see, that they were able to tell them the whole story—"

"Which I suppose you had told them," said Loring, with his fixed smile.

"Suppose so, if you like. They could tell them—and this is the point—that whatever they did or didn't tell, Doctor Loring was inevitably going to prison; and that they needn't be afraid of him any more. So Mrs. Stuart saw no reason, as they had made you no promises on the subject, why she shouldn't say that Trainor had come along and seen little Elias deposited in the camp, and that he had ridden behind you into the short cut. She merely stipulated—since their respect for you died hard—that they should be allowed to move. They did so at about seven thirty tonight. We were afraid you might hear about it, so I wangled Annie out of this house for the evening. You're so impetuous; I was afraid you might go berserk again, as you did last night."

"If we had had any hint of your activities we should have decamped; nothing more drastic."

"I was a little nervous."

"You're a nervous type, aren't you? I should be glad to know how you got an exhumation order through in less than a day, and on Sunday, too."

"It took some doing; but the powers were annoyed with you all. Now, Doctor Loring:" Gamadge sat swinging a leg, and regarding the other with intentness: "I've given you our case—the worst of it; and, as you have been aware since the beginning of this interview, I am giving you another break, which you best know the value of. Shall I now proceed to regularize the proceedings, or will you oblige me with a piece of information? You'll have to decide immediately; we haven't much time."

Loring said: "Know it all, don't you? I thought I was stalling you along. What do you want?"

"The motive, of course. What did old Mr. Bartram invest his four hundred thousand in?"

"Russian jewelry. It was in this country when he bought it, and the deal was a dead secret. White Russians were selling it, but there was something about a cut going to some of the Reds. Dangerous business for both."

"Heaps of diamonds and rubies, ropes of pearls?"

"Not forgetting the sapphires and the emeralds."

"I see. Thanks very much."

There was a commotion outside—cars driving up, motorcycle engines popping. Feet hurried up the flagged walk, and the doorbell rang. The sound of it seemed to set off an explosion, so instantly did a deafening roar answer it from upstairs. Miss Ridgeman screamed, her hands over her ears, and slid sideways in her chair. Hoskins and Schenck dashed for the hall; a crowd of people poured in, and made for the second floor.

Loring, his eyes on the ceiling, poured himself the last of the whisky. "I thought that shot would never come," he said.

"I thought so too," said Gamadge. "He waited a long time."

CHAPTER NINETEEN

The Queen Elizabeth Legend

"YOU AND HOSKINS beat all." Mitchell addressed Gamadge more in sorrow than in anger. He was facing him across the golden-oak table in Doctor Cogswell's dining room, on the glassy surface of which Mrs. Cogswell had set out coffee, a platter of homemade cookies, and a large dish of peaches. Cogswell was sitting at one end of the table, red with a day-long indignation; the lean, disillusioned sheriff was at his right, and Gamadge on his left. Mr. Schenck, still bemused, sat opposite Harold Bantz, who had his notebook open before him.

Hoskins spoke feebly, but he was loyal. "I thought I was supposed to watch Loring."

"Four of you in the house, and one of you a deputy; and you leave Bartram alone upstairs till he gets good and ready to shoot himself!"

Gamadge took a hot swallow of coffee before he answered: "The idea was that if I had half an hour with Loring I'd get him to give me what you wanted—their motive. I got it for you."

"Yes, but I didn't say you could bargain for it by letting Bartram kill himself!"

"The bargain was a tacit one. Loring thought that by telling us what we knew already he was giving his friend time to leave this earthly scene; I thought that you preferred the motive to Bartram. Was I wrong?"

"I can't understand why Loring wanted him dead."

"Bartram would have gone on the stand and sworn to the truth, that the whole plan was Loring's, from beginning to end; and that Loring engineered it for the sake of a third of the loot. I'm certain it's thirds. We might never have known for certain about that Russian jewelry; now we can hunt for it."

The sheriff drew slowly on his cigar. "It's better for Bartram's folks, this way," he said, "and better for his boy."

Cogswell poured himself another cup of coffee. "Speakin' for myself," he said, "I'll be glad to let Gamadge off with a warning. He says he ain't goin' to appear in the case at all; if we take advantage of his kind offer of all the evidence, we'll save part of our reputations. It's owin' to him that we have some of our credit left, as it is. When I think—"

"You forget about that, Cog. Nobody's going to blame you," said Mitchell.

"They fooled me into thinkin' I was bein' so darned hard on 'em. Oh, well. You know, I'm sorry for George Bartram. He's a mighty nice kind of feller; with all this trouble comin' down on top of him, all he worries about is that poor kid. I left him in the nursery, up there. The rumpus had waked the little feller, and he was settin' up on Adelaide Gibbons' lap, playin' with Bartram's watch chain. Bartram's hired her to go to New York with them tomorrow."

"I hope she won't call Mrs. Bartram by her first name—not for a week or two, anyway," said Gamadge.

"You bound and determined to go on to Boston tonight?" asked the sheriff.

"Yes, we all have to be in New York tomorrow morning."

"Hoskins will drive you as far as Boston."

"That's good of you. We'll take a train, or a plane, or something, and have a nice nap on it."

"I guess you don't feel like giving us the whole story now, before you start? I don't know the ins and outs of it yet."

"Glad to; it won't take long. Harold can write it down in shorthand, and he'll send you a draft tomorrow. Ready, Harold? All right. Let's see." Gamadge leaned back in his chair, crossed his legs, lighted a cigarette, and said composedly: "There was a story about Queen Elizabeth."

This opening was received in polite silence, and Harold transferred it to paper with a long-suffering air.

"Some people thought," continued Gamadge, "and for all I know some people still think, that she died young, was buried secretly by her terrified personnel, and impersonated thereafter by a boy. The boy was supposed eventually to rule all England, avoiding marriage, as you know, and exhibiting many unwomanly qualities during his long and successful reign. The whole thing was of course put over, according to the legend, because if King Henry the Eighth had been informed of his daughter's death he would have had the heads off her entourage. They had to produce a daughter for him.

"Yesterday morning, when I heard at the Bartrams' that old Mrs. Bartram required a female heir to inherit that jewelry of hers, I was vaguely reminded of the Queen Elizabeth story. But the Bartram jewels didn't seem worth committing a fraud for—they consisted of a bunch of picturesque junk, which might perhaps bring a few hundreds in cash. George Bartram knew all about them, and had seen them often.

"He didn't know, however, that a fabulous addition had been made to them. Old Mr. Bartram, badly hit in the war of 1914, and aware of what could happen to the most firmly established family business, had invested his savings in a princely collection of Russian jewels. I say princely; they may have been monarchical. The deal was a sort of international affair, and conducted with the utmost of secrecy; in fact, Mr. Bartram told nobody about it but his wife. When he died she annexed them—they were hers, her husband's provision for her—and placed them in a wall safe which she had installed in her bedroom.

"You will note that neither parent seems to have put much trust in the sons. George had offended by going off on his own; Carroll, by faults of character which we can only guess at. Note that old Mr. Bartram took the part of his son's enemy when that row occurred at the school, and afterwards made Ormiston his protégé; I considered the fact significant.

"The old lady probably confided her secret to Carroll Bartram after she had had her first stroke. He had settled down by that time, married the right sort of girl, and become very attentive to his mother. He, in his turn, no doubt confided in his broad-minded friend Doctor Robert Loring; and I am sure that they had many a discussion about the matter. George was married; which of the sons would provide Mrs. Bartram senior with the first granddaughter?

"We arrive at that spring evening, seven years ago, when they are all at the old house; Miss Ridgeman, Loring's choice as a nurse, is unpacking her bags, and there is no other resident servant but Annie, the old, lame, devoted cook. Loring gave us a highly dramatic account of what happened; he didn't care to have us find out the details, piecemeal, and ask a lot of questions. You know the events of that night; old Mrs. Bartram had her second stroke, a boy was born to the Carrolls, and Mrs. Carroll died. Confusion, tragedy, distress.

"Loring goes to his friend, with arguments all prepared; they must have gone something like this: 'Your child is a boy, old man; but that won't matter, if your mother only dies without regaining consciousness—in that case you simply take the jewelry, and nobody will ever be the wiser. But unfortunately we don't know whether she *will* die without regaining consciousness, and we can't wait to find out. Because, if she once hears that the baby's a boy, she'll get into communication with George.

"'My suggestion is this: tell everybody that the boy is a girl. You and Ridgeman and I can easily put it over—the place is isolated, the nursery is upstairs, Annie can't go up, and it's nobody's business to leave your mother and explore. You couldn't do it if you hadn't a doctor and a nurse at your disposal, and you couldn't do it if the Georges weren't settled in Europe—forever, so they say; as it is, the thing's easy. The moment your mother dies the four of us clear out for Europe, where you lose a daughter and adopt a son. What about it? Your mother probably won't live a week.'

"Carroll Bartram wanted that money—wanted it badly; and he didn't want George to have it. He made his decision; and for the next seven years he and Loring and the nurse were the slaves of their own invention; because old Mrs. Bartram didn't die—she lived on, bedridden, competent, and exacting; and the George Bartrams produced a girl.

"You know, I can almost find it in my heart to pity those three. They were tied to the place, haunted by the fear of accident, illness, death; vulnerable to all sorts of danger. They had to take the boy to Boston periodically and present him to his grandmother; though I imagine the visits grew less frequent as the years went on. They couldn't see their friends, go anywhere, call their souls their own. When the old lady died, in June, they must have swooned, almost, with relief. But their troubles weren't over. The situation in Europe made their first plan very difficult, if not impossible; they had to devise something else. Whatever it was, they were on the point of carrying it out; and then the Georges descended on them, at two days' notice.

"Well, they hadn't lived through all that without formulating some scheme or other, to be used in a crisis; they had their eye on a little girl up the road named Beasley, the same age as the Bartram boy, who could easily pass for a Bartram. They decided that it would look very odd if they removed little 'Julia' for those few hours on Tuesday; and they didn't want George Bartram to think them odd. They made up their minds to borrow Sarah Beasley.

"It wasn't too difficult. Her parents would be frightened, but Loring would 'find' her early in the afternoon, and she would never be able to remember anything more than that a lady in a car gave her some berries. Little Carroll Bartram—that's his name—could spend the interval in Loring's office.

"But the affair had an unexpected and frightful ending. It was to have been a passing mystery, with nobody the worse for it; it became a *cause célèbre*, with one child dead, another presumably missing, a panic, a hue and cry, and an enigmatic little boy at the gypsy camp, who required medication three times a day. The gypsies, who knew nothing about the nightshade case, and were never to have been connected with it at all, came in for questioning; Loring couldn't be sure that they wouldn't mention his bringing the child to camp, and that they wouldn't mention Trainor.

"But things settled down pretty well. Bartram got his boy back, Sarah Beasley was safely buried, the gypsies didn't talk, and the police seemed resigned to the theory of a wandering half-wit, who probably wouldn't do it again. And I left on the ten o'clock train; Loring or Miss Ridgeman saw me go." Gamadge reached for a cookie. "That's all."

"All!" Cogswell almost shouted it. "We want to know how you found out about it. Mitchell says you told him you knew by lunchtime, yesterday."

"I just got some impressions."

"Let's hear what they were."

"Well, if you're interested: the first ones arrived before I left New York. There was a faint flavor of coincidence about two of the facts Mitchell gave me; a gypsy child of the fatal age was ill, though perhaps not from atropine poisoning, and Trainor died violently on Tuesday evening.

"When I arrived, my first definite idea that something was odd about the Bartram household received confirmation; it was strangely understaffed. There was a scared old cook, who couldn't go upstairs; and there was a paragon of a trained nurse, who seemed to do most of the housework, besides her own job. Outside help seemed to be invoked only on great occasions, such as the unexpected arrival of relatives from Europe, who had never seen the daughter of the house.

"Next came Irma Bartram's extraordinary tale (communicated without prompting, and without words) that she had found the red bell under the pine tree. To me that meant from the first one thing, and only one; that Sarah Beasley had brought it into the Bartram grounds. Wadded up in her hand, it would have escaped notice; and she never let go of it until her hand relaxed in stupor. I was struggling with this conviction, when Annie conveyed to me *her* inalterable conviction—that magic had been at work, and very bad magic too. On top of that came the jewel scene, and on top of that George Bartram's story of the lost four hundred thousand dollars.

"The Queen Elizabeth legend lodged itself in my brain, taking the form of one of those hypothetical questions to which I am so passionately addicted: If old Mr. Bartram's missing money had somehow been added to his wife's estate, and if, therefore, a female child was required to inherit this large fortune, what would an unscrupulous parent do if his child turned out to be a son?

"I had no data as to the possibilities of such a substitution; but at least the word—'substitution'—gave me another word: 'changeling'; and Annie's behavior fell into the pattern. Suppose she had known, almost from the first, that the Bartram heiress was in fact an heir? She wouldn't mention her knowledge to the persons responsible for this strange deception; first, because she knew nothing of the financial end of it; secondly, because Bartram could do no wrong; thirdly, because her son in Ireland was completely dependent on Bartram generosity, and she wasn't going to offend them by asking questions that obviously would be more than unwelcome. But on Tuesday she had a frightful shock—Mrs. George Bartram came into the kitchen with the news that a little *girl* was ill upstairs!

"Somewhere, deep within, Annie knew that there had been a fraud and a swindle, and that it was now coming to its logical conclusion; but consciously, she wouldn't and couldn't face it. She took refuge in a horrible but less shattering theory—that the fairies had changed the Bartram heir into a girl, or had wafted him away and substituted a changeling in his place. She believed thoroughly in the possibility, of course—many of her race still do; and the Bartram child was peculiarly vulnerable to such an attack, since his mother had died when he was born. There was a magic herb in it, too; the Sidhe, or Little People, use such herbs in such magic. She could only be thankful that the changeling died, and even more thankful when the rightful heir inexplicably returned to his home. You're not to blame the old thing; she knows the truth now, and I swore you'd let her go to New York with George Bartram, tomorrow. Serena Turnbull is taking care of her as well as she can, for the Turnbulls are, as you know, practically comatose from shock.

"Well; Loring told us the interesting story of that tragic night, seven years ago; and I became aware that fantastic and grotesque as my theory might seem, all the known facts fitted it, and it only. I couldn't present such a welter of guesswork to Mitchell, however; the proof lay in the Bartram cemetery, and I should require something in the nature of fact to persuade him to look for it. So I telephoned to my assistant here, asking him to come up on the night train, and telephone me on his arrival. When he arrived, I had him canvass the vicinity for anyone who had ever laid eyes on Julia Bartram.

"Nobody had—tradesman, beach attendant, neighbor or occasional help—except two persons who caught a glimpse of the child in the family automobile. I conveyed this information, and my whole theory, to Mitchell. Within an hour he had that cleaner down from Bailtown, who operated not only on the Loring car, but later on the Humphrey disguise. The result you know. I am glad that you had confidence in me, and that your confidence was justified."

The sheriff said: "You've been put to expense. That bicycle you bought for the Stanley boy—"

"Don't mention it. If you think you owe me anything at all, let poor old Annie off without questioning. You don't need her testimony, and she certainly couldn't give it coherently in court. She'd mix the fairies all up in it."

"George Bartram's going to look out for her."

"I knew he would. He's had a horrid time ever since he saw that bell on Irma's kitten. He drove up to the Beasleys' this morning, as I knew he'd do, to condole and to thank them, and they told him all about the red ribbon and the red bell. When he saw them on Whitey, he came to my conclusions; he had no illusions about his elder brother, you know. He was tempted to tell me all about it this afternoon—nearly pulled the bell out of his pocket; but of course he couldn't, when it came to the point. Well, his financial troubles are over; and if Irma ever comes into her property, they're all rich."

CHAPTER TWENTY

Strong Gypsy Wish

"THERE IT IS." Mr. Albert Ormiston placed a smallish framed picture on the mantelpiece in Gamadge's library, and stepped back to get a view of it. "Nice little thing, isn't it? I must say the cleaning process makes it look less like a Vermeer than it used to do."

"Not so much depth, and not so much mystery. There's virtue in dirt," agreed Gamadge. Stretched out in an armchair, with the cat Martin lying at extreme length across his knees, he squinted at the painting through half-closed eyes.

"Oh, it's seventeenth century Dutch, all right; and plenty of people would be glad to give five hundred for it."

"I would, for one."

"You mean that? It's yours!"

"I'll write you a check."

"Just for that, I'll tell you a secret; the old lady gave it to me."

"No! Good for her."

"And all the other daubs. They all were daubs, except this, but perhaps I can persuade somebody they ain't. Old man Bartram meant to leave me something, and she knew it; but being just a teeny bit close with her money, she presented me with all the things she had no use for, instead. I did hope she'd make a mistake or two, and include a little chipped Chinese lacquer, or some odd pieces of that ugly blue Doulton; but no, she didn't make any slips."

"Wasn't this Dutch interior a slip?"

"Terrible, but I wasn't including it. That wasn't really her fault; the old man and I had joked about it so much that she thought it wasn't worth a nickel. George got his business sense from her. How're they getting on, by the way?"

"I had a nice note from Mrs. Bartram; they're coming through it all pretty well, and I actually believe we'll see them in the old house again, some day."

"No imagination."

"She says Irma and her cousin Carroll are very thick. Irma sent me a picture of him; at least, I thought at first that it was a picture of him, but she seems to have given him a tail, so perhaps it's a sketch of Whitey."

"Those brothers couldn't stand each other; that was the principal reason why George pulled out for good. By the way, my wife wants to see you again; wants you to come to dinner. She thinks you're the original hound of hell, but you fascinate her."

"Any night next week. I'm not aware of having hounded Mrs. Ormiston."

"She thinks it was miraculous, the way you guessed Tom was Millie's boy; can't imagine how she came to give the show away."

Theodore came in with cocktails. Gamadge said: "Oh—sorry; I forgot you don't drink. How about some tomato juice?"

Ormiston seized a cocktail with alacrity. "Matter of fact, I do," he confessed, "but I was in such a confounded temper that morning, and I find nothing annoys people more than to say you're a teetotaller."

"Nothing except making caricatures of them."

"You heard about that, did you? I never could stand Bartram at school; such a Brahmin! But I didn't think he'd bust me on the nose; the others didn't mind their pictures so much. You know, I believe my caricature showed him something none of the rest of us saw in him—something he couldn't face. Have you found the Russian jewelry?"

"Bushels of it, in all their safe deposit boxes. I suppose they counted on scattering it all over Europe and America; but it wasn't the best time to liquidate, exactly. How are the Brecks?"

"Booming. Breck got himself transferred to Boston, and they're living in that flat Miss Walworth gave them, and Millie's painting away for dear life. Walworth is getting more sensible every minute; they tell me she's torn up her Great Purple literature, and gone back to her pew in the Unitarian church. I looked into her mental condition, for Millie's sake, and the doctors tell me she never was dangerous, and now that she has an interest in life, she'll probably improve steadily."

"I thought her a touching old thing."

Harold came into the room. "That woman's on the wire again," he said. "She says, can't you make that Walpole letter a Walpole letter?"

"We've told her six times it was written by his secretary." Gamadge's annoyance communicated itself to Martin, who allowed himself to drop sinuously to the floor. "Tell her again."

"She still thinks it must be a Walpole letter."

"Tell her this is one of the times when thinking doesn't make it so."

Ormiston said in a commiserating tone: "Hanged if I can see how you ever do make any money; and you must be out of pocket over that Maine trip."

"Not at all. I'm fixed for life." Gamadge took a dirty envelope out of his pocket, and handed it to Ormiston, who read aloud:

"Mr. Henry Gamadge
Police
New York City."

"And this reached you?" he inquired, somewhat respectfully.

"Yes; they looked me up in the telephone book."

Ormiston unfolded a ruled sheet of paper, and stared bemusedly at a formula arranged in the shape of a vase or urn:

TO WIN AT CARDS
Make
the
STRONG GYPSY WISH
And Burn Salt
In a Silver
SPOON

Signed:
MARIA STUART
GEORGINA STANLEY
MARTHA STANLEY
WILLIAM STANLEY
X (THE BABY)